MURDER
BY
POISON PEN

A completely unputdownable cozy murder mystery

VERONICA HELEY

The Ellie Quicke Mysteries Book 2

Originally published as *Murder by Suicide*

JOFFE
Ostara
CLASSICS

Revised edition 2023
Joffe Books, London
www.joffebooks.com

First published by HarperCollins in
Great Britain in 2002 as *Murder by Suicide*

This paperback edition was first published
in Great Britain in 2023

Cover art by Dee Dee Book Covers

ISBN: 978-1-83526-069-2

CHAPTER ONE

From things that go bump in the night,
Good Lord, deliver us . . .

Turn the lights off and the name of the game changes to Danger.

The click of the light switch sounded unnaturally loud. Darkness enclosed them. Ellie could hear her own breathing.

A whoosh of heavy coat over trousers. She must move, or she would be trapped. She took a cautious step back and banged into the wall behind her.

She blinked, trying to accustom her eyes to the dark. A dim light seeped around the edges of the blind at the window. Something — someone — was standing between Ellie and the window.

Ellie slid to her knees, trying not to make any noise. She told herself not to panic. But which way was the door to the outside world?

A key snicked. She was locked in.

Someone was moving around the desk. Feeling the way. Arm raised.

Light caught the edge of a weapon. Ellie would have screamed, if there had been anyone to hear.

The heavy arm fell . . .

* * *

'But Ellie, didn't you know he'd been sacked?'

Ellie nearly spilt coffee down her best blue skirt. 'What? I don't believe it!'

She had been staying with her daughter and son-in-law over Christmas and had returned home late the previous night after a cold, slow journey south. Oversleeping, she had been late for church. She had only joined the choir recently, so she had dressed in a hurry and braved disapproving stares to stumble into the choir pew as the first hymn was announced.

Over coffee in the church hall after the service, Ellie had remarked in all innocence, 'I was surprised to see the curate taking the service. Has Gilbert gone on holiday?' Only to hear that Gilbert had been sacked!

Up came Archie Benjamin, church warden, swarthy, five-o'clock-shadowed at noon, beaming his pleasure at her return. 'Good to see you again, Ellie. You were asking about Gilbert? He wasn't sacked. Just transferred.'

Archie fancied Ellie and as usual tried to stand too close to her. She endured this only because his information was likely to be accurate.

Ellie's informant — another soprano — sniffed richly. 'Transferred, sacked. The same difference.'

Ellie rubbed her forehead. 'Nothing was said before I went away for Christmas, and I've only been gone two minutes . . .'

'Dear lady, you've been away nearly three weeks. Believe me, I have been counting the days!'

Put in the wrong, Ellie felt she had to explain. 'My grandson had flu and then my daughter Diana caught it, so I stayed on for a while. I know Gilbert's been here for some years and must be due for a change, but why transfer him so quickly?'

The soprano's protuberant eyes glittered. Ellie decided that she really did not like the woman. 'Scandal, dear! It all came out in a letter to the bishop . . .'

Archie was pretending to be horrified, but he was enjoying the drama, too. 'And others. I got a letter as well. It said, "Ask that slut Nora about vice at the vicarage."'

They both tittered. Ellie was repelled.

She knew Gilbert well. Apart from the fact that he loved his wife dearly, in no way could he have been involved in anything as tacky as a liaison with Nora, their limp little organist.

The soprano said, 'I was going to tear my letter up and throw it away, but I'd never received a poison-pen letter before, so I showed it to my mother and she said . . .'

Ellie felt as if she could do with a sit down. Quickly. She looked around for a chair, but the church hall was crowded and there were no seats available. A man's hand inserted itself under her elbow and steered her to the foyer where there was room to breathe. With equal efficiency, the hand disposed of her empty coffee cup.

'Roy Bartrick,' said the hand's owner, introducing himself. 'Widower, newly of this parish.'

Ellie blinked. She wondered if she, too, were going down with flu, because for a moment she thought she was seeing double. She blinked again and the double image disappeared. What nonsense, she thought. This man was not at all like her own dear husband Frank, who had died precisely three months ago tomorrow . . .

'Ellie Quicke,' she said, with a social smile. 'Widow, of this parish.' And nobody very special, she would have added, if asked. She was neither tall nor particularly slender, and at fifty-plus no model agency would have looked at her, despite the fact that her short curly hair had turned a most attractive silver and she had good skin.

This man was taller than Frank had been. Slimmer, almost gaunt in a handsome, silver-haired way, with black eyebrows over deep blue eyes. Frank's eyes had been blue too, but . . .

She tried to smile again at the stranger, because it was rude to drift off into her memories when in company. Really, this man was nothing like Frank.

'I must apologize,' she said. 'The Reverend Gilbert Adams and his wife are among my oldest friends and it was a shock to hear he'd been transferred.'

'Scandalous goings-on, I gather,' said Roy. 'Something about "vice in the vicarage"? Who would have thought it, in this quiet suburb?'

He was inviting her to laugh with him, but Ellie couldn't bring herself to do so.

Their curate — known to the parish as 'Timid Timothy' — was doing the rounds, still in his cassock. Shaking hands, smiling, nodding. No, not smiling. Beaming. One very happy little bunny at being in charge in Gilbert's absence.

'You look a little tired,' said the stranger. 'May I give you a lift home? My Jag's outside.'

'That's kind of you, but I live just the other side of the church.'

'Let me see you home, then.'

Archie was ploughing his way through the throng. In a moment he would ask to take her home, too.

Annoyed rather than flattered by his attentions, Ellie was pleased to see Mrs Dawes, formidable head of the flower-arranging team and another member of the choir, also surging towards her.

'Ellie, are you coming? Nice to meet you again, Mr Baltic . . .'

'Bartrick.'

'Of course, Bartrick. Ellie, are you coming? You've heard the news, I suppose. I was never so shocked in all my life. Do up your coat, dear, these January winds can be really cutting, and there's so much flu about. Did I hear that your daughter had it, too? I was ill all over Christmas, couldn't even get out to take down the tree at church, and then when I did, that silly little . . . I mean, our curate . . . came in and told me that he'd be taking the services in future and he didn't want any of our big flower stands at the side of the altar, which we've been doing, as you know, dear, ever since I can remember . . . mind your step, this path is icy . . .

'So I said to him — to Timothy, I mean — that I expected the bishop would be appointing someone new pretty quickly, and he said no, he was going to apply for the vacancy himself, which, as I pointed out to him, he's not going to get, seeing as this is his first curacy . . .'

Down the path under the towering trees around the pretty Victorian church they went, and through the gate into the alley that ran alongside the church grounds. Once in the alley, they were opposite another gate which led into Ellie's garden and so up to her house. A dog walker was having trouble with his terrier, which had spotted a neighbour's small boy up a tree.

Ellie waved at Tod, who was a special friend of hers. He waved back. He was probably pretending to be a detective. Tod was a solitary soul with a taste for the dramatic.

Mrs Dawes paused as they reached Ellie's gate. Ellie knew what was expected of her. 'Will you come in for a while?'

'I shouldn't, really, but perhaps . . .'

* * *

In a green and yellow kitchen, a woman drew the blind down over the window so that nobody could see in. She pulled on some Marigold yellow gloves and took a pad of multicoloured paper out of a drawer. She assembled a ruler and biro beside her mug of coffee. The slut must be punished, driven out of the parish. Only then would justice be done.

The woman in the yellow gloves enjoyed the sense of power this letter-writing gave her.

As she reached for the biro, she jarred her mug of coffee and spilt some on the table. She mopped it up quickly. Only a few drops stained the edge of the pad.

Nothing to worry about. No one was going to trace the letters back to her.

* * *

As Ellie closed the gate behind her, she looked back up at the church and saw that Roy had followed part of the way to see that she got safely home. She waved to him before ushering Mrs Dawes up the garden path and through the back door into her cheerful kitchen.

'Another cup of coffee, or perhaps something stronger?'

'No, I won't stay, dear,' said Mrs Dawes, shedding her padded olive-green jacket and tartan scarf while patting her improbably jet-black hair into place. 'Well, perhaps just a small sherry, then.'

Ellie led the way into the cool green living room which stretched from front to back of the house, overlooking the garden and church on one side and a quiet side road on the other. 'Apologies for the mess. I only just got back last night from Diana's, and I haven't had a chance to dust yet.'

Mrs Dawes felt the earth in a flowerpot nearby. 'You should have asked me to come in and look after your plants while you were away.'

'I didn't mean to be away for more than a week, but then . . . the flu . . .'

'You missed all the fun.' Mrs Dawes gulped sherry and set the glass down with a click. 'Well, no; it wasn't funny. First Gwyneth got a letter — you know her, don't you? You were talking to her just now — big bosomy soprano, thinks herself another Brunnhilde, God's gift to the parish, part-time receptionist at the doctor's, very keen on the vicar, and you know how kind he always is — was — when people were in trouble . . .'

Ellie nodded. She didn't know how she would have coped after Frank's death if it hadn't been for the kindness and understanding of Gilbert and his wife Liz.

'Gwyneth showed us her letter. Nasty. She took it as a joke, but I didn't like it. Left a nasty taste. It said, "Stop the vice at the vicarage! Sack the slut, now!"'

Their meek little organist had acted like a hen whose head had been cut off after her elderly father had died; even before she'd discovered that he'd left her penniless and in danger of being evicted from their flat. Gilbert had been endlessly kind to her, making time in his busy schedule to try to help. Nora in turn had become dependent on him.

Ellie had known Gilbert for years. 'He would never have done anything . . .'

'No, dear. Of course not. But perhaps Nora would have liked him to, eh?'

Mrs Dawes caught Ellie's eye and they both smiled indulgently. Gilbert had a habit of hugging those in trouble, which was very comforting to the bereaved, but which might perhaps — to a censorious eye — be misinterpreted.

Poor middle-aged, unprepossessing Nora, thought Ellie. A delicate touch on the organ and no dress sense. Never had a job. Never worth one. No wonder she'd missed the service today.

Nora's absence was the first thing Ellie had noticed when she got into church. The sub-organist was the local scoutmaster, and he had a heavy foot on the pedals. You could never mistake his thumping chords for Nora's delicate trills.

Mrs Dawes stared at the carpet while the grandmother clock in the hall ticked softly away, and a couple of dead leaves fell from the dehydrated azalea plant. With a shock Ellie realized that for once the formidable old woman looked vulnerable.

'It's horrible, wondering who's going to get a letter next,' said Mrs Dawes suddenly. 'They're all on coloured paper, different colours, red, purple, blue, green. Written in capitals, in biro. No spelling or grammar mistakes, so it must be someone who's had a reasonable education.

'I haven't had one, but several other people got them after Gwyneth. I said they should take them to the police, but nobody wanted to do that, because they thought the papers would get hold of it and the last thing anybody wanted was to get Gilbert into trouble. Nora, perhaps. But not Gilbert.

'Our beloved curate got a particularly virulent one. He showed it around, asking everyone if it was his duty to tell the bishop. Trying to look as if he weren't pleased about it. Nora got several and took them to Gilbert, who also got one. It was Gilbert and Liz who took them to the bishop in the end. Liz was marvellous; but then she always is, isn't she?

'The next thing we knew, Gilbert and Liz were packing up. The bishop had a vacancy the other side of London which he needed to fill in a hurry. I don't think he believed what the letters said. I'm sure he has more sense. But there it is. You'll always get some people to say there's no smoke without a fire.

'Gilbert came round to see me. He looked . . . old. But you know how he is. Always springing back. He said the new parish was a welcome challenge, that he'd been here too long. He said he was sorry he wouldn't have time to say goodbye to everyone. He mentioned you, particularly. He said he'd drop you a note as soon as he knew what his telephone number was.'

Ellie looked at the pile of unopened letters she had found on her doormat when she got back the night before. Mindful of good manners, she said to Mrs Dawes, 'Shall I just have a look?'

'Go on, then.'

There were the usual late Christmas cards and letters from friends, circulars and bills. Then a note from Gilbert in his distinctive scrawl. Ellie tore it open, noted the address and said, 'Yes, it's here.'

There was nothing from her solicitor, Bill Weatherspoon, and there should have been because Ellie had asked him to look after Nora in her absence.

Ellie had got involved in trying to help when Gilbert had discovered that Nora's flat — together with others in that block — were owned by Ellie's aunt-by-marriage, Miss Drusilla Quicke. This redoubtable lady had always pretended she hadn't a penny in the world apart from her old age pension, and it had been a shock to discover that she was in fact very well off.

The mere thought of crossing swords with the older woman had made Ellie's pulse rate leap into triple time, but at Gilbert's urging she had tackled Aunt Drusilla on Nora's behalf. Ellie did have one great advantage when negotiating with her aunt. Her late husband Frank had left Ellie the Quicke family's large Victorian house in which Aunt Drusilla had lived for ever. Although, in general, averse to blackmail, by threatening to sell the house over Miss Quicke's head, Ellie had made some progress towards renewing Nora's lease. Before going north for Christmas, Ellie had asked her solicitor to finalize the lease for Nora.

Yet there was no letter from him in the pile, and there hadn't been any message on the answerphone, either. Ellie sighed. 'How is Nora coping?'

Mrs Dawes raised pudgy hands in a gesture of resignation. 'Weepy. Everyone's furious with her. If she hadn't behaved so stupidly, we'd have kept Gilbert. He was a good vicar, and we're going to miss him. Timid Timothy's not got what it takes to keep this parish together. Officially, Nora's off sick with a virus. I did think about going round to see her, but the weather's been bad and my leg's been playing up something diabolical. Still, now you're back you can pop in to see her, can't you?'

As she waved Mrs Dawes goodbye, Ellie thought that visiting Nora was the last thing she wanted to do. Her stay up north with Diana and Stewart had been unrestful, to put it mildly. Her daughter and son-in-law wanted Ellie to sell up and move to a small flat near them. They were hoping, Ellie knew, that she would then be able to act as an unpaid baby-sitter.

Diana and Stewart were in a mess financially. As her late father had remarked, Diana's eyes were bigger than her stomach. Frank had given Diana and Stewart a large sum of money to help them buy a small starter home, but the young couple had landed themselves instead with a crippling mortgage on a large, executive-style house. Stewart was only middle management and likely to remain so, while Diana had been unable to return to full-time work because of the baby. Each month they fell further behind with the mortgage payments.

Diana's solution to the problem had been to ask her father for a further large sum of money. Frank had refused, believing that young marrieds should cut their coat according to their cloth. Ellie tended to agree with him, but since Frank died, she had been making Diana an allowance for child-care so that she could go back to full-time work. Only so far Diana had not been able to find a full-time job that she liked.

Frank and Ellie had been joint owners of their house in London. Under the terms of Frank's will, his half of the house went to Ellie for life, and only after her death would it pass to Diana. Hence Diana was putting pressure on Ellie to move north, hoping to latch on to some of the capital which would be released by the sale of the house.

One moment Ellie felt she ought to move north for the sake of peace and quiet, and also for baby Frank's sake. On the other hand, Ellie's baby-sitting sessions were never a suc-cess, since Diana forbade Ellie to pick the little boy up when he cried. And he did seem to cry a lot.

Ellie loved her daughter; of course she did. But there was no doubt about it: Diana wanted her own way in everything. She was perhaps a bit of a bully, Ellie reflected — like Aunt Drusilla.

Now that she was back home, Ellie realized that she really did not want to move. She loved her own little house and garden, she had many friends in the parish, and she was still toying with the idea of building on a conservatory. If only she didn't miss Frank so much! Three months was noth-ing. The house had felt so cold and empty last night when she returned. She had hardly known how to keep from weeping her eyes out.

And now this trouble with Nora.

It sank the heart, rather.

*   *   *

'St Thomas's Rectory.'

'Gilbert? It's Ellie.'

'Thank the Lord you're back! Ellie, we can't do this over the phone. Can you come over straightaway? Stay the night.

Come by tube, and I'll pick you up at the station, any time after seven. I've got Evensong at six.'

'You want me to come over tonight? But Gilbert, it's raining and—'

'I wouldn't ask if it weren't important, Ellie.'

Ellie held back a sigh, thinking of the nastiness of travelling across London by public transport on a chilly January Sunday. Then she remembered that she had money in the bank now, thanks to Frank's foresight in leaving her comfortably off.

'I'll take a minicab. Be with you by seven.'

* * *

Fat, capable hands poured wax granules into a double boiler, and inserted a thermometer. The wax must melt, but not boil. Meanwhile, the hands prepared a very special candle-making mould, a mould for a cat.

There was an unusual feature about these preparations: this candle would have no wick in it.

At the right moment, when the wax was liquid but not too hot, the molten wax was poured into the mould and set aside to cool. Soon the mould could be removed. Then the competent hands would tie a wire tightly round the neck of the wax cat and leave a long loop.

* * *

Ellie put up her umbrella as the minicab drove away. A fine drizzle was falling over the leafless trees in the deserted park nearby. A stand of laburnum trees in a raised bed divided the brightly lit, modern church from its attendant hall and parish office. In either direction stretched rows of sixties' housing, backed by high-rise flats, while a flickering neon light down the road advertised a large shopping centre.

Even as she looked around, the double doors of the church were thrust open and the organist within pulled out all the stops on the final chorus. Unlike poor dear Nora, this organist liked a lot of noise. Evensong was over. People began to leave the church, putting up their umbrellas. Ellie could see Gilbert shaking hands with his new parishioners, smiling, bending his spider-thin body over to listen to a woman, or help an elderly man put up his umbrella.

It was a fair-sized congregation.

Good for Gilbert.

Ellie picked up her overnight bag and turned left into the driveway of the two-storey vicarage — modern, like the church. Security lights flicked on, and she was able to see neat beds of wallflowers on either side of the glassed-in porch.

Liz Adams opened the door and gave Ellie a bear hug. 'Thank God you've been able to make it. We were at our wits' end!'

Horse-faced, carefully blonded, Liz was a highly respected counsellor who seemed to be suffering badly from anxiety. Recalling her role of hostess, however, she took Ellie's bag and drew her into the centrally heated warmth of the hall.

'Dear Ellie, I didn't mean to pounce on you like that. It's lovely to see you. Come in and get warm. We'll talk later. Supper's in half an hour and the spare bed's made up for you. And look! Central heating that works!'

Slipping off her coat, Ellie congratulated Liz most sincerely on the improvement in her living conditions. What a contrast to the inconvenient, cold and draughty Victorian monstrosity of a vicarage which Gilbert and Liz had left! Here a wall-to-wall speckled brown and cream carpet in the hall led through open doors into a spacious sitting room with lined gold brocade curtains shutting out the night. A spitting noise off to the left indicated that there was a roast cooking in the bright, modern kitchen.

Stairs climbed to a first-floor landing from which white-painted doors led off to bedrooms and bathrooms. From a den to the rear came the noise of a computer game; pop music seeped from above, but, muted by good carpets and curtains, the sounds were not as intrusive as they had been in the old vicarage.

'We have so much to be grateful for,' said Liz, ushering Ellie into the sitting room. At one end a coal-effect gas fire made a focus for the old vicarage furniture, while the dining table was laid ready for supper at the other. Liz's pleasure in showing off her new home was clearly real, but surely the lines on her forehead were deeper than they had been the last time Ellie saw her?

The vicar's wife put on an over-bright smile. 'No draughts, no smells, the plumbing all works, there's an efficient secretary in the parish office, I have a new job with better pay so we can afford to replace some of the old furniture, the kids love their new schools, and Gilbert is as happy as the day is long.'

'If everything in the garden is so lovely,' said Ellie, 'why did you have to drag me over here tonight, chop chop, no delay? Not that I'm not delighted to see you both again.'

Liz's smile disappeared. 'Gilbert will explain after supper. You will stay the night, won't you?'

* * *

Gilbert sipped his coffee, poured in another two spoonfuls of sugar, stirred again, drank deep and stretched out his long legs.

'Well, Ellie, as you've probably guessed, it's about Nora. The bishop gave me the benefit of the doubt before Christmas, but if anything else happens and the whole thing goes public . . .' he shrugged, 'well, you know the way some of the tabloids would seize on a scandal in the Church. I would probably have to resign.'

'But surely, now you've moved away . . .'

'That doesn't stop her. We think she's gone round the twist. Do you think you can do something about it?'

CHAPTER TWO

Ellie took a deep breath. 'Look, I didn't get back till late last night. Mrs Dawes told me about the letters this morning after church, but she didn't say anything about Nora going round the bend. Surely you exaggerate.'

'I don't think so. You saw for yourself before Christmas that she had become dependent on me. I blame myself. I ought to have been more careful, involved Liz more, perhaps. I thought I was helping Nora, but as it turned out . . . well, anyway, I don't think her feelings for me in the beginning were anything more than sisterly, or daughterly, if you prefer. Understandable if you remember how much she was under her father's thumb.'

Liz broke in. 'After the letters started, Nora began to act as if she and Gilbert *were* secret lovers. She seems to think that he's as much in love with her as she is with him. She claims that he moved away from the parish to this place, so that the two of them could be together.'

'As if I would!' In his indignation Gilbert shot out both arms, dislodging his spectacles. Liz put out her hand to touch her husband's shoulder. He retrieved his glasses, returned her smile and put his own hand on top of hers.

Ellie felt a twinge of jealousy. As old married couples went, Gilbert and Liz were quite something, while now that Frank had gone . . .

Where had she put her handkerchief?

Liz said, 'Gilbert, dear, I know you wouldn't! But you really must learn to keep your hands to yourself in future.'

She was turning it into a joke, but undoubtedly she meant what she said. She turned to Ellie. 'Luckily the bishop had been talking to Gilbert about moving over here for, oh, a couple of months. We felt bad about not being able to tell our friends, but we had to keep it quiet till it was all settled. The previous incumbent died suddenly and the curate and two readers were making do. It's a thriving parish with lots going on — out-reach, Alpha courses, disciple courses, seminars. It's a great opportunity for Gilbert and he's just the man for the job. Oh, and by the way, Ellie, do congratulate him. He's got his book on modern saints accepted by a publisher!'

'Oh, how wonderful! Congratulations!'

'Yes, we're thrilled about everything, even though we miss some of our old friends. You in particular, of course.'

'Flatterer.'

'Truth,' said Gilbert, winking at her. 'We tried to ring you as soon as we knew we were moving. Then we heard on the grapevine that you were tied up nursing the sick. The original plan was for us to move after Easter, but when the letters started coming, the bishop said we'd better get our skates on because that sort of thing escalates . . .'

'. . . and now,' said Liz, 'it's getting worse, which is why we need your help, Ellie. Last week Nora turned up here with a suitcase, hair all over the place, coat buttoned up wrong. I invited her in to wait for Gilbert. He was taking a confirmation class at the time. Nora got more and more agitated. Finally she dashed down to the church hall and broke in on the class, which luckily was just about to leave.'

Gilbert threw out both his arms again, reddening with embarrassment but trying to pass it off with a laugh. 'Consternation! She tried to kiss me . . .'

Liz said, 'I had followed, of course. Only to see her leaping at him, trying to get her arms round his neck.'

'Don't laugh,' said Gilbert. 'It really wasn't funny!'

Liz met Ellie's eyes. Both women spurted into laughter, quickly smothered. Gilbert was not a handsome man, though some considered his profile aristocratic. He was also very tall and thin, while Nora was under average height.

Liz shook her head. 'It's tragic, really. There's nothing new about maiden ladies of an uncertain age falling for the vicar. Very Victorian melodrama. We were sorry for her at first. But now . . .'

Gilbert put his hand on his wife's knee. 'Let's keep the record straight. Ages ago you said the way she was acting wasn't healthy, but I thought I knew the difference between her being somewhat dependent on me and paranoia.'

Ellie jerked upright. 'You think she's paranoid?'

Liz pulled a face. 'She was furious when I tried to pull her off Gilbert. She was not reasonable.'

'And you want me to deal with her in case she causes another scandal,' said Ellie. 'How?'

'You'll think of something,' said Gilbert.

* * *

A nasty, cold, wet Monday morning. The white van drew up in a side street while the driver consulted his A-to-Z map. He was in his mid-twenties, with a close thatch of dark hair, wearing paint-stained overalls.

Satisfied that he wasn't far off his destination, he opened the back of the van and scrabbled around for one particular half-empty tin of paint. He levered off the lid to double-check the colour. No good wasting paint he could use again.

He hoped there wouldn't be much security at the entrance to the flats, but if there was, he would ring the bells until he found someone who would let him in. He'd say he was delivering a package.

Which he was, in a way.

* * *

Ellie decided that this was the sort of morning when it would be easy to fall into a depression if you didn't turn on all the lights and bump up the central heating. Or perhaps go out for coffee with a friend.

Instead, she stood outside the front door of the flats in which Nora lived and rang the bell on the intercom beside the organist's name. The front door remained firmly shut, and no one answered her ring. She waited. Then she rang again.

Perhaps Nora was out. Ellie wished herself elsewhere, preferably a long way away. How much longer should she give it?

She thought of all the pleasant things she could be doing, such as shopping for some new clothes. Roy Bartrick was taking her out to dinner that evening. What a nice man he was. She wouldn't normally have accepted a dinner invitation from a stranger so early in their acquaintance, but he had said he needed to tap her knowledge of the area for his work, so she had agreed.

Alternatively, she could be looking at catalogues for a conservatory, or eating chocolates and wallowing in a cosy crime novel from the library.

She wished she had put on a thicker woolly under her coat. It was cold and draughty out here. She found the exterior of the flats repellent, resembling as it did a land-locked ocean-going liner with its rounded corners and cavernous balconies. No doubt the block looked charming on a sunny day, but today it looked as if it were glowering down at passers-by. Ellie thought it typical of Frank's Aunt Drusilla to own property in a building which glowered at you.

She wondered if a block of flats could really take on the personality of its owner, as some houses did. If so, Ellie thought she rather fancied a country cottage with roses round the door and a decent patch of good earth for growing vegetables. With all mod cons inside, of course — including central heating, and perhaps a garage for the car which she was one day going to learn how to drive.

She really must get on with her driving lessons. The first one before Christmas had been a bit of a nightmare.

The instructor was rather too obviously of the opinion that a woman of her age would never pass the test. Daunting, that.

On second thoughts, scrub the cottage. What would she do living in the country miles from the nearest shop, without being able to drive? Or even when she did learn to drive, come to think of it?

She rang the bell again. She had enjoyed her evening with Gilbert and Liz. She had been amused but a little saddened that Gilbert was already beginning to look back on the years at his old church without regret.

Early that Monday morning Ellie had taken herself back to her own house by minicab, noting as she walked down the drive to her front door that her garden could do with a bit of a tidy up. She had looked to see if her young neighbours Kate and Armand were at home. No, no car outside. No lights inside. She hoped everything was all right there. It was not an easy-going marriage.

Ellie felt rebellious. Why should she sort out Gilbert's problems for him? Or Nora's, for that matter. The only interesting thing in the post was a note from Roy asking her out to dinner that evening at the hotel where he was staying temporarily. She had phoned a message through to the hotel, accepting.

She had put a load of washing in the machine, checked what food she had in, made a shopping list, paid some bills, done a little dusting, rubbed up the silver. She decided she was not going to visit Nora. No. But she would ring her solicitor, Bill Weatherspoon, and check how far he'd got with the renewal of Nora's lease on the flat.

When first consulted, Bill had not held out much hope of Aunt Drusilla performing such an uncharacteristic act of charity as renewing Nora's lease on favourable terms. Yet he had promised that, if the deal fell through, he would help the organist find somewhere else to live.

So Ellie had rung Bill's office to find out what the state of play was. Unfortunately, it appeared that Bill was away at some conference or other and his secretary had been unhelpful, disclaiming any knowledge of the case.

Bother. It meant that Ellie couldn't put off action herself.

Well, she could, of course. It wasn't her fault that Nora was in such a state. But Ellie couldn't quite still a pang of guilt. She had known that Nora was in trouble before Christmas. She had asked Bill to do something about it, but she hadn't made sure that anything had been done. Truth to tell, she had forgotten all about Nora while she was up north with Diana. Also, Gilbert's description of Nora as 'gone round the twist' kept bobbing up in her mind.

* * *

Ellie rang the bell again. She'd give it just five minutes more.

A middle-aged woman bounced up the steps to the front door of the flats, taking out her key. A resident, obviously. Her hair, clothes, fingernails and make-up were all rather too bright for Ellie's taste, but she looked good-natured.

Ellie gestured towards Nora's name on the intercom. 'Do you happen to know if your neighbour is in?'

'I expect so. She lives on the same landing as me. Doesn't go out much nowadays. Come on up and see if you can get through to her upstairs.'

On the third floor she tried again. Still no reply. The helpful neighbour pounded on Nora's door, shouting, 'Open up, Nora! It's me! You've got a visitor!'

Nora's door opened on the chain just as a telephone rang in the flat opposite. With a muttered excuse, the neighbour left Ellie to it.

'Nora?' said Ellie. 'It's only me, Ellie Quicke. May I come in for a moment?' The door began to close again. 'I've a message for you from Gilbert.'

Nora took the chain off and opened the door wide enough to let Ellie slide in. Then she put the chain on again. More than a little paranoid, perhaps?

Nora led the way into a large sitting room which should — if Ellie's calculations were correct — overlook the river.

Yet the curtains were still drawn and the only light came from a dim table lamp.

The room smelt of old man. How long was it since Nora's father had died? Surely the smell should have abated by now? It was better further into the room. A window was open somewhere, blowing in cold air off the river.

Ellie said brightly, 'It's awfully dark in here, isn't it! Shall I open the curtains?'

Without waiting for a reply, she drew back the curtains to let in the grey morning light. Nora put up her hands to shield her eyes. She was wearing a man's shabby grey dressing gown that trailed on the floor behind her. Everything in the room was either grey or brown, or a mixture of both. Nora's straggling, greyish hair looked as if it hadn't been washed for a long time, and from the unhealthy look of her skin, Ellie could well believe that Nora hadn't been out of the flat for days.

Not allowing herself to feel distaste, Ellie took Nora's hand and led her to an overstuffed, greyish settee covered with an assortment of crocheted blankets. Ellie tried not to think about the origin of the aroma that emanated from the upholstery as they sat down. Possibly this was where Nora's father had spent his final days.

'Nora, when did you last have a square meal?'

Red-lidded eyes, red-tipped nose. The eyes watched Ellie as the hands clutched at the buttons on her dressing gown. 'Gilbert sent you?'

'Both Gilbert and Liz are very worried about you,' said Ellie, her voice seeming far too loud and positive in these faded surroundings. This is Miss Havisham all over again, she thought. Rejected as a lover, double-locked into her flat.

'You've seen him?' The faded eyes flared into life. The mouth wavered into a smile. 'Oh, thank God! He hasn't forgotten me! When will he be here?' Her hands left the buttons and clutched at Ellie. The fingernails were clawlike, none too clean.

'No, dear, no.' Ellie tried to free herself but failed. She told herself to keep very calm. 'Listen. Gilbert and Liz asked me over to their new place last night. They're both concerned about you. They asked me to come to see you—'

'It's all right, I understand!' Nora gabbled, all feverish gaiety. 'He can't speak in front of . . . her! He's given you a letter for me, hasn't he?'

'No. Listen to me, Nora. You're not well. Who's your doctor?'

'I don't need to see the doctor again. She gave me some pills. They don't help. It's the waiting, you see.' Nora began to cry.

Ellie extricated herself, saying she'd make a cup of tea.

The kitchen was not in much better state than the sitting room. Apparently Nora had been living on bread and cheese for some time, leaving the loaf and the cheese out on the table between meals. A couple of cracked saucers on the floor hinted at the presence of a cat. A cockroach lurked by the cooker. Ellie shuddered, but told herself that she was a lot larger than the cockroach and she would not let herself be intimidated by it.

Kettle. Tea. A two-pint bottle of milk in the otherwise bare fridge. No sugar. Wash two stained mugs, very carefully. Make the tea. Ignore the cockroach. Where's the cat? Do cats eat cockroaches?

There was some junk mail on the table. And a lilac-coloured piece of paper with a message on it in wobbly, back-slanting capital letters. Ellie read it in appalled fascination. Across the top was written one word,

SLUT!

And then,

> *YOU'VE LOST HIM HIS JOB,*
> *SO HE DOESN'T WANT YOU ANYMORE.*

'You've seen it, have you?' said Nora, reappearing.

Ellie nodded. It was one thing hearing about poison-pen letters, but quite another reading them. She felt sick.

'There are lots more. I used to tear them up and flush them down the loo, but I don't bother now. The papers are such pretty colours. All colours of the rainbow. Blue and red and green. There's a yellow one, too, somewhere.' Nora sounded detached, as if the letters had been sent to someone else.

'Nora, dear, this is awful. You must take them to the police. They'll soon find out who's doing this.'

Nora almost smiled. 'I would never do that. Gilbert mustn't have his name dragged into the papers.' She took a mug of tea, cradling it in her hands. 'You've got a message for me from Gilbert?'

Her eyes begged for comfort, but Ellie had none to give. 'He's really worried about you. He asked me to see you, to find out what's going on with the flat and you having to move.'

'No letter?'

Ellie shook her head. 'Nora, you know there's not going to be a letter. Gilbert and Liz have done all they can for you.'

Nora whimpered. She dived back into the hallway and opened a door. Into a bedroom? The bathroom? Ellie could hear Nora blowing her nose. She also heard a strange thump from the hallway, and wondered if Nora had heard it, too. It sounded as if someone was at the front door, but Nora made no move to open it.

Ellie shrugged and took the two mugs through into the sitting room. Putting them down, she nearly spilt the contents. Sitting on the back of a high armchair was a long-legged ginger cat. The cat inspected Ellie with golden eyes. Then it disappeared.

Ellie sat down on the nearest chair. *Alice in Wonderland*, she thought. The Cheshire Cat. Then she felt smooth, warm fur brush against her legs from left to right, and a poker-stiff tail tickled her hand.

'Oh, good. Midge has come back. I was getting worried about him.' Nora was looking almost normal. She had discarded the dressing gown, pulled on a sand-coloured jumper and skirt, and run a comb through her hair.

Ellie queried the cat's name. 'Midge?'

22

Cats are given unsuitable names from time to time, but this was ridiculous. Tiger, Killer or Cheetah would have been more appropriate for a cat which looked as if it could take Olympic records in its stride. She moved her feet as Midge sniffed over her shoes. Had she stepped in something inappropriate on the way?

'His previous owners called him Midge. They'd had him from a kitten, you see, when he was always dancing about, trying to catch flies.'

Nora picked up her tea and sipped it. Her voice was so matter of fact that you wouldn't have suspected anything was wrong with her, except for the way she clutched her mug with tense, cramped hands. She even pulled back her lips in an effort to smile. It was not a great success.

'You see, when Daddy died, I was lonely. Gilbert suggested I get a little dog to make me go out for walkies. Daddy didn't like animals around the place. He said they smelt. I went down to the Pet Rescue place, who needed to find a home for Midge, urgently. Like me, he'd always lived in a flat, but his people said he was very clean. Which he is. But I have to leave a window open for him all the time.' Her voice trailed away.

That explained the open window.

Midge was now weaving back and forth around Ellie's legs, purring. He had a very loud purr. Ellie had never had much to do with cats and didn't think she liked them. She tried to bat him away.

Nora said, 'Pardon?' and jerked back to attention. 'Midge used to get out and kill birds, you see. Pigeons. Most people don't mind, but these were racing pigeons. The owner said he'd sue if Midge wasn't got rid of. So I took him and it's true, he does kill things. I see him from my window. But he doesn't bring them back in.'

Ellie squeaked as Midge decided he'd now like to try her lap. He dared her to turf him off, treading on her skirt, turning round and round before settling down. Would he scratch her if she tipped him off? He looked very determined.

Nora watched without jealousy. 'He likes you. That's good, isn't it . . .' Her voice trailed away again.

Ellie tried surreptitiously to shift the cat, who adhered. He was quite a weight. 'Nora, about the flat?'

'The flat? Oh. Yes. Well, the lease is up at the end of January.'

'I asked Mr Weatherspoon to see if he could get the lease renewed for you.'

'Is that your solicitor? I think he came round to see me. He said he'd tried to get the lease renewed, but it was no good. He asked if I had any family or friends who would help me. I told him I have a half-brother somewhere, but we've never met. He wrote after Daddy died, hoping he'd been left some money. I had to laugh. He wanted me to help him financially! I wrote and told him, Daddy's pension died with him, and all I've got left is . . .'

She gestured around the room. 'Mr Weatherspoon wanted to know if I needed any help putting in for a council flat, but I couldn't do that. No, I really couldn't. Then he said, hadn't I got any friends I could go to? I said I'd ask around. He said he'd send me a list of other flats I might rent, but I don't think he has. It doesn't really matter. Not now.'

'Nora, you really mustn't expect Gilbert to help you any more. He will always be your friend, but you mustn't trade on his kindness any longer.'

Nora's face broke up. Ellie looked away. She felt as if she were hitting a small child, but somehow she had to get Nora to face reality.

Ellie found that a bullet-head was pushing itself under her hand. Midge wanted to be stroked. Agitated, Ellie removed her hand. She tried to make herself into an uncomfortable seat for Midge. Midge didn't seem to notice. Many years ago, when Diana was seven or eight, she had asked for a kitten, but Frank had been slightly asthmatic so it had been out of the question.

Ellie tilted forward on the chair. The cat gave her an indignant look and removed himself. One moment he was there, and the next he was up on the windowsill. Ellie brushed hairs off her lap — that was another reason why Frank had vetoed having a cat — and stood up.

'Nora, I meant to come to see you immediately after Christmas, but I got held up at Diana's. I asked Aunt Drusilla to see if she could get something sorted out for you, but . . .'

'I've spoken to her. We came to an understanding. Don't worry about me,' said Nora, gazing into space again. 'I've made my own arrangements.'

'You have?' Ellie looked around the room, which was filled with heavy, unfashionable furniture, glass-fronted bookcases filled with old-fashioned books, china cabinets, and an eight-seater dining room set. Most of it must have been bought pre-war, and it didn't look as if anything had been shifted since it was first installed. It was going to be quite a job to pack all that lot up.

Presumably Nora had made arrangements to go to live with a friend. Ellie hoped the friend had a capacious room to let, because this lot took up a lot of space. 'Do you need the name of a good removals firm?'

'I told you, everything's arranged.'

'That's all right, then.'

Nora was gazing into space again. The cat had disappeared. Ellie hoped it was chasing cockroaches, but perhaps that was too much to expect.

'I'll be on my way, then.'

Nora nodded, but didn't get up. Ellie wrestled the chain off the door and let herself out with relief. It was so much lighter on the landing.

She paused, frowning. Nora's front door, which had been a uniform grungy brown when Ellie arrived, was now splashed across with vivid lilac paint. Ellie stared at it. She looked across the landing to the neighbouring flat, but the door there was plain brown.

So she *had* heard someone at the front door when she'd been in the kitchen. This was persecution indeed.

Ellie rang Nora's bell again. And again. And again. No reply. What ought she to do? Leave it to Nora to sort out? Inform the police? Yes, but Nora had said she didn't want the police involved . . .

Ellie rang again. Still no reply.

Turning to go, Ellie almost fell over a cardboard shoe-box which had been left at the top of the stairs. It had Nora's name on it, printed in bold capital letters. Well, Nora would have to come out sometime. She would see it then.

Ellie made for the stairs, feeling that she ought to have been clever enough to think of something constructive to do about the paint. Frank would have known what to do, she was sure of that. She stifled a sigh. She did miss him. He had been so capable, had always taken charge in difficult situations. It was three months ago to the day since he died.

Well, he was gone and she was left to make the best of it. She tried to put Nora's problems out of her mind as she descended the stairs. Without success. It was going to take some experienced removals men to shift all that furniture down three flights of stairs.

She must make a list of what she needed to do in the next couple of days. And it was choir practice tonight. Mustn't miss that, especially since she'd not been for some weeks. She'd told Roy she wouldn't be free till eight o'clock.

She felt slight unease at the thought of going out to dinner with Roy. A nice man, of course, but what would the neighbours say? She thought her own particular neighbours were too intelligent to misunderstand her, but she was not so sure about others in her circle. Not everyone who went to church was so discerning.

She braced herself against the cold wind in the street. Forget chattering tongues. Do something you want to do, for a change. Look forward, not back. What should she wear? Her best cream and blue jersey suit, perhaps? Or the dark blue velvet that Frank had always liked so much?

CHAPTER THREE

Choir practice and an evening out with a personable man were to have been the high points of Ellie's week, and neither was an unalloyed delight. The scoutmaster took choir practice for Nora and spent more time talking at them than letting them sing. Infuriating. And although Roy was amusing and the food was good, he seemed to suffer from the same defect as the scoutmaster, being a good talker and a bad listener. On both occasions Ellie had to suppress a yawn.

About halfway through the evening, Ellie realized that she was being looked at by Roy as if she were a blonde bimbo, instead of a widow in her early fifties. This flustered her at first. Then it amused her. Then she was annoyed, and finally amused all over again.

Well, who would have thought it? At her age! What would Frank have said? She made a mental note not to be caught alone with Roy.

After those two pieces of excitement, it was back to the daily round. When you've been away for a time, household jobs crowd in on you — not to mention clearing up in the garden. Ellie made lists, cleaned and dusted, shopped for food, and changed library books.

A considerable amount of mail needed answering, and she nerved herself to do this on Frank's all-singing, all-dancing computer — with variable success. Letters would keep running themselves off upside down and on the wrong side of the paper.

She persevered. The first time she managed to print off a letter which looked decent, she awarded herself a small sherry by way of congratulation.

She rang the driving school to book some more lessons and was given somebody else's cancellation dates — flu, you know, dear — to resume that week. She wasn't sure whether she was pleased or anxious about that. If she were to be absolutely honest with herself, the prospect of driving in London streets frightened her a lot. Perhaps she ought to take a herbal tranquillizer before her lessons.

Sometimes she missed Frank terribly.

Life would have been more bearable if she could have got out into the garden, but the weather continued to be foul. Even the boy Tod — who usually popped in to see her a couple of times a week — seemed to have deserted her.

She had stopped work at the charity shop after Frank died, partly because it had become increasingly difficult for her to work under their particular supervisor. This loud-voiced but inefficient lady — known to her staff as 'Madam' — had resented Ellie's popularity with the other volunteers. Ellie missed the structure that working in the shop had given to her life. She also missed the friends she had made there.

At least she could do something about that.

She called in at the charity shop, hoping that Madam would be out. She particularly wanted to see John, who was in charge of the books, and little Rose, who sorted clothes in the back room. Ellie's plan was to ask them to have lunch with her one day, but, although John was on the till, Madam was also in evidence.

Madam was not pleased to see Ellie. 'Well, just look who's condescended to visit us! Slumming, are we, Ellie?'

Ellie smiled and let the jibe pass. It was obviously not going to be possible to chat to her friends that day. She chose a couple of whodunits from the bookshelves, and paid for them.

'How are you?' John muttered, tendering change.

'All right,' she replied, also low-voiced. 'Would you and Rose like to come to lunch one day? Your wife, too, of course.'

'Love to. I'll ring you, right?' said John.

'What's that?' Madam's sharp nose intervened. 'An invitation to lunch. Oh my! Our Ellie has turned into a Lady Who Lunches!'

John rolled his eyes. Ellie made her escape, thankful that, even if she no longer had a job to go to, at least she didn't have to put up with Madam's pinpricks.

* * *

Late that night a woman in a hooded raincoat left her car on the corner of the road by the flats and walked through the drizzle, stalking one particular cat.

Cats are said to have nine lives. This particular ginger tom accepted one too many titbits. The figure in the raincoat watched as the cat arched its back and died.

She fitted a loop of wire around its neck, and lowered the corpse into a large plastic bag.

Balked by the security system on the front door of the flats, the woman hesitated. How was she going to get her present up to the flat? A group of four middle-aged people were descending the staircase after a convivial evening. The woman in the raincoat whipped herself and her burden around the corner of the flats.

Returning when the revellers had departed in their cars, the killer tried the front door again. It was firmly locked.

She abandoned her original idea of taking the present right up to the flat, and left it tied to the handle of the front door.

That would teach the evil slut!

* * *

Ellie was half-amused and half-annoyed by Roy Bartrick's pursuit of her. Dinner on Monday had been followed by the gift of a basket of hyacinths in bloom and an invitation to lunch on Friday.

As she explained to her young neighbour Kate on Wednesday evening, 'I only met him on Sunday. He took me out Monday night and wants to take me out Friday lunchtime, too. He says he'll take me to the new Holiday Inn restaurant. I'm flattered, of course. But also a bit, well, flustered. I feel like a heroine in a melodrama exclaiming, "Oh sir! This is so sudden!"'

Kate pushed back her mop of dark hair, trying and failing to hold back a giant sneeze. 'If I've caught another cold . . . !'

'Take zinc tablets. Frank always did when he thought he'd a cold coming.'

Ellie peeled potatoes with enthusiasm. Kate's husband Armand was out at a school function that evening, and the two women planned to eat an enormous, fatty, carbohydrate-stuffed meal to ward off the January blues.

'Sherry's nicer,' said Kate, stirring natural Greek yoghurt and double cream into blackberry puree. 'Go on about this Roy. Is he that smooth geezer that's been sending you flowers?'

Ellie went pink. 'Actually, it was only a basket of hyacinths. You've met him?'

'He knocked on my door. Got the number of the house wrong. I've met types like him before.'

Ellie frowned. 'What type do you mean?'

'Second-hand car salesmen.'

Ellie laughed, and knew her laughter sounded forced. 'Oh, really, Kate! Roy's an architect, taken early retirement, house in Surrey, was visiting relatives locally, came to church and that's where he met me.'

Kate added more sugar to the mix, and licked the spoon. 'He doesn't strike me as being a regular churchgoer. There's something too devil-may-care about him. A bit like Martin

Kemp playing the baddie. His Jaguar's four years old. Good suit, though. I bet he makes a reasonable living at it . . . selling second-hand cars, I mean.'

She laughed as Ellie threw a piece of potato peel at her.

'Seriously, though,' said Ellie, putting the potatoes on to boil and checking the chops cooking in the oven. 'What do you really think of him?'

'Seriously?' Kate refilled their glasses with sherry, and then tipped some into the dessert. 'How serious do you want to be?'

Ellie sighed. She was in a tangle about Roy. He had started off by saying he needed her advice on neighbourhood properties. Fine, as far as it went. But she couldn't be mistaken in thinking he was also sexually interested in her. She still wasn't sure how she felt about that. Most of the time she thought it was ridiculous, so soon after Frank's death.

On the other hand, she'd felt so bruised, so 'joggled', since Frank died, that any distraction was welcome, and she had to admit it was soothing to be appreciated by a personable man. She told herself that she had to build a new structure into her life, and if Roy wanted to take her out on a friendly basis, well, why not? Provided she kept it light.

Then again, he didn't half talk too much about himself. And too little about her. A long-term relationship was right out. She'd had enough of that sort of behaviour in the long years of her marriage to Frank.

Perhaps she would have told Kate all this, if only Kate hadn't been so rude about him. As it was, perversity took over.

'I must say, it's very pleasant to be taken out to dinner at a good restaurant and worry about which dress to wear, to take trouble with my hair and make-up. Roy is excellent company.'

'Mm.' Kate dipped her finger into her mix and licked it. 'I realize I ought to be pleased for you. And I suppose I am.'

'But?'

'Mm. A speck more sugar, I think. Shall I put the sprouts on?'

31

'But?'

'Dunno.' Kate sighed. 'A feeling. Feelings don't count, do they? "Give me the facts, ma'am." Where does that come from? What are the facts, Ellie? He says he's a widower. Is he? Or is he going through a messy divorce and looking for sympathetic company? What do the relatives say? Do we know them?'

'I don't think so. I got the impression they lived some distance away. He doesn't want to be a burden on them — I gather they're pretty ancient — so he's putting up at that big hotel opposite the tube station.'

'What's wrong with his house in Surrey?'

'He felt restless after his wife died, wanted a change. He took early retirement but accepted a roving commission from his firm to find new projects for development. After he'd visited his relatives, he drove around to get a feel of the area and spotted the potential for development of four or five big old houses around here. That's why he wanted my advice. How would the neighbourhood feel if a developer moved in? He's particularly interested in that big house opposite the church that's been empty for ever. This week he's been making enquiries about planning permission, etc. It makes it a lot easier if he's on the spot. It's all quite above board.'

Kate stretched out long limbs and yawned. 'If it were all above board, Ellie, you wouldn't be asking my advice.'

'I'm not asking your advice,' said Ellie, getting cross.

'Mm. You helped me through a bad patch when my darling hubbie was doing my head in last year . . .'

'Not to mention beating you up . . .'

'No, we don't mention that, nowadays. We're very, very careful about not referring to that, and he really is on his best behaviour.'

'Long may it last!' said Ellie in a sour tone.

Kate dimpled. 'Yes. Long may it last. And if it doesn't, I'll move out again and take him for every penny he's got in a let-it-all-hang-out divorce. As head of department in a high school, he can't afford that, can he? Not to mention that, with the bonuses I'm getting, I can buy him a top-of-the-range car

32

and treat us to expensive foreign holidays. So he's being very careful of my feelings — and my skin — at the moment.'

Both women laughed, because, although Armand had a wicked temper, there was no doubt that if it came to a battle of brains, he would lose out to Kate.

'Well, then,' said Kate. 'Your looking after me last year gives me the right to tell you to "Watch it". I don't trust smoothies. Shall I run a financial check on him for you?'

Ellie hesitated, sipping sherry. Kate was something in the City and it made sense to check on Roy's background, but it felt like spying, didn't it?

'That's tacky. Taking me out is just his way of passing the time while he's away from home. He's not close to his relatives. He's at a loose end . . . the weather's foul . . . no particular friends in the area . . . he'll be off again soon, I expect.'

'Meanwhile, you enjoy making your old friend the church warden, jealous?'

Ellie giggled. 'Poor Archie.'

'Ellie, you astonish me! Can it be that you actually enjoy having two men fight over you?'

'You think I'm being pursued by two separate men because I'm a reasonable cook and own my own house?'

'I wonder,' said Kate, in an unusually diffident tone, 'whether the news has got out somehow that you've been left very comfortably off?'

'Ouch,' said Ellie, sitting down with a bump. 'And here was I thinking it was for the sake of my blue eyes and sympathetic nature.'

'That too, I shouldn't wonder,' said Kate.

When Ellie had discovered that Frank had left her a small fortune, her solicitor had advised her not to tell anyone about it. But Bill Weatherspoon had been unavailable on so many occasions recently, that Ellie had asked Kate to help her with an investment which had fallen due.

So far as Ellie knew, no one but Bill and Kate were aware of her good fortune. Certainly not her greedy daughter

Diana. It was a horrid thought that perhaps Archie and Roy were asking her out just because she had money.

Ellie rallied. How could they possibly know? No, they couldn't. Archie had a good income and wanted a new wife to cuddle. As for Roy . . . no, the idea was absurd. He was interested in her, yes. But not for her money, because he didn't know about it. He hadn't tried to kiss her or anything like that. Yet.

She wouldn't have let him kiss her, anyway. It was too soon after Frank's death.

'A-a-a-choo!' Kate fumbled for a tissue.

'Feed a cold and starve a fever.' Ellie dished up.

* * *

Ellie did a little shopping every day in the Avenue, but every now and again Kate would put a large order through to Tesco's on the Internet for her. Loo paper, bottles of sherry, pasta and potatoes — anything too heavy or too bulky for Ellie to carry back easily.

Ellie was slowly, very slowly, coming to terms with Frank's word processor, but the Internet still frightened her and, as she didn't drive, this was the easiest way to get her supplies in.

The next order was delivered just before noon on Thursday. Ellie unpacked the bags, humming along to the radio. This in the freezer, that in the fridge. These in the cupboard. Have they forgotten the plain flour? No, it's here.

Something was not quite right, though.

She thought they'd forgotten the ice cream, but it was there after all. Everything checked out on the list. Ellie stood at the kitchen window and looked down her garden, across the alley and up towards the church.

The wind was getting up and it was still spitting with rain. The trees around the church were tossing around, reminding her of unpleasant Channel crossings before Eurostar came into being. Long live Eurostar.

There was a light on in the church.

Really?

She pressed her face close to the glass. It was a dark day. Yes, there was definitely a light on in the church.

She checked the clock. Noon. Thursday. There was a flower-arranging class at the church hall on Thursday mornings, which usually finished about now. Soon Mrs Dawes would come along the path by the church, into the alley, and turn right on her way up to her own little house.

It was none of Ellie's business. Perhaps Timid Timothy the curate was in the church practising for his next sermon. Or . . . who knew?

Thieves, perhaps? There'd been reports in the papers about thieves breaking into churches and stealing candlesticks, old tables, anything that wasn't actually nailed down.

Ellie thought about phoning the police. No, stupid. You couldn't phone the police just because there was a light on in the church. There could be a hundred good reasons why it was on.

She didn't have a key to the church, but Mrs Dawes did. And here came Mrs Dawes, head down, dark green windcheater over heavy coat, National Trust golfing umbrella buffeted by the wind.

Ellie seized her old gardening anorak and went down the steps into the garden to intercept Mrs Dawes. 'Mrs Dawes, am I being very stupid? There's a light on in the church. Have we got the workmen in again, or . . . ?'

Mrs Dawes turned, awkwardly manoeuvring the umbrella between herself and the wind. She looked back up at the church, her eyebrows twisting with the same anxiety which had prompted Ellie to take action.

'No,' she said, pulling her windcheater closer round her neck, and raising her voice to be heard over the wind and the rain. 'Nora was practising. I heard her at it earlier, when I went up to take the flower-arranging class. I expect she's gone home and forgotten to turn the light off.'

'That's not like her.'

Mrs Dawes shifted her bulk from one foot to the other. 'I'm not going into that church by myself. Finding one body there was bad enough.'

Ellie felt a tingle go down her spine. 'You think she's in there, dead?'

'Of course not. What an idea!'

'I haven't got any keys, or I'd check myself,' said Ellie, trying to feel as brave as she sounded. 'But I'll come in with you if you like.'

Ellie took Mrs Dawes's arm and steered her back up the path to the side door of the church. There the two women stopped to listen. No sound came from within.

Sighing, Mrs Dawes felt around in her pockets for a loaded keyring, selected one particular key and opened the door into the church. Still there was no sound.

Ellie went through into the nave. The light was on in the organ loft above and to one side of the altar, but nowhere else. 'Nora, is that you?'

A listening silence. A stealthy movement that might have been caused by someone sliding off the organist's bench.

A hard-breathing silence.

'Nora, it's me. Ellie Quicke. Are you all right? We saw the light on and wondered if you'd been taken ill or something.'

Nothing. Except for a hint of something dark in the corner of the organ loft. Ellie was not tall, but she could see that no one was seated at the organ. Perhaps Nora was hiding in the shadows beyond, where a door let onto the stairs?

But perhaps it wasn't Nora, after all. Perhaps it was some stranger who had broken into the church and . . .

'Keep away from me!'

That was Nora, all right. She sounded so like a frightened child that Ellie automatically assumed a motherly tone of voice. 'Nora, are you not feeling well? Shall I come up?'

'No!'

There was the scrabbling sound of someone climbing steep stairs. The short flight up to the organist's loft continued on and up to a narrow gallery under the roof.

Ellie darted back to Mrs Dawes. 'What do you think?'

Nora was crashing along the gallery, uttering little cries of distress.

'Nora, it's all right!' called Ellie. 'Mrs Dawes, do you think we should fetch the curate?'

'It's not the curate she wants.'

'No, but . . .'

Nora screamed. The sound resounded around the stone vaulting of the roof. A large and heavy object plummeted down from the gallery and landed in the pews with a thud which would echo in Ellie's mind for weeks.

'Oh, God!' whispered Mrs Dawes.

Ellie froze.

Nora was lying jack-knifed between two pews with her legs over the one in front and her head over the back of the one behind. She had lost a shoe. She had broken . . . Ellie didn't know how many bones, but she looked like a rag doll. And she was still conscious.

Nora mewed like a kitten, and tried to raise her head.

Mrs Dawes began to shake. Ellie said, 'Sit down, Mrs Dawes. Don't look. I'll phone for an ambulance.'

'Don't you dare leave me here with her! I'll go. You stay with her.'

'Can you manage? My back door's open. You know where—'

'Yes. Oh, my God!'

On shaking legs, Mrs Dawes fumbled her way out of the church.

Ellie would have given anything to have followed her. This is not real, she thought. In a moment I'll wake up. She forced herself to touch Nora, to brush the hair out of her eyes.

'Hold on. Mrs Dawes has gone for help.'

Nora's eyes wandered around the church, perhaps only half-aware of her surroundings. Perhaps saying goodbye to a place in which she had been someone of importance, the church where Gilbert had befriended her. The pallid lips moved.

'What is it?' said Ellie, bending closer.

'It was taking too long . . . I didn't think it would take so long . . .'

'What would, Nora?'

'. . . dying . . .'

So she had meant to jump, thought Ellie. She had meant to kill herself.

This is terrible. Dear Lord Jesus, help her. Help me to say the right thing. The poor, deluded creature.

How much longer would the ambulance be?

Nora's lips moved and again Ellie bent to listen. 'I wanted you to have Midge, but they killed him, you know.'

Rambling, thought Ellie.

Nora closed her eyes.

The old building waited. Ellie imagined that it was looking down on them, holding them safe, saying that it had seen worse than this in its hundred-odd years of life, and that this too would pass.

The ambulance team arrived with a clatter of normality. The paramedics gave Nora oxygen, immobilized her on a board and took her away. They asked Ellie if she wanted to go with them. Mrs Dawes was nowhere to be seen.

Ellie recollected that her own house was open, that she had only a light anorak on to stave off the cold, that she was shivering, thirsty, and had a headache coming on. She also realized that someone was going to have to turn off the lights and lock up the church. And tell Gilbert. No, tell the curate. Both.

'I'll lock up here, get my handbag, and come along as soon as I can.'

She climbed the stairs to the organ loft, feeling stiff and unwell. Nora's bunch of church keys and her handbag were lying on the bench. The handbag was open and inside was a large white envelope addressed to 'The Coroner'.

A suicide note?

Now what? The police?

But no. Nora wasn't dead yet. Perhaps she was not badly injured, after all. Suppose she recovered. She would be given treatment for her depression, and as soon as she felt better, she would want to tear up the letter. It would be best to take the handbag to the hospital, and leave it with Nora.

* * *

Ellie's little house was a haven of warmth and light. Mrs Dawes was in the living room, with a glass of sherry.

'Thought you wouldn't mind my helping myself. I saw the ambulance team carry her off.'

'Good idea.' Ellie poured one for herself. 'I've got her handbag here. I'll take it along once I've got warm again.'

Mrs Dawes slurped sherry. Poured herself a second glass. 'Stupid girl! Couldn't even kill herself neatly. Mark my words, she did it this way to cause the maximum trouble for Gilbert.'

Ellie thought of the letter in Nora's handbag. 'She isn't dead yet. Perhaps she'll be all right.'

'If she thinks that trying to kill herself will bring Gilbert running to her bedside . . .'

'Won't it?'

Mrs Dawes gulped more sherry. 'Well, what I say is, that it ought not to. But there, he's that kind-hearted, he might . . . drat the woman!'

Ellie tipped the last of the bottle into her own glass.

* * *

Sitting in Casualty, Ellie wondered how the nurses could be so cheerful. She looked at her watch for the umpteenth time and thought that if she drank any more coffee from the machine, she'd be sick. And then the nurses would have to look after her, as well.

Eight o'clock. Nine o'clock. One of the nurses approached her.

'You were waiting for your friend? May I have a word? The paramedics say she was conscious and talking when they found her, but she's drifted off and we're having difficulty rousing her. In the ambulance she said something about not wanting to be pumped out. Do you know if she's taken something? The injuries from her fall are severe, but if she's taken something as well, then . . . is that her handbag?'

Ellie guessed what this meant. 'Oh dear. She has been under a lot of stress lately.'

Nora's handbag was large, scuffed, smelling of menthol. It bulged with the detritus of a solitary, unhappy life. The envelope gleamed white amid a chaos of unpaid bills, tissues, a couple more poison-pen notes written in capital letters on coloured paper, two bunches of keys, cough sweets, a make-up pouch with a torn plastic cover, pencils, rubbers, hair grips, a packet of Rennies, and an empty packet that had once contained paracetamol.

The nurse pulled out the envelope, read the superscription and sighed. She weighed the empty packet of paracetamol in her hand. 'If she's taken more than a couple of these . . .'

'Can't you pump her out?'

'It depends how long ago she took them. Hasn't she any relatives?'

'None, now. Look, I'll have to go home. I'll leave you my phone number in case anything happens. But I'll ring later, anyway.'

CHAPTER FOUR

Returning from the hospital, Ellie regretted all over again that she had never learned to drive when she was young. Frank hadn't thought she would be capable of learning and had discouraged her from doing so, but since his death, Kate next door had encouraged Ellie to have a go. Ellie was trying — with limited success. But for the time being it was back to minicabs.

She thought how lovely it would be to find the house all lit up with her dear Frank back from work, fussing about when his supper would be ready. Instead the house was shut up and dark, and none too warm.

The answerphone light was winking. It was Thursday, so it would be a message from her daughter Diana, of course. It would be, 'Mother, where are you? Why aren't you there to answer the phone when I take the trouble to ring you?' Or something similar.

Wearily Ellie listened to the predictable message and phoned Diana back.

'Mother, where have you been? I do have to go out tonight, you know!'

'At the hospital, dear. Our organist Nora — you remember her? — fell from the gallery at the church and landed up in hospital. I took her handbag in and waited, but she hasn't regained consciousness and they very much fear . . .'

'Oh, mother. You're always fussing around some lame duck or other, when I need to talk to you.' A heavy sigh. 'I don't know how we're going to keep up with the mortgage. If only you would help . . .'

Ellie stiffened. 'Now, Diana, we've been over that several times. You'll just have to sell that big place and get something that you can afford.'

'Think how bad that would look! Besides, we wouldn't need to, if Stewart would only pull his finger out. I've been on and on at him to ask for a raise at work, and . . .'

Ellie thought, but did not say, that Diana had chosen Stewart because she could bully him. Poor Stewart. Ellie was fond of her rather stolid son-in-law.

'. . . and then baby Frank is still not himself. Stewart would keep getting up in the night to see to him . . .'

Bet *you* didn't! thought Ellie. And immediately felt ashamed of herself.

'. . . and I do wish you lived nearer, mother. At times like these . . .'

You only want me, thought Ellie, when I can be of use to you. I wish it weren't so, but it is. More's the pity.

'. . . sometimes I feel so desperate!'

Ellie stiffened her backbone. This was emotional blackmail, and she would not respond.

Eventually Diana rang off. Ellie sat there, thinking about poor Nora. No kith or kin. No one to mourn her loss. Except, hadn't there been a long-lost brother — no, half-brother — who'd written asking for money after Nora's father died? Someone on the dole, probably. No help there.

* * *

In the morning Ellie phoned the hospital. They said Nora was about the same, but the prognosis was not good. She rang Gilbert. He was out and so was Liz, so Ellie left a message with their answering service.

She also rang Timothy the curate and told him what had happened. Timothy sounded annoyed that Nora should have tried to commit suicide in 'his' church. He said he'd try to make room in his busy schedule to visit her in hospital later on. He also said that as soon as he could find time, he wanted to have a quiet word with Ellie about something.

Ellie said, 'Of course!' She hoped he wasn't going to ask her to take on some time-consuming job for the church. She rather feared he might. Well, so long as it didn't require her to use Frank's word processor, she would see what she could do.

As she cradled the phone, Ellie remembered Nora saying, 'It was taking too long.' Perhaps Nora had intended to commit suicide by taking too many paracetamol tablets, but death hadn't come quickly enough. When Ellie and Mrs Dawes had found Nora in the church, the poor woman must have feared being taken to hospital and pumped out. And so she had jumped. 'It was taking too long . . .'

Ellie felt guilty. She ought to have realized what Nora had meant when she said she'd made her own arrangements. The phone rang, making Ellie jump.

'Ellie, is that you?' A harsh voice accustomed to striking terror into inferiors — and Aunt Drusilla Quicke considered almost everyone else an inferior. Ellie had been counting herself fortunate that she had not heard from her husband's aunt for some time. A phone call from her meant she wanted something — now!

'Ellie, I wish to see you. Now!'

Ellie tried to make excuses. 'It's raining and I think I have a cold coming . . .'

'Take a cab. You can afford it.' The phone was replaced.

It would be more wearing to ring back and argue than to go. Besides, Ellie thought she might — if she were brave enough — do something to soften Aunt Drusilla's stance towards Nora. So she took a cab.

As usual she felt depressed at the sight of the dense laurel shrubs that lined the semicircular driveway. The house itself was pure Disney, she thought. Victorian Gothic, turrets and all. Bracing herself, she mounted the slightly tatty stone steps under the peeling stucco of the porch and rang the doorbell.

Remember that you own this house, she told herself, and you could turn Aunt Drusilla out if you wished! To which a small voice replied, Ah, but you wouldn't dare, would you?

Ellie was let into the house by the usual scared-looking cleaner. She tried not to slip as she skated across the polished wooden floor of the hall. How on earth did the elderly Aunt Drusilla manage not to fall and break a leg on that surface? The sitting room looked cavernous on that dark morning, despite the fact that its tall windows overlooked the severely trimmed garden at the back of the house. Aunt Drusilla was enthroned in her usual high-backed armchair, with a luxurious fur rug over her knees. Hot air billowed from the efficient central heating.

Ellie bent to kiss the air a couple of inches from the old woman's paper-thin cheek. 'How are you, Aunt Drusilla?'

'None the better for being kept waiting. I see you've put on weight.'

Bone china coffee cups were laid out on a tray with a cafetiere and kettle nearby. Ellie's first task was to make some coffee and place it on a pie-crust occasional table at Aunt Drusilla's elbow.

Aunt Drusilla sipped, observed that Ellie had never been any good at making coffee, and then got down to business.

'I have received a most peculiar phone call about a cat from one of my tenants at the flats. I can't possibly go down there in this weather and the estate agent who manages the property for me is unfortunately away — on a Caribbean cruise, if you please! He has no business taking time off and leaving that flat still fully furnished. But there it is, you can't trust anyone nowadays.'

Ellie sighed, knowing that whatever it was that was bothering Aunt Drusilla, it was about to be dumped in her lap, and she would probably agree to do it. Frank had been brought up by his aunt after his mother's early death, and he had expected his young wife Ellie to jump to the old lady's bidding, too.

Ellie had obliged, believing — as everyone else did — that the old lady was penniless and dependent on their charity.

Frank had discovered, only a short time before he died, that Aunt Drusilla had squirrelled enough money away over the years to purchase, one by one, the block of flats in which Nora lived. What a shock that had been! Since then, Ellie had tried to stop being a doormat to the old bat. Without much success.

Ellie leaned back in her uncomfortable but no doubt valuable antique chair and wondered if Aunt Drusilla felt any guilt over what had happened to Nora. Probably not, she thought. She's as likely to feel guilt as Attila the Hun.

Aunt Drusilla said, 'Pay attention, girl!'

At just turned fifty, Ellie very much disliked being called a girl. Aunt Drusilla probably knew it, too.

'I'm listening. What was that about a cat?'

'How on earth should I know? One of my tenants at the flats — Mrs Bowles, divorced but with excellent alimony — rang me to say she is flying to Australia on holiday tomorrow and wants to know what I want done with her next-door neighbour's cat, seeing as how that shiftless woman has ended up in hospital, and she, Mrs Bowles, will not be there to feed it any longer. Mrs Bowles is, of course, perfectly aware that there is a clause in her lease forbidding the keeping of pets.'

Ellie remembered the long-legged Midge, the cat Nora had adopted after her father's death. She said, 'Nora did take in a stray cat, but it got killed. I expect it's another stray. Mrs Bowles had better take it to Cat Rescue or something.'

'Of course she should, but she seems to think *I* should give it a home. Go down there, get the keys off Mrs Bowles — who seems to have acquired a set purely in order to look after this stray, if you please — take the cat to the vet, and have it put down. And don't send the bill to me. Send it to the vicar who caused all the trouble in the first place.'

Ellie bit back the words, 'Oh no, he didn't.' Arguing with Aunt Drusilla would be as effective as spitting in the face of a tornado.

Aunt Drusilla continued, 'Now, since you're having to go there anyway, I've arranged for two antique dealers to be at the flat, one at eleven o'clock sharp and one at twelve, to value the furniture. Once I have their written quotes and have decided which one to accept, they will arrange with you to collect the best pieces. After that you can send in the house clearance people. The flat has to be ready for new tenants in three weeks' time. Between now and then it will have to be emptied, professionally cleaned and redecorated.'

Ellie put a hand to her forehead. 'Aunt Drusilla, you can't do this. Nora is gravely ill . . .'

'Don't tell me what I can and can't do. I haven't had a penny in rent for the last nine months. It's all perfectly legal. I've been through the small claims court and obtained judgement and costs in my favour. My solicitor informed the woman that I would have to send the bailiffs in if she did not pay up, and what did she do? She telephoned me, saying that she was leaving this week and that I could take all her furniture and books in lieu of what she owed me, if I agreed to pay off the gas, electricity and telephone people for her. I told her to put her offer in writing and enclose all the outstanding bills, but I haven't received them yet. You'd better look for them when you go there.

'I imagine she's arranged some accommodation for herself with the council. She can go straight there when she leaves hospital. Meanwhile, I need to turn that flat round and put some more tenants in. I will, of course, let the woman have any balance over after I've cleared her debts.'

I bet there won't be much over, thought Ellie. Aloud, she said, 'Can't you wait till she gets out of hospital?'

'No, I can't. Now Ellie, I don't suppose there is anything there of much value, but I am relying on you to see that I am not cheated. By rights, everything there belongs to me, but I am not made of cast iron . . .'

Aren't you? thought Ellie, suppressing hysteria.

'. . . and you may arrange to have her clothes and the odd item of sentimental value put in storage for her.'

'Aunt Drusilla, don't you care that she tried to commit suicide?'

A snort. 'Taking the coward's way out. Just like her father.'

'What?'

'Don't forget, the valuers will be there at eleven and twelve o'clock today. And get rid of that cat. See yourself out.'

Ellie felt like telling the old . . . bat to stuff herself. But then what? Aunt Drusilla would find someone else to do the dirty work, someone who wouldn't take care to preserve Nora's clothes and intimate possessions. No, it would be best if Ellie did it, but how she hated the task.

She was now on a tight schedule. She was not dressed warmly enough for hanging around in a cold flat, so she would have to go home to change first. Rather daringly, she used the phone in Aunt Drusilla's hall to call a taxi.

Back home, she asked the taxi to wait while she pulled on her thickest winter coat and warm boots. Scooping the post off the mat, she chucked the letters at the table to be looked at later. One fell to the floor — a large white envelope, addressed to her, in Nora's writing.

Ellie tore it open. The writing sloped all over the place, but was easy enough to read.

. . . because everything I touch turns to evil. If I hadn't taken Midge in, he'd have survived. If I hadn't loved Gilbert, he'd still be with us. And now I've got cancer and I can't carry on.

I took the pills after you told me Gilbert didn't want anything else to do with me. I was going to wait a while then tell him what I'd done, give him a good scare, make him acknowledge his true feelings for me. And then I would let them pump me out. But after I heard about the cancer and Midge was killed I decided it was best if I died.

Miss Quicke is going to sell everything from the flat to pay off my debts. I promised to send her all the bills but I haven't got a big enough envelope so I left the papers in my father's briefcase under his bed. The woman who lives opposite — for lady I will not call her — has keys to the flat. Will you get the papers and send them to Miss Quicke for me? You're the only one who's been kind to me. I'd like you to have my mother's pearls, if Miss Quicke doesn't need them. They're in the top drawer of my dressing table.

The tablets take some days to work, I gather. I don't know how many, but it shouldn't be much longer now. I did think of dropping this letter through your door, but then you might try to save me, so I'll put it in the post on my way to church, and you won't get it till I'm gone. I want to play the organ one last time.

God forgive me.

Ellie found a tissue and had a good blow.

Oh misery. I ought to have helped her, but I didn't realize how bad things were. Ten o'clock. I must hurry. Dear Lord Jesus, look after poor, unhappy Nora, please . . .

Just as she was about to leave, the phone rang. It was Roy wanting to confirm their lunch arrangements. She had forgotten all about it. No time now to fetch her skirt from the cleaners or sew on new buttons. 'I'm so sorry, Roy. I wish I could, but . . .' Ellie explained what had happened.

Roy was sympathetic. 'My dear, how dreadful for you. Can't you get someone else to do the dirty work?'

'How can I? Aunt Drusilla wants her pound of flesh, but at least I can rescue Nora's clothes. Also, Nora's told me where she left some important papers and . . . oh dear, I feel so guilty . . .'

'No need. Listen, I've got a couple of phone calls to make and then I'll meet you there, give you a hand with the valuers. We don't want them pulling the wool over your eyes, do we? And then we can go out to lunch, a bit late, but it will blow the cobwebs away. What do you think?'

'Bless you, Roy! The flat is down by the river . . .'

Once in the taxi again, she tried to recover her sense of humour. Doing something for Nora — even such a nasty job as this — would assuage the feelings of guilt which still hung around her. That letter! Ellie could quite understand that to hear you had cancer on top of everything else would push you over the edge.

Some householders had planted up their window boxes for spring with ivies and polyanthus. There was a shower of yellow winter jasmine down a house on the other side of the road. Children were singing in a school playground. Ellie hoped little Frank was getting over his last cold.

She paid off the taxi — ouch! She must draw some more money from the bank. Brrr! The air off the river was always colder. She looked for Roy's car, but he hadn't arrived yet.

What a kind man he was. How silly of Kate to doubt him — and he was very attractive, too, with those deep blue eyes. A pity about the cat, Midge. He'd given poor Nora some comfort in her last days.

Bowles, Aunt Drusilla had said. Would that be the woman in the flat opposite Nora's? The one Ellie had met the other day? Ellie found her name on the intercom opposite Nora's, rang the bell, explained who she was and why she had come. Mrs Bowles released the lock on the front door and Ellie climbed the stairs.

Nora's door was still splashed with paint. What a nasty colour! Who on earth would want to use such a colour in their house? Imagine a bathroom painted in that overpowering shade of lilac, or a hallway . . . Mind you, some interior designers thought it great fun to inflict these violent colours on their clients. Nora had made no attempt to clean the paint off. Another little job for Ellie.

Mrs Bowles was waiting in her open doorway, dangling some keys in her hand. Her eye shadow was emerald-green today, matching her fingernails.

'Excuse me, but I'm just on the phone. I'll pop over later, right?'

Nora's key turned in the lock. It was dark inside the flat. All the curtains seemed to be closed and it was very cold. There was no heating on. Perhaps a window was open somewhere? A shuffle of letters on the floor, mostly bills. Dust. A feeling that things were lurking under the skirting-board.

Ellie shuddered, remembering the cockroach. Aunt Drusilla had been right about professional cleaning and redecoration. Kitchen. Much as she had last seen it, but with a fresh bowl of milk and some cat food in a dish. Aha, the stray was still around, then.

The master bedroom. Large, looming furniture, still smelling of old man. The curtains were stuck on their track and would not draw back. She hooked one heavy curtain back over a chair to let in some half-hearted morning light. This must have been the father's bedroom.

Blackened silver photo frames on the chest of drawers. A heavy, old-fashioned wardrobe, full of expensive, heavy, old-fashioned clothing. Nora ought to have cleared the clothing out ages ago, but Ellie could understand why the poor creature hadn't. After Frank had died, clearing out his clothes had been the very worst job she'd had to do. Ellie turned her mind away from that particular memory.

Nora's bedroom. Probably the smallest room in the flat, no bigger than the bathroom. The thin curtains drew back easily enough. Neat and tidy, except for an indentation on the bed and some cat hairs.

Hating this, Ellie pulled out the drawers under the mirror and found a small pile of trinkets, including what looked like a very dirty string of tiny beads. The pearl necklace which Nora had wished to leave to Ellie, no doubt.

Some of the other trinkets might fetch a few pounds. Ellie tipped them all into a plastic bag. She found a canvas holdall and a couple of light suitcases at the top of the slender wardrobe, and started packing Nora's clothes. There weren't many.

The holdall took Nora's nightdress and toiletries for delivery to the hospital, and as for the rest — well, honestly! Even the charity shop would turn up its nose at the cheapness of Nora's things. Ellie thought of the excellent quality of the clothes hanging in the master bedroom. The contrast with what Nora owned made her angry.

On Nora's dressing table was a leather-framed photograph of her father, which Ellie crammed down on top of her clothes, wishing she knew some really bad swear words to throw at his pompous, self-satisfied, fat face.

Pillar of the church and OBE for services to charity. Frank had never liked the man, saying that OBE in this case stood for 'Other Blighters' Efforts'. Nora's father had been a clever, sarcastic brute, headmaster of a private school who in his retirement had pontificated on any committee that would put up with him. He hadn't wanted his only daughter to train for any job other than that of looking after him. And then he had left her without a penny. Some men!

The first of Aunt Drusilla's valuers was late. Ellie moved into the sitting room, where the drab curtains shifted in a cold wind because a window had been left open. Ellie pulled back the curtains and tried to close the window, but it had been wedged open so tightly that she failed. She must find some sort of tool, a screwdriver or hammer or something, to get it closed.

This room was much as she had last seen it, except for a pile of coloured papers on the table, which turned out to be more poison-pen letters. There was also an open shoebox containing a crudely made but recognizable waxen figure of a cat, with a piece of twine round its neck and a wire stuck through its body.

Ugh. How could anyone do that — and then kill Midge, and leave him to be found by someone as fragile as Nora?

Something brushed across Ellie's legs and she screamed, collapsing into the nearest chair. The cat jumped up onto her lap and began to rub his head against her hand. His purr was so loud it was almost like a growl.

'Midge?'

Long-legged, ginger, handsome, golden-eyed. Wearing a blue collar with a name tag on it. The tag said, 'This is Midge. Phone number . . .'

The front doorbell rang and Ellie jumped. The cat gave her a reproachful look and disappeared into the kitchen.

Shaken, Ellie hurried to the door to let in the first of the valuers, and also Roy. The valuer was an antique dealer who seemed to be on excellent terms with Roy already, and Ellie was more than happy to let them get on with it. She retired to the kitchen to reassure herself that Midge was no ghost — which he certainly wasn't, judging by the rate at which he was wolfing down the food left out for him.

'Ellie love, how do you feel about a cuppa?'

Ellie jumped again — and thought how kind it was of Roy to think of that. She certainly could do with one. Someone, presumably Mrs Bowles, had left half a bottle of milk on the table, and there were a few tea bags left in the tin.

Ellie washed out some mugs, made tea and took it through to the men, who were happily making lists in the sitting room. They had swept the poison-pen letters and the shoebox off the table, in order to inspect it for woodworm.

While Roy and the valuer looked at the other rooms, Ellie picked up the letters, put them into the shoebox on top of the wax cat, and stowed them beside Nora's belongings in the hall.

Didn't men together talk loudly! Women conducting business didn't seem to feel the need to shout like that. Luckily, they were in agreement that only the suite in the master bedroom was worth looking at apart from the stuff in the living room.

The papers in the briefcase! She remembered that Nora had said the briefcase would be under the bed in the main bedroom. She must hand that over to Aunt Drusilla.

Had Roy finished in the master bedroom? He had. Good. She retrieved the briefcase and put it with her pile of Nora's things in the hall.

Now for the old man's clothing. She was pretty sure that he would have had some good, solid luggage. She had just located some suitcases at the top of a broom cupboard in the hall when Roy showed the first dealer out.

'Let me do that. You don't want to strain yourself.'

Roy said they'd found some papers in the bureau which would need looking through. He'd like to put them in the cardboard box that had been on the table if Ellie knew what she'd done with it. Ellie transferred the wax cat and the bundle of poison-pen letters into a plastic bag and gave Roy the box just as the second valuer arrived, ten minutes early. Roy dealt with him, too, while Ellie made a start on piling the old man's clothing into his suitcases. He had really had some excellent clothes and they could all go to the charity shop, if Nora failed to make it.

Another ring at the doorbell. This time it was the next-door neighbour, Mrs Bowles.

'Can you make us another cuppa, Ellie love?'

Ellie felt a stir of impatience. Couldn't Roy see that she was busy?

'Do come in, Mrs Bowles. You've been feeding Midge, I think.'

'Oh yes, the poor thing!' Mrs Bowles was a twitterer. She sat down in the kitchen and filed her nails while she gave Ellie the history of her acquaintance with Nora — which was not great because Nora kept herself to herself, didn't she, and then her father didn't like her hanging around the stairs and gossiping.

By easy stages Mrs Bowles passed on to her hysterectomy, what her son had said about her taking a holiday, and how she and her husband — unfortunately parted, my dear, by circumstances, not love — had been to Madeira and Tenerife, but this time she had to steel herself for such a long journey, by way of Hong Kong if you please, all the way to Sydney, Australia.

Ellie nodded, made some more tea and took it in to Roy and the dealer, who had their heads close together over the furniture in the master bedroom.

'Sit down and drink your tea, dear,' said Mrs Bowles. 'You look worn out.'

The dealer went and Roy put his head around the door to say he'd just finish packing up the old man's clothes, all right? Midge jumped up onto Ellie's lap, and Mrs Bowles remembered why she'd called in.

'. . . and what a terrible thing that was, killing that other cat. Poor Nora was distraught when Mr Pedler

— ground-floor flat number one — found the poor little pussy strung up with string and tied to the handle of the front door. The cat was exactly the same colour as Midge, though perhaps not quite so large, and of course Mr Pedler thought it was Midge, and he went up and told Nora, and Nora screamed and said it was all her fault, though how it could be I really don't know. Mr Pedler told me, and we decided it would be best to drop the body in a plastic bag and put it out with the rubbish, which is what we did, dear, for we've got no garden here as you've probably noticed . . .'

'But it wasn't Midge.'

'Well, no, dear. As it turns out, it wasn't. It was one of the cats belonging to that woman with the fuzzy hair across the road. She has four cats, and her ginger tom looked exactly like Midge, but of course he wasn't. When Mr Pedler saw her out looking for her Tibbles, he wondered if there'd been some sort of mistake, so he fished out the bag that we'd put the pussy in, and she let out such a scream when Mr Pedler showed her the body. No collar on it, so it was really all her fault, wasn't it?

'But of course we didn't find out that it was Tibbles until after Nora had been taken to hospital. Midge came back yesterday afternoon. I had such a fright when I saw him, walking along the window ledge. My flat has a balcony at the back which links up with Nora's balcony, you see. Not that you can grow anything much on the balcony because of the wind. But Midge always came in that way. He climbs that big tree at the side, then leaps across to the balcony, ever so clever, just like a squirrel, it's a treat to watch him.

'Nora gave me a key to her flat when she got Midge. She wanted to make sure someone would be able to get in and feed Midge if she was kept at church with rehearsals and that, because he does stay out at night sometimes and you never know when he'll turn up, but when he does turn up, he's that hungry! So I had a key, and when I saw him on the balcony I came in to feed him and bring him some milk — and then I thought, what's going to happen with Nora in hospital and me about to fly to Australia?

'So I rang the agents and they said the usual man that deals with these flats was away, and I should write in. That wasn't good enough, as I said to them, considering it was an emergency. Then they mentioned Miss Quicke's name and there's only two of that name in the phone book, so I took a chance this morning and rang the first number and luckily it was the right person, and I told her she'd better send someone down to see to the cat, which was rather clever of me, I thought, wasn't it? And how is Nora, do you know?'

'Not good, apparently. She gave Miss Quicke carte blanche to clear the flat, so I'm just packing up a few things to take to the hospital for her.'

'I did think about visiting her, but I haven't had a minute. Oh, and the cat's things are in the airing cupboard. It's a load off my mind, that you can take him.'

You assume too much, thought Ellie. I've been ordered to have him destroyed. At which Midge looked up at her with his golden eyes, purring, treading money on her skirt. She made a face at him. He nudged her hand, and she rubbed his head behind his ears.

'If I did that to him,' said Mrs Bowles, 'he'd bite! Nora always used to say that he liked people to admire him, but only from a distance. She reckoned he was an excellent judge of character, though how she would know, poor dear, I really can't imagine!'

Ellie wafted Mrs Bowles out of the flat and went to see what Roy was up to. He was in the old man's bedroom, hammering down an over-full suitcase.

'This is so good of you, Roy.'

He sat on the bed, looking tired. 'It's hell, clearing out after a death. I had to do it for both my parents. And then for an aunt. It doesn't get any easier, does it? You told me you had a good charity shop in the Avenue. Would they like this stuff? If so, I'll drop it in to them. Don't you try lifting any of those bags. They're heavy.'

He took the bags down to his car while Ellie washed out the cups they had used. She didn't want to think about taking Midge to be destroyed, but what else was she to do with him?

Midge was yowling somewhere. Ellie found him clawing at a cupboard hidden behind the kitchen door. Inside was a stout wicker cat basket, some tins of cat food, dishes and a box of flea powder. Midge delicately clawed open the door of the cat basket and climbed into it. He turned round and hunkered down, his eyes on Ellie.

The cat command was easy to interpret. *Take me, I'm yours.* Or perhaps, *Get a move on. I'm all done here.*

Ellie thought, I'll have to take him with me, because there's no one left to feed him now Mrs Bowles is off. I'll drop him off at the vet's on the way home.

She closed the lid of the basket and heaved it out into the hall for Roy to take down to the car. Gathering up the things to take to the hospital, she made sure all the windows were shut. Roy had obviously managed to get the sitting room window closed — trust a man for that; he probably had a Swiss army knife with ten blades including one which took stones out of horses' hooves. She pulled the door to behind her.

Roy leaned against the car door, panting. 'Is that the lot? What a day. I could do with a drink, couldn't you?'

'Mm. I was just thinking, we'd better not get rid of anything till we know whether Nora's going to make it or not.'

'Well, I'm getting rid of the old man's clothing. She ought to have done that ages ago. I'll drop you at your place first, deliver his stuff to the charity shop, and pick you up in an hour for lunch, right?'

'You're very good to me, Roy.'

'No more than you deserve, my dear. So it's "Home, James, and don't spare the horses!" That's what my father always used to say. Odd how these little sayings persist in a family, isn't it?'

As Roy unloaded the baggage into Ellie's hall and disappeared with a wave, the phone rang. It was Gilbert, who had just returned from a conference and got Ellie's message.

'Prepare yourself, Ellie. Not good news, I'm afraid. I've just been on to the hospital. Nora died this morning.'

CHAPTER FIVE

Ellie had expected the news and while she had never been that fond of Nora, she still found herself crying. Perhaps she was just overtired.

'Are you alright?' asked Gilbert.

'Are you?'

'Well, no.' He sighed. 'Poor Nora. What a sad life.'

'Yes,' said Ellie, her thoughts zigzagging between recent memories of the nasty, cold, smelly flat, of Nora saying that she had made her own arrangements, and of Nora at the organ, playing a complicated piece of music with panache.

Gilbert sighed again. 'Well, I suppose it solves a difficult situation for me, but . . .' Another heavy sigh. 'I'll be in touch, right?'

'Yes.'

Ellie felt for her hankie. Bother. There were no pockets in this skirt. She seemed to remember tucking a tissue into her waistband, but it wasn't there now. She went into the kitchen to blow her nose on a piece of paper towel, and screamed as the head of a ginger cat turned to look at her across the table.

Midge! She had forgotten all about him. She had been going to take him to the vet's on the way back, but what with this and that, she had forgotten. Roy must have unloaded the cat basket in the hall along with the rest of Nora's things, and somehow Midge had got out and found the chair nearest the fridge.

Well, she could take him to the vet's tomorrow. Meanwhile, he ought to be fed. She opened one of the tins left by Nora and gave him some milk. When she sat down to have a cup of tea, the cat jumped up onto her lap and started to pat her cheek with his paw.

She wept, partly for Nora and partly for herself. She missed Frank so much. Presently the cat's warmth on her lap began to take effect and she started to stroke him. He purred in return. She held him tightly, wondering if he had comforted Nora in the same way.

What a poor, unloved creature Nora had been. What a pitiful way to go. Those awful poison-pen letters! Ellie hoped the person responsible would be ashamed of him- or herself when the news of Nora's death came out. And whoever had sent that nasty practical joke of a wax cat and killed Tibbles . . . What a pity you could never really get to the bottom of such situations.

Or could you? Suppose she gave the matter some thought, asked around among her friends and acquaintances? Presumably it was someone at church who had written those letters, because only they would know so much about Gilbert and Nora. Horrid to think that someone she knew might have written them.

It might be worth asking around, although — she sighed — punishing the letter-writer wouldn't bring Nora back and Christians weren't supposed to be vengeful. However, in this case Ellie wished him or her — and she seemed to remember it was usually a her who wrote poison-pen letters — some unquiet nights.

Yes, she would certainly see what she could do about it. For a start, how about that lilac paint? It was a most unusual colour. Had she seen anything like that recently? No. But if she asked around, she could soon find out who'd had some decorating done recently, and then she could check on the colour.

Then there was the paper on which those letters had been written. Such bright colours, really rather unsuitable for ordinary letter-writing. She'd seen something like it somewhere, she was sure of it. Give her time, and she might come up with a lead or two.

When the phone rang she jumped, startling Midge into springing off her lap. It was Roy again. 'My dear, I'm so sorry, but something has come up business-wise. Would you be very disappointed if we postponed our lunch date?'

Trained by her husband to fall in with men's business arrangements, Ellie said, 'No, of course not, Roy.'

'But good news! I've managed to get tickets for the opera tomorrow night. *Carmen*, English National Opera. Wear your prettiest dress, and we'll have supper in Soho afterwards, all right? Pick you up at six.'

'Oh, but . . .'

He'd already put the phone down. Ellie was left with mixed feelings. She was relieved she didn't have to go out and be sociable immediately, but . . . opera? She hadn't been to an opera for years. Frank had been dismissive of opera, and she had never felt strongly enough about it to go by herself.

Well, this was a new world she was entering. Roy's background was far more cosmopolitan than hers. She should take advantage of it, instead of feeling intimidated. Well, not precisely intimidated, but wary, perhaps. And ought he not to have *asked* if she would enjoy an evening at the opera before getting tickets? Everything was such a muddle.

She felt the need to be quiet for a while. The grandmother clock in the hall ticked along, measuring the minutes away. The sun would set and rise as usual. Nora was gone, but everyone else must get on with their lives as best they could.

She felt depressed. A reaction against all that tragedy, she supposed. Depression was best treated with carbohydrates, hot sugared tea and a cat that purred on your lap. But Midge had vanished, and she could no longer hug him for comfort.

Ellie was alarmed. He couldn't have got out of the house and got himself run over, could he? No. He was giving himself a thorough wash, sitting in the middle of her bed.

While Midge made himself at home, Ellie stood by the window, looking out on the quiet road, wishing . . . longing . . . for something, hating herself for her inactivity when so much needed to be done. She felt quite unable to make a start on the spring-cleaning, or turning out her wardrobe, or going to fetch her skirt from the cleaners — anything practical.

She could almost hear Frank saying, 'Let sleeping dogs lie'. He'd always hated it when she got involved in other people's troubles. Perhaps he was right. 'A trouble shared is a trouble doubled' as he used to say.

Nora was gone, and nothing could bring her back. It was useless to think she could track down the writer of the letters. Or someone who'd recently had some decorating done. No, she would leave well alone.

* * *

That might have been the end of the matter, if dear Rose at the charity shop had not been of an inquisitive turn of mind and Ellie, both conscientious and hospitable.

* * *

They met at the café as usual.

'You've heard?'

She of the Marigold gloves giggled until she gave herself hiccups.

The heavy-set woman frowned. 'Control yourself, dear.'

The third woman tidied the pepper and salt to one side and slotted the menu between them. 'Did she really take a dive in the church? How like her to cause trouble right to the end. She couldn't have acknowledged her guilt more clearly if she'd trumpeted it from the rooftops. A job well done.'

The heavy-set woman nodded. 'A service to the community. Now, is there anyone else?'

'My vote goes to Ellie Quicke. You know? The Merry Widow. Her husband's hardly been dead five minutes and she's gallivanting around with all sorts.'

'I second that.'

Conversation was suspended as the waitress approached. They ordered chicken and mushroom pie, a portion of vegetarian quiche and a salad by way of celebration.

* * *

A week later Ellie returned from poor Nora's ill-attended funeral service and stood at the window looking up at the church.

The forsythia and the early camellia were beginning to come out in her garden. Midge was winding himself round her legs, and there was no denying the comforting effect of a warm cat on your lap when you were suffering from the February blues. But Ellie failed to appreciate the beauty of the flowers or the attentions of the cat, for the morning post had brought a Royal Command from Aunt Drusilla.

Aunt Drusilla's letter was written on such thick paper that it crackled in Ellie's hand. Aunt Drusilla was the only person Ellie knew who used paper of such quality.

> *. . . I have decided to accept an offer for Nora's effects — including the few trinkets which you have passed on to me already — from the antique shop in Kensington. The list of what they will buy is attached. Would you kindly arrange to be at the flat to let the men in and see that they take nothing they have not contracted for. Then get the house clearance people in, followed by the cleaners, and then the decorators. Time is, of course, of the essence.*
>
> *I append details of the firms I use for this.*

* * *

With rain spitting at the window, Ellie glanced at the clock. She was expecting John and Rose from the charity shop to

61

lunch. She had asked John to bring his wife, but the poor woman very rarely accepted invitations — nerves, or something — so it was unlikely she would come. Ellie thought what a long time ago it seemed since she had worked at the shop, although it was only just over four months since Frank's illness had struck and she had stopped working there.

The table was laid in the bay window, the casserole was sizzling quietly in the oven, and a home-baked apple tart awaited a dollop of *crème fraiche*. Ellie supposed she ought to check Aunt Drusilla's list, but it was far more interesting to wonder if there was anything she could spread on the garden to deter the squirrels from digging up the early tulips in the tubs outside the French windows. Luckily Midge enjoyed chasing squirrels away.

Ten minutes until her guests were due. She would just run her eye down the list.

Midge jumped up onto her lap as Ellie sat down. Aunt Drusilla had accepted Ellie's assessment that none of Nora's clothes, kitchen utensils and bed linen were fit for anything but the rubbish bin, and she acknowledged receipt of the briefcase full of bills, and the box of her papers which had been missing for some days until Ellie had eventually retrieved it from under an old waterproof in the boot of Roy's car.

Aunt Drusilla declined to take any interest in the poison-pen letters which, with the wax cat, had drifted into the cupboard under Ellie's stairs.

Aunt Drusilla did not, of course, go to the lengths of thanking Ellie for the hours she had spent so far in Nora's flat, and would continue to do in the future. At least this meant that Ellie could now get someone to take away the contaminated upholstered three-piece suite and mattress. The place would smell sweeter without them. 'One oak dining table with two spare leaves, six matching dining chairs . . .'

At church the sub-organist had replaced Nora, and Timothy the curate was throwing his weight about in a way which Mrs Dawes described as 'childish'. Roy had treated Ellie to a night at the opera with a splendid supper in Soho afterwards. Ellie thought she'd have to watch her waistline, or her new blue and cream two piece would get too tight to wear.

The news from up north was still unsatisfactory. Diana was going for interviews for a better-paid job. She said she was fed up with Stewart moaning about the cost of running two cars. But how, complained Diana, could she go for interviews if she didn't have a car of her own? Ellie had nobly refrained from pointing out that their second car was really Ellie's, co-opted by Diana after her father's funeral.

'Three Victorian prints of scenes from Shakespeare in original frames . . .' and very dull they were, too. Perhaps they were so dull they were now fashionable again.

Ellie turned over the page. There was nothing to claim the attention of the antique dealer in Nora's bedroom, but it would be interesting to see how much her father's heavy old bedroom furniture would fetch nowadays: high-backed bed, armoire with mirrored doors, high chest of drawers, matching low chest of drawers, dressing table . . . and there were all those silver photograph frames, as well.

Except that there was no mention of the photograph frames in the list.

Ellie made a cross noise. Why was everyone so inefficient nowadays? Her late husband Frank would have been on the phone straightaway, demanding to know why the silver frames had been omitted from the list. Ellie, of course, wouldn't do that. There would be some very good reason why they were not on the list. A separate page had probably got itself detached.

The weather was deteriorating. She hoped Rose would have remembered to bring her umbrella. Ellie had given her a new one for Christmas.

No driving lessons for Ellie in this weather. Too depressing. Her driving tutor was depressing, too. Each time they went out he made the same remark about women of a certain age finding it exceedingly difficult to learn. It didn't do Ellie's self-esteem any good to hear that. Perhaps she could find someone else to teach her.

She went back to the list. No, the silver frames had not been listed. The total for the rest of the furniture was there. For some reason they had excluded the silver frames from their valuation. How had Aunt Drusilla missed them? Answer: she hadn't known of their existence.

Ellie had a sharp struggle with her conscience. It was hard for her to fight Aunt Drusilla's corner, but she supposed she couldn't let the old bat be cheated.

And talking of valuations, she really must start to get quotes for a conservatory extension at the back of the house . . .

Ellie laid the papers aside with a sigh of relief as down the path from the front gate came her old friend, that dear little brown mouse Rose, with the brand-new, gaily striped umbrella that Ellie had given her for Christmas wavering around her in the wind. She was closely followed by stalwart John, catching her up with giant strides, flat tweed cap pulled well down and a tartan wool muffler — also a Christmas gift from Ellie — concealing the lower part of his face. Poor John suffered badly with his teeth and sinuses.

'Dear Rose! So lovely to see you. John, let me take your coat. So sorry your wife couldn't make it, but in this weather and her being so susceptible to colds, perhaps it's as well.'

Rose shook herself, a button flying off her coat. 'What terrible weather! "February Filldyke" my mother always used to say, though I suppose she really meant "ditch" not "dyke", and perhaps it ought to be "gutter" nowadays? And what a lovely smell of cooking. You're so clever, dear Ellie, and how are you coping?'

John handed over a box of chocolates, and treated Ellie to a hug and a chaste kiss on her cheek. 'You're looking well, my dear.'

Midge bounced in from nowhere, sniffed at the visitors' shoes, and disappeared with a flick of his tail about some business of his own. 'I must apologize for Midge,' said Ellie. 'He has no manners. He comes and goes as he pleases, especially since I've installed a cat flap for him.'

'Oh, he's beautiful!' said Rose. 'You must find him a great consolation.'

With two such good friends, Ellie could speak the truth. 'I would never have thought of myself as a cat person, but yes, he is a great help. Of course I have my bad days, but I am determined not to fall ill. You should both be very proud of me, making all sorts of plans to go to exhibitions and garden centres and even some walks with the local historical society. You don't belong to the historical society, do you, John? They sound dull, but I've been assured the lectures can be quite fascinating. I remain unconvinced, but I'll try anything once.'

Rose shuddered and John laughed. Ellie drew her two friends into the warmth of the sitting room and poured out sherry for them.

'I don't usually, but in this weather . . .'

'Just a small one.'

'Think of it as medicine, a protection against flu,' said Ellie. 'Now, do tell me how things are at the charity shop. I don't really miss it, you know. I miss seeing you two, but I don't miss having to, be polite to everyone all the time. And somehow my time seems to have got mopped up.'

'Yes, we heard about your new beau.'

Ellie reddened. 'Hardly that. He's at a loose end, here on business, likes to have someone to take out and about . . .'

'If you say so, dear,' said Rose with obvious insincerity.

'Anybody know where he comes from?' asked John.

Ellie laughed. 'Oh really, you two! He's very charming, but I will admit to you that he's not Frank. Sometimes I feel a bit claustrophobic because he never asks me what *I* would like to do, but always assumes I'll fall in with his plans.'

'Just like Frank,' said John with a sly smile.

Ellie laughed again. 'Yes, just like Frank. But he took me to the opera the other night. *Carmen*. A new experience. Of course I knew most of the tunes from listening to the radio, but I couldn't compare performances as he can. Apparently his parents were opera buffs and he expects everyone else to be equally at home with it. But enough of me. Tell me, how is Madam getting on nowadays?'

Rose and John were delighted to fill Ellie in on the latest gossip. After a short period of super-efficiency in which Madam had driven them all mad with a new rule every day, things had gradually lapsed into their usual state of mild muddle. Rose spent much of her time sorting clothes in the back room, while John was in charge of the books and banked the takings. Between them, they could have run a mini-MI5 intelligence survey for the neighbourhood.

'Now, Ellie,' said Rose, delicately scraping the last of her portion of apple tart off her plate, 'tell us about the poison-pen letters. I've never seen one. They were saying in the shop that it was the letters which drove poor Nora to commit suicide.'

John protested. 'She must have been unbalanced already. Surely you don't commit suicide because you receive a few silly letters?'

Ellie shuddered. 'Not so silly. Rather nasty, really. Also she was given a wax cat with a pin through it, and a neighbour's cat was killed in mistake for her own. As a matter of fact, I'd been thinking I might show you the letters. I've got some in a bag under the stairs. Coffee, anyone? Tea?'

Piling plates onto the tray, she looked around for Midge, who could hear a fridge door open from the other end of the house and usually had the scraps off everyone's plate. Prompt on cue, Midge leaped down the stairs and followed her into the kitchen.

The bag of letters also contained the wax cat, which gave Ellie a frisson nowadays, thinking how easily it might have been Midge who had been left hanging from the front door of those flats.

Rose scooped up some of the letters and read them. 'Goodness!'

'"Goodness had nothing to do with it,"' quoted John, who had always been a fan of Mae West. 'You're right, Ellie. These are nasty. It takes a twisted mind to think this way. But I still maintain that Nora must have been fundamentally unsound to be driven to suicide by a batch of letters, however ugly.'

Rose squeaked, having taken an incautious sip of scalding-hot tea. Waving a clutch of the letters around, she fanned her mouth. 'Paper!' she managed at last. 'Look at the paper they're written on!'

'A bit bright for my taste,' said John. 'Lurid, even.'

Ellie smiled. So her hunch had been correct — the paper had passed through the charity shop.

Rose was getting excited. 'But that's just it, don't you see? Take one or two of the letters, and you just see bright colours, but if you put a whole lot together — like this — you see a pad of multicoloured paper.'

John nearly spilt his coffee. 'You're right, Rose! We sold pads of multicoloured paper like this in the shop just before Christmas. There was — oh — maybe a couple of dozen pads. They went like hot cakes. I even bought a couple myself for when the grandchildren came to stay.'

Ellie refilled everyone's cups. 'I thought I'd seen that paper before, but I wasn't sure. Do you think we could trace the others? No, I suppose not. So many people come in and buy things. But we ought to tell the police, perhaps. Are there any pads left?'

Rose shook her head. 'No, because Joyce — my daughter, you know, who's going out with the scoutmaster at church — well, she asked me only the other day if I could get some more for them to use in some craftwork at Scouts, and I looked and there weren't any left. I gave her mine, of course, but it wasn't enough.'

'Could we make a list of how many we can trace?' asked Ellie. 'If we asked everyone who serves in the shop if they remember selling them . . .'

'Would anyone remember, especially in the chaos just before Christmas?'

They all shook their heads. John put the letters back into the bag and anchored them with the wax cat. 'You ought to take that lot to the police, you know.'

'I thought about it, but what's the use now Nora's dead?'

Rose said, 'That poor pussy, dying for someone else's cat. You know, John, we might be able to get some idea of who bought the pads, if there were only a couple of dozen packs. You and I had three between us. Then Joyce had two . . .'

'I rather think that Irish woman who comes in on Tuesday mornings had a couple of packs for her children. I remember because she asked for a discount and of course we had to refuse.'

'That's seven,' said Ellie, counting on her fingers. 'Though I can't see Joyce's Cub Scouts writing poison-pen letters. That was a joke, Rose!'

'Well!' said Rose, flushing. 'I mean, Joyce takes her work with the boys very seriously indeed.'

Ellie hastened to divert her. 'Any news of the wedding date yet?'

'And are we both to be invited?' asked John.

'Yes, of course! And your dear wife, too, if she feels she can manage it.'

It's always good to be positive about things, to look forward to a wedding, rather than to think back to a funeral.

* * *

Timid Timothy's sermon that Sunday seemed even less interesting than usual — a mere repetition of the Gospel reading. Ellie was not alone in sighing for the Good Old Days of Gilbert and his sparky, thoughtful, ten-minute talks.

At coffee after the service, Ellie avoided Roy's eye because she knew he wanted to take her to inspect a decrepit Victorian house which fronted onto the Green beside the church. He said he'd got his firm to actively consider the site for development, but he wanted Ellie's advice on the matter. He would treat her to lunch, of course.

Ellie was not sure that she wanted to be taken out to lunch, and she definitely didn't fancy trudging over the house. Anyway, she was wondering if she were courageous enough to approach Rose's daughter about the pads of multi-coloured paper. Joyce was a handsome enough girl, Ellie supposed, if you liked them dark and sulky looking. Evidently the scoutmaster did.

Ellie herself had always found the girl intimidating, even when not meeting her eyes over the counter at the bank where she worked. 'Forgive me,' said Ellie, smiling as sweetly as she knew how. 'Can you spare a minute?'

Joyce's eyes said 'No', but her lips muttered acquiescence.

'It's about the poison-pen letters. You didn't have one, by any chance?'

'What? No, of course not.' Joyce tossed her hair back impatiently, and looked around to check on her fiancé's whereabouts. Ellie wouldn't give much for the chances of anyone wanting to come between Joyce and her prey. She checked the unworthy thought.

'Have you seen any?'

The girl frowned. She shook her head.

'Seen what?' Gwyneth's magnificent bosom intervened.

Joyce shrugged. 'Those poison-pen letters. You had one, didn't you?'

'Mm. Nasty. Why are you asking?'

'She . . .' Joyce indicated Ellie, 'wanted to know.'

Two pairs of dark eyes regarded Ellie with mild annoyance. 'Whatever for?'

Ellie fidgeted. 'Well, it was just that it looks as if the paper used came from some pads of multicoloured paper sold at the charity shop before Christmas, and I know that Joyce . . .'

'You thought I had something to do with them?' Annoyance deepened.

'No, of course I didn't think that, but . . .'

'But what?'

Ellie mumbled something about being sorry for poor Nora. Knowing that she had gone red, she excused herself and dashed off to the loos. There she scolded herself for cowardice. How was she ever going to find out the truth about the letters, if she couldn't even question Joyce about the pads she had bought? Nonetheless, Ellie waited till she was pretty sure that Joyce would have gone before emerging.

Roy was hunting for her, looking strained. 'Thought I'd been stood up.'

She smiled at him. He really was like Frank in so many ways, hating to be kept waiting for a minute. Unlike Frank, Roy expected her to take an interest in his business affairs. Frank had been almost secretive about his finances, but Roy was forever reeling off facts and figures about his various projects.

They walked together across the grassy island on which the church stood, and crossed the road to meet the estate agent in the drive of the old house. It had been on the market for years and looked as if it would be quite happy to disintegrate where it stood.

Ellie shivered a little as the agent unlocked the mock-Gothic panelled door in the cavernous porch. 'Dracula's castle,' she said, trying to lighten the atmosphere.

'What?' said Roy. 'Can you smell the damp? Ought to have been pulled down years ago.'

'The old lady who owns it is in a nursing home now,' said the estate agent. 'Needs a sale to fund her weekly bills. It's for sale at a bargain price. Would make a splendid conversion into flats.'

No, it wouldn't, thought Ellie, negotiating the wide wooden floorboards of the hall. She suspected the house harboured woodworm, woodlice, dry rot and possibly mushrooms. Massive holes gaped where the original fireplaces and surrounds had been torn out by enterprising thieves.

A sapling had thrust up through the derelict conservatory at the back, and the garden looked as if it were about to attack the house. Up the sweeping, creaking staircase they went, with the estate agent still talking in a falsely optimistic voice about the splendid height of the rooms. Paper drooped from the walls of the bedrooms, and the bathrooms — yes, there were actually three — looked like something out of a museum.

'Ripe for redevelopment,' said Roy, twitching aside a torn net curtain to assess the extent of the garden.

'Just consider the position! Primary school opposite! Library, bus route, shops around the corner!' said the estate agent with enthusiasm. He pushed a door wider to usher them into what had been the master bedroom. The door toppled off its hinges and fell sideways onto the floor.

'I've got an appointment at the Town Hall to discuss planning permission,' said Roy. 'What do you think about pulling it down and putting something else in its place?'

The estate agent's smile wavered. 'My client would prefer the house retained, perhaps turned into flats. I know she doesn't want it pulled down.'

Ellie shivered. 'It isn't a listed building, is it?'

'Clever girl.' Roy grinned at her. 'That's the crux of the matter. Are there likely to be any local objections to clearing away this building and putting up a two-storey block of flats with off-street parking? Or perhaps a row of town houses, integral garages, small patio gardens? What do you think, Ellie?'

'I think I'm hungry and thirsty and getting cold. It's even colder in here than it is outside. If you're going to be some time, then I'll just go home and wait for you to finish, shall I?'

'Sorry, sorry. Didn't think.' And to the estate agent, 'I'll call in tomorrow, talk it over, right?'

Ellie stamped her feet in the drive, waiting for Roy to have a final word with the agent. It was beginning to rain again. Of course.

Roy was delightfully, boyishly, full of what they'd seen, as they had lunch at the carvery. Did she like the idea of flats for the site, or town houses? He valued her opinion, as an old-time resident of the area. He didn't want to put forward suggestions for redevelopment that might offend the neighbours. This particular site was the best he'd found so far, but if she felt it was wrong to pull down a Victorian building, however unworthy, then he would look elsewhere.

'Of course I don't mind,' said Ellie, savouring the first mouthful of beef and Yorkshire pudding. 'And if the owner is in a nursing home, it sounds as if she'd have to sell without strings. The house is an eyesore and in such bad repair I'm sure no one could object to your putting up something modern in its place — provided it fitted in with the neighbourhood, of course.'

'That's where your opinion is so valuable, my dear. You know what people would like, and what they wouldn't. So, a Georgian-style terrace, perhaps?' He raised his glass in a toast to her. 'To our partnership.'

Ellie laughed, and clinked her glass against his. It was fun to be consulted. Frank had never done that. And perhaps she could be of assistance to Roy in this, having lived in the neighbourhood for so long.

'Penny for them?' said Roy.

'Mm. No good thinking about the past.'

The roast potatoes were not, perhaps, quite as good as those she cooked herself, but the beef, the cabbage and carrots were delicious. And perhaps a portion of apple pie to follow? Lucky she had worn one of her old skirts with an elasticated band at the back.

'So you'll come with me to the estate agents tomorrow?'

'Wish I could. I've got to be at Nora's flat by ten o'clock. They're coming to collect the good furniture. Then in the afternoon I've got the house clearance people taking the rest. Which reminds me: do you remember the silver photograph frames in the old man's bedroom?'

Roy dropped a piece of roast parsnip and swore. Ellie didn't mind a mild swearword now and then. Frank had used far worse words than that.

'You may not remember them, but they're probably worth something, and the antique dealer who's taking the rest of the good stuff hasn't got them down on his list, so I suppose I shall have to make myself unpleasant about them tomorrow.'

'As if you could ever make yourself unpleasant!'

Ellie sighed, putting knife and fork together with reluctance. That had been an exceptionally good meal. 'Well, if I have to, I will. I can't let Aunt Drusilla be cheated out of the price the frames would fetch, can I?'

'No, of course you can't. But Ellie, if anyone's to be called to task for the missing frames, then it's me. I know a bit about silver, and I thought the antiques chappies offered far too low a price for them. So I said I'd take them to a friend of mine and send the cheque direct to Miss Quicke.'

Ellie was immensely relieved. She had been thinking, no, fearing . . . well, it was all perfectly above board. 'I thought there must be an explanation. Frank would have been on the phone to the antique dealer, shouting about incompetence.'

'And that's really not your style, is it?'

Ellie shook her head, smiling at him. What a nice man he was. So kind and thoughtful. 'And how much did you get?'

'Can't remember, exactly. Two hundred and something. I've got the receipt back in the car, I think. Miss Quicke should be pleased, anyway.'

'Miss Quicke is never pleased, as I think you may have realized by now.'

Roy refilled her glass. 'Fancy a sweet?'

Ellie had a sudden unwelcome memory of one of the silver-framed photographs. She thought she had only given them a passing glance, but now it seemed that she remembered one particular picture only too well. A smiling, middle-aged man holding a young girl of perhaps eight years of age. The girl was standing on the parapet by the river and he was holding on to her, making sure she didn't fall. Nora and her father. Ah me.

'You've gone away from me again,' said Roy.

'Who was it who said that the saddest words in the English language are "if only"? I was thinking of poor Nora's unhappy life. I hope that when I die, I shall have had more happy memories than her.'

'I'll drink to that.' He put his warm hand over hers.

After a moment, she removed her hand to pick up the menu. He really was going rather too fast for her. Flattering, of course, but . . .

And there it was on the mat, waiting for her when she got back home.

CHAPTER SIX

Midge bumped his head across her legs as she bent to pick up the envelope. He was trying to pretend he had been waiting inside for her to come home, but his fur was wet, so she knew he'd been out. She also knew she would be unable to do anything else until she'd fed him, so she left the envelope on the kitchen table while she dished him up some duck-and-turkey mix.

It smelt horrible, but Midge seemed to like it. All the time she was thinking, there's no Sunday delivery. No stamp. Hand delivered. Her name written in large, wobbly capital letters.

Ellie hadn't seen any of the envelopes the poison-pen letters had come in, but she guessed that this was one. She knew in her bones that there was something extremely nasty lurking inside that envelope. She was half-inclined to tip it straight into the bin. She wondered if Nora had felt like that, too.

She gulped a bit and made a dash for the envelope. She tore it open and out fell a lilac-coloured piece of paper with a message in the familiar, large capital letters.

SLUT!
OPENING YOUR LEGS
FOR ANYONE WHO ASKS!

Trembling, Ellie let herself down into a chair.

How dared they!

She was so angry she could have bitten a piece off the table. She crunched the letter into a ball and threw it into a corner of the kitchen, narrowly missing Midge, who was too intent on his meal to notice.

She was breathing so hard she almost didn't hear the telephone ring. She let it ring on and on. And on. Finally the answerphone clicked in. She couldn't think straight.

Shock.

Hot chocolate? Tea with sugar? She wanted to cry. Her face was so hot that she ripped open the neck of her top to get some air.

Did people really think . . . that . . . about her?

It was intolerable. She hadn't given them the slightest reason for thinking that.

Well, she supposed she had, rather. Totally innocently, of course. Roy had made a dead set at her and needed someone to talk to. So she had fallen into the habit of accepting his invitations, using them as a sort of defence against thinking too much about Frank and how much she missed him.

There was no one else. Well, there was John from the shop. She'd had him to lunch, but only with Rose. She had asked his wife, but his wife hardly ever accepted invitations, so it was understood that John occasionally went out without her.

This was *ridiculous*! They had made her feel guilty, and she was quite, quite innocent.

They would be saying next that . . .

No, she would not even allow herself to think it. They were quite wrong!

Midge jumped up onto her lap. Ellie bent her head down into his soft fur and breathed deeply. He began to purr, but she was too distraught to be calmed so easily.

She jumped up, tipping Midge into the chair on which she'd been sitting, and went to make herself a cup of tea. She must phone someone up and tell them about it, have them laugh about it with her.

She put her head out of the back door, to see if Kate were by any chance having a rare bout of housewifery, perhaps cooking in the kitchen. Then Ellie would pop round there and they could have a good laugh about it. There was no light on in Kate's kitchen, and — she checked on the street side of the house — her car was not there. She sometimes had to work at weekends, of course. But why now when Ellie needed her?

It was still raining, though not as hard as before. She would go out for a walk. Yes, that's what she would do. Tramp round the park. Feed the ducks or something. Perhaps she'd meet a friend, someone from the church — anyone. And then they could have a good laugh about how absurd it all was.

How cringe-making, though. Suppose she met the redoubtable Mrs Dawes and told her? Suppose Mrs Dawes didn't laugh, but took it seriously? That would be awful.

Perhaps other people were gossiping about her. 'And with Frank not in his grave four months . . . !' Suppose dear little Tod heard about it — or his mother. Tod would never be allowed to come near her in future. Or perhaps . . . had she heard already, and that was why he hadn't been round lately? It didn't bear thinking about.

She could ring up Gilbert.

No, not on a Sunday, the busiest day of his week. Besides, people might think that if she ran to Gilbert with this, well, he'd always been fond of her, and perhaps Liz might not like yet another silly little woman phoning him at all hours with stupid notions, wanting him to spend yet more of his precious time with them. It wasn't even as if she was one of his parishioners anymore. He had a whole new parish to deal with now.

The winking light of the answerphone caught her eye as she went to fetch her walking shoes. She pressed 'Play' and heard the fruity voice of her *bête noire*, the church warden Archie, wanting to know if she were at a loose end and fancied a night out at the cinema, 'or if you prefer to be cosy, come and sit with me by the fire and we'll open a bottle of something good'.

She recoiled. She'd forgotten about Archie. Come to think of it, he had been making rather a nuisance of himself since Frank died, wanting to hold her hand and pray with her and take her out. His attentions had been pointed. She had always declined his invitations, but it was possible that a number of people knew about them, while not realizing that she'd declined. Especially people at church.

She felt herself going hot again . . . and then cold. Menopause? She pulled on a thick winter coat and a warm hat and scarf. Key. Umbrella, just in case it turned out worse than it was at present. Out of the house. The wind fair took your breath away on a day like this. She had forgotten her gloves. Well, she wasn't going back for them.

Up the path, round the corner, across the road and into the park. It was a truly nasty, cold, wet day. Branches whipping around. Sludge edging over the sides of the paths. Hardly anyone about.

Slut!

She wasn't. She really wasn't. Oh, Frank! Why did you have to die so young?

She'd been angry with him so often since he'd died. She'd told herself she was better off — which she was financially, of course. In some ways it had been good to be able to order her days according to her own wishes. Yes, she had to acknowledge that she had enjoyed a new feeling of independence, having people to lunch, buying little treats for herself and making plans for the house and the garden.

It didn't stop a hollow ache inside. And now this!

She could scream, she really could. Except that people would think she was being extremely odd, walking around the park in the rain, screaming.

She put up her umbrella and tried, distractedly, to turn her mind away from the letter. She tried to pray. Please, dear Lord . . . you know how much I miss Frank. This hurt is unbearable . . . am I really guilty of a crime, just having lunch with a friend . . . friends? Please, Lord. Help me. I'm not going to be able to cope with this.

She remembered that Jesus had suffered far worse from his enemies. That made her laugh. A little.

She was getting things out of proportion. She would ignore the letter, but be more careful about accepting invitations in future.

A pity, that. In spite of certain misgivings about him, she had enjoyed being taken out by Roy, and she had also enjoyed the feeling that she was of importance to someone else. She wondered if perhaps she had been getting too fond of him, on the rebound, so to speak, from Frank's death. Widows in Charles Dickens's novels were always remarrying in what seemed to the modern reader to be indecent haste. She had never understood it, before. Now perhaps she was beginning to understand.

Well, the letter had certainly made her reassess her relationship with Roy. A nice man, she thought. Kind, helpful. Very like Frank in some ways. She could see how it was that she had allowed herself to become fond of him. But . . .

She pulled her mouth into a grimace. There was something inside her which had refused to fall down and yield everything to Roy. If she dug around in her mind enough, she would be able to track it down.

He had homed in on her as if she were the answer to all his dreams. That was ridiculous, considering their age and the short length of their acquaintance. He was very self-centred, assuming that she would always fall in with his plans, which were usually delightful, though not necessarily what she would have chosen for herself.

There was a certain steely quality in Roy, neatly masked with urbanity. She could understand how he had been so successful in business, but once or twice she had wondered what would happen if she crossed him in a major decision. She sighed.

She had been leaning on the bridge over the river which wound its lazy way through the park. Today, though, the river was swirling under the bridge, carrying the usual detritus found in London parks — tin cans, plastic bags, underwear, condoms, general yuck. Plus branches torn from the trees which bordered the river. She realized she was wet, in spite of the heavy coat and umbrella. And she was cold.

She began to retrace her steps. There was something at the back of her mind which Roy had said . . . She shook her head. She couldn't quite recall it now. No doubt it would come back to her later.

She decided to cool her relationship with Roy. And if she got a cold as a result of this excursion in the park in driving rain, she would curse the anonymous letter-writer.

* * *

She did get a cold. She made herself attend choir practice on the Monday night, even though her voice had almost gone. Everyone else was out of sorts and out of tune. Ellie felt she ought to make herself inconspicuous in a corner all evening, but no one seemed to be casting meaningful glances in her direction, so it seemed that no one else knew about the letter she had received.

No one referred to Nora. There was an exchange of views about which builder Ellie ought to use for her projected new conservatory, and that was about it.

Ellie struggled through the following days attending to the clearing of Nora's flat, and seeing none of her particular friends. The weather might have accounted for that, being as nasty as February gales usually are. But of course they might be avoiding her, if the gossip hinted at in the letter had been circulated. She tried not to think that this might be the case, although the suspicion lingered at the back of her mind.

The cleaners used by Aunt Drusilla were troublesome, because Ellie insisted that they wait for the pest control people to deal with the cockroaches before they could start on the kitchen. They made veiled remarks about never having had this problem with the man who usually managed the letting of Miss Quicke's flats. It was tiresome, soothing them down, listening to their troubles.

Then she developed conjunctivitis in her right eye. From experience she knew that only something on a doctor's prescription would clear it up, so she made an appointment and sat surrounded by coughs and sneezes and what looked suspiciously like a case of chicken pox, waiting to be seen. She knew the doctor's receptionist, Gwyneth of the impressive frontage, from the church choir. Ellie smiled at Gwyneth, who looked right through her. Oh dear. Gwyneth must have heard the gossip.

She saw the lady doctor in the practice, who was unexpectedly warm and helpful. Dr Mehta had hawk-like eyes and long, slender hands. Ellie liked her.

How was Ellie coping, apart from the conjunctivitis? Up and down. Only to be expected. A prescription was scribbled, but Dr Mehta seemed in no hurry to let Ellie go. I expect you're a bit run-down, are you? Any problems with anything else? Throat, tummy, periods all finished, no more hot flushes? Perhaps it might be a good idea to have a blood test, rule out anything nasty? Dr Mehta phoned through to the practice nurse to fit Ellie in with that before she left the surgery.

Ellie knew she ought to go and let the busy doctor get on with her day. She had determined not to speak of the letter, but found herself poking around in her handbag and passing it over the desk.

'Ah! Upsetting.'

'Yes. But in a way, salutary. I had been receiving a lot of attention from a newcomer to the area — perfectly harmless, I thought, though someone seems to think I'm taking him seriously, which I'm not. I still miss Frank dreadfully.'

Dr Mehta leaned back in her chair, smiled, shook her head and exuded encouragement. Ellie gave her a rather tentative smile. 'The letter has been weighing on my mind, rather. I was so shocked when I got it. You're the first person I've been able to talk to about it. I haven't seen Roy since, and I imagine everyone else is gossiping about him. Stupid, really!'

Doctor Mehta pushed a box of tissues towards Ellie, who mopped up tears and blew her nose. She tried on a better smile for size. 'One solitary little letter, and I'm reduced to jelly!'

Doctor Mehta's smile widened. 'You're lucky only to have had one. I gather they were zizzing around the area like mad. I know Gwyneth had one. Luckily she brought it to me. Some of my other patients have had them, too.'

Ellie sighed. 'Yes, poor Nora. I wish . . . but we didn't realize how bad she was, and then I suppose the cancer was the last straw . . .'

'What?' Doctor Mehta straightened.

Ellie blinked. 'She said that she had cancer in her farewell letter.'

The doctor leaned forward. 'Ellie, sometimes people imagine they have terminal diseases when they haven't.'

Ellie blinked again. 'You mean, Nora didn't have cancer?'

The doctor shook her head.

'Oh. I don't know whether that makes it better or worse. Poor Nora. I've been lumbered with the job of clearing out her flat, you know.'

'Book yourself onto a cruise, look up friends or family in Australia or somewhere exotic. Isn't there somewhere you've always wanted to visit?'

'Frank always wanted to go to the Galapagos Islands to see what Darwin wrote about.'

'But what do *you* want?'

'I don't know.'

'Give some thought to that. A week in Paris? A fortnight at a health farm?'

Ellie giggled. 'I couldn't. So self-indulgent.'

'Perhaps that's what you need.' The doctor rose, indicating that Ellie's time was up. 'Look after yourself, and if you get any more of those letters, take them to the police.'

Until that moment, for some reason Ellie had not considered the possibility of there being any more letters. The prospect made her feel at once belligerent and afraid. She told herself that if there were any more, they would go straight into the bin. So there!

* * *

Manicured hands flicked over the keys on the computer, setting a bold-type message in large capital letters. The nails were painted shell pink, the slender wrists shown off by a matching pink blouse with ruffled cuffs. Short-sighted eyes checked the message on the screen, centred it, and used the mouse to print it out.

The typist hesitated over using an office envelope and finally put her note into a plain brown one. She would post it through the door on her way home. It wasn't very much out of her way.

* * *

Conjunctivitis pulls you down, so as soon as the eye drops began to work, Ellie started to feel better. She would not be intimidated by one nasty-minded person's poison. She would be brave and ask her friends if they had received any letters about her, and if they hadn't, she would think no more about it.

To be on the safe side, however, she refused a further lunch invitation from Roy. She was very busy attending to Nora's flat, anyway.

The only bright spot in her life that week was a fleeting encounter with Tod, who waved to her on his way home, shouting that his mum had got him a computer with games on it, so he was in a hurry to get back. At least he didn't seem to have heard any gossip about her.

The second letter arrived by post on Thursday morning. Green paper, untidy handwritten capitals, as before.

SLUT!
SOON EVERYONE WILL KNOW YOU FOR
WHAT YOU ARE!

She thrust it into her bag, shaken but determined not to let it ruin the plans she had for that day. Shopping. Library — the last couple of books she had taken out were extremely dreary, leaving her feeling worse than before she started them.

She would get something extremely light. Something to make her laugh. Something by Terry Pratchett, or an old Dick Francis to re-read. Frank had laughed at her for wanting to re-read old favourites. He had been a Bernard Cornwell and Wilbur Smith man himself.

Also, she was due at Nora's flat. The cleaners had been through the flat and now it was the turn of the decorators, who were complaining because the windows in the old man's bedroom wouldn't open, so Ellie had needed to get a carpenter in to deal with that.

She would not let the letters throw her off balance again.

'Magnolia paint throughout,' Aunt Drusilla had decreed. 'It wears better than white. I always have my flats painted in magnolia when a new tenant moves in. After that, if they've a long lease — and I don't like short lets — they can do what they like. Provided, of course, that they pay to have the flat repainted in magnolia before their lease is up.'

Aunt Drusilla had used these painters before. They were the best in the business, or so they informed Ellie. Ellie was inclined to believe them, partly because they appreciated her helping them out in the matter of the windows — which was more, they said, than the usual man did. With the carpets and curtains removed, the flat looked spacious, smelt clean and would undoubtedly be appreciated by the new tenants.

All traces of Nora and her father had gone. It was only in Ellie's imagination that they lingered in the shadows. While the painters worked away in the sitting room, Ellie carried out a final check to see that the kitchen cupboards had been properly cleaned. She didn't entirely trust those cleaners. No cockroaches remained, thank goodness.

The bedrooms were bleak on this cold February day. The decorators had obliterated the darker patches on the wallpaper where the old man's heavy furniture had once stood.

She checked that the windows now opened easily. They did. Nora's father had had rotten taste in wallpaper, anyway.

She thought of all the distress these walls had witnessed. Even Roy had been affected by it as he had helped her to clear out the old man's clothes. Ellie remembered how he'd talked of clearing out his own family's things after they died. She sighed. The poor man was completely alone in the world. It seemed harsh to refuse his invitations when all he wanted was a friendly face to chat to. Well, almost all. But that second letter reinforced her resolution to keep her distance from him.

As she left the flat, now busy with decorators clanging around, slapping paint on the ceiling, adjusting ladders, radio blaring on some chat show or other, she ran her finger down the faint traces of lilac paint on the door. What a strange colour to choose. She wondered why the vandal had used it. It wasn't as if it were a colour you would come across easily.

She couldn't remember ever having seen it used, herself. Whatever would you use it for, anyway? A bedroom? Hmm. A front door?

No! Who would want to use that in-your-face colour for a front door? She smiled at the absurdity of it.

Then she paused with her hand on the front door downstairs, that very front door from which a cat had been strung. Something stirred in the undergrowth of what passed for her mind these days. Front door? No, nonsense. Nobody she knew would paint their front door lilac . . . would they?

She shook her head and stepped out into the cold, adjusting the silk scarf around her throat and putting on her gloves to face the walk back home. She would be glad to see the last of Nora's flat. If she had another letter, she would take them all to the police. Until then, she would put them out of her mind. She must look forward now, not back.

Oh, Frank. Why did you have to go away and leave me? At this time of the year we'd be planning our summer holidays, and . . . enough of that! Yes, but who does a widow go away on holiday with? Answer: other widows. Or spinsters.

She sighed. She couldn't think of a single person with whom she would like to go away on holiday. Not anyone compatible, anyway. Except perhaps her next-door neighbour Kate, who was not only much younger but also married. What an absurd thought. Of course Kate wouldn't want to go away with her, for all sorts of reasons. Not least of which was that she appeared to have tamed her delightful husband's habit of knocking her about whenever he felt threatened by his wife's superior earning ability and — let's face it — brains.

Ellie decided that, on the way home, she would call in at the travel agency and get some brochures for holidays in exotic places. Singapore, perhaps. Hong Kong? The Great Wall of China? Well, why not?

She treated herself to lunch at the Sunflower Café, served by Mrs Dawes's granddaughter, Chloe. Chloe was dressed from head to foot in denim today, with five gold earrings in one ear and a dangler in the other. Colourful. Ellie liked Chloe and, remembering her ambition to travel for a year round the world, gave her a big smile and said, 'I expected you'd be off to Australia before now.'

Then she recalled that Chloe might have heard some gossip about her, and might not respond. To her enormous relief, Chloe beamed back. 'I've got my ticket, leaving end of April. It's nice to see you again, Mrs Quicke. Thought you might be laid up with flu, with your not being around lately.'

Ellie grew voluble with relief. 'I was kept up at my daughter's after Christmas — they had flu, you know — and now I'm having to clear up after our organist's death.'

'Yes, poor thing. Gran told me about her falling from the gallery in church. She said she didn't know what she'd have done if she'd been by herself, but being with you, she was all right. I said it was just like a film, where the person dies in the place they used to be happy, but Gran said I was talking nonsense as usual. Fish and chips is best today.'

'Fish and chips it is, then. And I agree with you. Nora was happy playing the organ at church. Thanks, Chloe.'

The café was popular, as always. A sudden shower of sleet drove a married couple in whom Ellie knew slightly. They hesitated in the doorway, since all the tables were taken. Mr and Mrs . . . Ward? Lock? Key? Ellie cleared away her brochures and asked if they'd like to sit with her. Then she worried that they might have had a letter about her, and would refuse.

'Thanks,' said the man, helping his wife off with her mac and putting their dripping umbrellas in the stand. 'Thought we might be turned away.'

'How are you, Ellie?' asked the woman. 'Planning a holiday, I see. Where are you going?'

'Trying to decide.' Ellie felt the need to blow her nose. Absurd to want to cry just because someone was nice to her.

'Best to keep busy.' The woman nodded. Ellie noticed that she looked very frail.

'Are you OK?'

'Mustn't grumble!' said the man, in a warning tone of voice.

The woman grimaced. 'I've decided not to have any more treatment, so we're taking each day as it comes.'

Ellie glanced at the soft woollen scarf the woman was wearing around her head, noted the absence of eyebrows and eyelashes, and remembered. Cancer. Inoperable. Oh. There were lots of people worse off than she was. Another salutary lesson. Mr and Mrs Guard, that was the name.

The ever-efficient Chloe materialized at their elbows. 'Fish and chips is best. Or stew of rabbit. He calls it friccy-something, but that's what it is. Very tasty, too.'

The Guards ordered one of each, and conversation lapsed. Ellie couldn't think of anything to say which wouldn't be tactless.

'Bad business, that,' said Mr Guard. 'Your organist.'

Ellie nodded. Chloe delivered the fish and chips, which were excellent.

The man sighed. 'We had a couple of letters, too, some months back. Wish now we'd taken them to the police, but we had more important things on our minds.'

'I was in hospital at the time,' said his wife. 'I did think of going round to see Nora when I heard, after I came out, but I didn't get a chance.'

'Oh, you!' said her husband, with affection. 'Always thinking of others, never of yourself.'

Mrs Guard laughed, and shook her head at him.

'I was up north staying with my daughter,' said Ellie. 'I did go to see Nora when I got back, but she was too far gone to be helped.'

'We do hope it's stopped now. The letter-writing. Very nasty.'

Ellie forced herself to be brave. 'I've had a couple and yes, it is nasty.'

Two pairs of eyes eyed her in silence while Chloe delivered their food. Then Mr and Mrs Guard consulted one another wordlessly. 'You've taken them to the police?'

'I was ashamed.' Ellie felt herself redden. 'The letter-writer said I was far too friendly with men.'

Their eyes were kind. 'You must take them to the police. This simply must be stopped before any more harm is done.'

Ellie tried to smile. 'I'm not likely to commit suicide. Although I must admit it has shaken me. I never thought that going out with this man — he's a newcomer to the parish and he's lonely — I never thought it could be misunderstood.'

Mrs Guard was toying with her food. 'This fish is good.'

'Eat as much as you can, dear.'

Mrs Guard laid down her knife and fork. 'I can't bear to think of it all starting up again.'

'Don't upset yourself, dear.'

When the Guards said they'd had a couple of letters, Ellie had thought they meant they were about Nora. But they might not have been.

'You mean, the letters you had . . . ?'

'. . . said my wife had cancer because she married me. She was married to my brother first, you see, but after he died she did me the honour of marrying me.'

Ellie protested. 'Surely no one thinks that's wrong, nowadays!'

'Someone does.' He pushed back his plate and gazed out of the window.

Mrs Guard touched a tissue to her eyelids. 'We're not going to let it upset us all over again. Are we, dear?'

'No. We are not.'

Neither of them made a good job of eating their meal, though. They left without having a coffee, but Ellie sat on to drink hers, trying to think. When Chloe came to clear the table, Ellie asked her if she was still going out with her policeman friend, Bob.

Chloe pulled a face. 'Yes and no. He's on a course this month, which gives me a bit of space. I've told him I'm too young to commit myself, but he won't listen. So sometimes I go out with other people, just to make the point, you know.'

Ellie had no further questions for Chloe — which was rather a pity, as it turned out.

CHAPTER SEVEN

The second post had come by the time Ellie returned home. Before she could collect the mail from the mat, however, Midge arrived and banged against her shins until she picked him up and stroked him. He smelt of fish.

'You awful cat, you!' she said. 'Where have you been stealing from? I didn't give you any fish this morning.'

He purred even harder, and rubbed his head against her jaw. When she put him down, he made straight for the big chair in the living room, to give himself a good wash and enjoy a doze.

Ellie opened the mail, dreading to find another poison-pen letter, but there was none. Notification about an investment due to mature — she must try to get through to Bill; it was ridiculous that he hadn't fixed her up with an accountant yet. Seed catalogue. Estimate for building on a conservatory at the back, with a drawing which made her gasp.

She had asked for a plain lean-to right across the back of the house, using part of the existing patio as a base. They had drawn a semicircular rotunda which would take up far more space than the patio occupied, and which took no account of the steeply sloping garden.

She could almost hear the man saying, 'She's only a woman, doesn't really know what she wants. We'll give her our usual.' That went straight into the bin.

There was a note from Timothy the curate about having tried to contact her several times and would she ring him, please, it was urgent. There was also a note from Roy.

Hi, partner . . .

That made Ellie smile. 'Partner' indeed. What a flatterer the man was!

> *. . . I've tried ringing you, but you never seem to be in. What a busy little person you are! I hope you're getting paid for the work you're doing, clearing out that awful place. How about supper tonight? I've got some good news to report on the housing scheme we discussed. Ring me?*

Ellie sighed. It would be pleasant to dine with Roy and talk houses, but she had made up her mind to keep her distance in future, and so — no dinner. Besides, she had other things to do. She tried phoning her solicitor, but Bill was busy and unable to take her call. His secretary promised he'd ring back, but he didn't.

Timothy, when reached, turned out to need someone to produce the weekly church notices on a computer, since the parish secretary was off sick, and her back-up had moved away. Ellie was gradually taming Frank's computer into producing the occasional letter, but she could hardly be said to have mastered it. Timothy had become much more assertive since Gilbert's departure and, though Ellie tried to tell him that she had hardly progressed beyond the first steps in learning to operate the machine, he persisted. Would she at least give it a try? He was at his wits' end, etc.

Eventually she agreed to ask her computer-literate neighbour Kate to help her. Timothy said he'd bring round the draft notices for her to do, straightaway. 'I thought that by now you'd have signed yourself onto one of those starter courses for computers,' he said, putting her in the wrong.

Ellie thought, but did not say, 'And what about you? I *hate* computers.'

She reflected that if Timothy went around trying to bulldoze people like this, he would soon lose what little good-will he had in the parish. What a contrast with their own dear Gilbert, who would have flattered and flannelled her into trying without feeling badgered. Ah me. Happy days. It made her need to contact Kate even more urgent. Hastily she scribbled a note to her neighbour and pushed it through her front door, before telephoning a message through to Roy's hotel to say that she was sorry, but she was rather tied up at the moment.

Housework. A great panacea, or a great bore. Perhaps she would get someone to come in to clean for her, once a week or so. She could afford it, and it would be heaven never again to have to hoover the stairs or clean the silver.

The rain had stopped, so she gathered some sprigs of winter jasmine and some tightly furled buds of iris *stylosa* — no, wait a minute, it was called something else now. Iris *unguicularis*, or something like that. She did wish they wouldn't keep changing the names of flowers. She put the sprigs in a small china vase Frank had bought her on an Austrian holiday. What was she going to do about a holiday this year?

The silver vase looked dirty, so she put it at the back of a kitchen cupboard. She was *not* going to clean it any more. She did buff up Frank's old christening mug and replaced it on the coffee table. She couldn't put that away. Not yet.

When it was time for her weekly call to Diana, Ellie nearly funked it. She loved Diana, of course she did. But there was no denying her daughter's greed and her tendency to bully people. But if the child was really desperate . . . ?

Ellie wished she could consult Bill about this. He would advise her. Ellie could not allow Diana to get into real financial difficulties. Perhaps a loan? Frank had been against it, though.

Oh dear. She phoned Bill at the office, hoping to catch him at the end of his working day, but his secretary said he had already left. So Ellie rang Diana's number, only to find that the answerphone had been switched on. Well, at least that was one problem which could be put on the back burner.

Kate came home early and invited Ellie round for supper. Armand was going to be out, so she'd just get a takeaway if Ellie didn't mind. Ellie didn't mind. She took a bottle of wine round.

The two houses had adjacent hallways and staircases, but were arranged differently. On the ground floor Ellie had one long through room with a dining table at the end overlooking the garden. In Kate's house the sitting and dining rooms were still separate rooms, because Armand used what was Ellie's dining area as his study. What was the small kitchen and smaller study in Ellie's house had been thrown into one large kitchen-diner in Kate's house, and it was there they ate their Chinese meal.

'Don't look at the garden. It's a mess,' said Kate, wielding chopsticks as to the manner born.

Ellie used a spoon and fork. 'You haven't the time.'

'We should get you to redesign it for us. That rockery is so old fashioned.'

'Me, set up as a landscape gardener? I haven't the training for it.'

'Yes, but you know what needs to be cut back and what needs to be taken out. You could tell me what shrubs to get, to make it low maintenance. Look at it! Everything's either overgrown or dead.'

'Perhaps when I've finished with Nora's flat, I'll have time to come in and do something about it.'

'Yummy. I do like ginger and spring onions with beef. Can I finish it up?'

'Bless you, dear. I've had more than enough already.'

Kate gave a tiny belch, patted her stomach, and invited Ellie to come clean.

Ellie was startled. 'How did you know . . . ?'

'You wanted the lowdown on Roy. Well, I asked around and found a guy in our office who lives down that way, and he asked around and found someone at the golf club who knows the senior partner in Roy's firm. According to him, your Roy's got a good reputation as an architect, was a partner in the practice until recently, when he retired. Big house, member of the golf club, social whirl.

'Now for the gritty bit. He married the much younger daughter of the senior partner in the firm, no children, and they're in the process of being divorced. Yes, divorced, not widowered. She's claiming half the value of the house, which is now on the market.'

'Ah,' said Ellie. That was a shock. Thinking back, she remembered that Roy had told her he was a widower when they first met, but while he'd referred later to clearing houses after his mother and father and an aunt had died, he hadn't mentioned a wife.

Kate said, 'Sorry to give you bad news. It wasn't all his fault — the divorce, I mean. His wife was much younger, didn't want children, liked the company of a toy boy even younger than her and eventually ran off with him. The gossip is that Roy was persuaded to resign from the partnership when the marriage came unstuck.

'I don't think he'll have to pay her as much as she's demanding, but he may not be able to keep the house, which, incidentally, was his family's home. The other thing is that you thought his partnership had asked him to look out for properties to develop. My informant says this is unlikely. I think he's on his own here.'

Another blow. Was Roy so unsure of himself — or her — that he couldn't tell the truth? Ellie said, smoothly, 'I expect he'll go into partnership with a developer. That's what architects usually do, isn't it? He thinks that big derelict house on the Green has potential.'

'So it has. But has he mentioned a developer, Ellie? I worry that he's looking elsewhere for his finance. He hasn't asked you to—'

'No!'

The word 'partner' floated into Ellie's mind.

'No,' she repeated, unclenching her hand from her wine glass. 'He hasn't.'

'I hear you saying "but . . ."?'

Ellie forced a laugh. 'Mm, yes, maybe. I'll be careful. I really like him, Kate, and I believe he likes me. I expect I shall go on seeing him.' But perhaps not as often as before, she added to herself. She smiled at Kate. 'But I really didn't come here to talk about Roy. I need your advice on several counts. To tackle the easiest one first: can you find me a trustworthy accountant?'

'Trustworthy or clever? I know one of each.'

'Keeps his mouth shut, but knows how to sort out my finances.'

'I know a guy who'll do that. Older man, small partnership of chartered accountants. He does the books for my dear Armand's father's firm, but we won't hold that against him. I'll give you his number. Next problem?'

'The curate at church wants me to produce the weekly notices for him. Someone has to type them out, add the odd picture and pass the bumf on to someone else at church to duplicate. An A4 sheet, doubled over. Should I tell him to take a running jump, or is this the right time for me to sign on for a computer course — or will you show me how?'

'Of course I will, if you'll help me with the garden here. Fair exchange?'

They clinked glasses. 'Done!'

Kate frowned. 'You still look as if you've got something on your mind.'

Ellie nerved herself. She took the handwritten poison-pen letters out of her handbag and handed them over. Kate read them and said 'Ouch!' to herself. She turned the pages over, scrutinized the envelopes, and shook her head.

'Nasty. It's about Roy, of course. A woman who fancied him for herself?'

'His wife, you mean? A woman scorned? No, I don't think so. You see, they're written on the same sort of paper

95

and with the same awkward-looking capital letters as the ones Nora received. I found out that the paper probably came from the multicoloured jotting pads we sold through the charity shop before Christmas. I've been trying to find out where they all went to, but it's a bit of a forlorn hope. When I got the first letter, it . . . it . . .' She felt for her handkerchief.

'It did your head in.'

'I felt guilty. As if I had deserved it. I thought all my friends would have received the same letter, because so many of Nora's circle got them, too. I could hardly bring myself to look people in the eye, afraid that they would be judging me. I began to understand how it had affected Nora. I know she was unbalanced as well, and I'm not. At least, I hope I'm not . . .'

'You're not.'

'No. But that letter did upset me. Then I got the second one. It looks as if the first one was a warning, sent to me only. The second letter is to tell me that other people are soon going to get the gossip about me. Then at lunchtime today I learned that Mr and Mrs — no, you won't know them, so I'd better not say their name — they received nasty letters too, and I realized that I have to fight this thing. A couple of days ago I decided that I wasn't going to take any further action, that it wasn't worth it. I'm pretty bad at questioning people, anyway.'

'No, you're not.'

Ellie blew her nose. 'Yes, I am. You should have seen me run away from Joyce at church last Sunday. That girl intimidates me. I knew she'd had a couple of the pads of paper, you see, to use for the Cub Scouts' craftwork, and I wondered if . . . but of course that was a stupid idea. Kids don't go in for this sort of poison.'

'You've been to see the police about it?'

'Not yet. I cringe at the thought of anyone seeing the letters and saying there's no smoke without fire, and of course Frank hasn't been in his grave that long, and in a way I can understand people thinking badly of me when I went out with Roy. But I do realize that I've got to take them to the police, however embarrassing it might be. Though what they can do about them, I don't know.'

Kate said, 'Tea or coffee?'

They moved into the sitting room. The décor was modern, with lavender-painted walls over a bright green dado, but the prints on the walls were in subdued greys and browns. Lots of candles, pine cones, strangely angled lights. 'Do you like it?' said Kate. 'I had a decorator friend in to do it. Not sure about all that lavender, though.'

'It's like you. Stimulating, but comfortable to be with.' Ellie tried out one of the odd-shaped chairs and found that it was surprisingly comfortable.

'Plan of campaign?'

'All right, I know I have to go to the police. I'll ring tomorrow and make an appointment. I don't want to have to tell my story to the desk sergeant and then someone else, and finally reach a man who'll actually have any power to do something about it. I was thinking about it after lunch. I will check around to see if we can trace where any more of the pads went to. Then I'll see if I can find out who might have thrown paint at Nora's front door — it was a rather bright lilac, brighter than yours here. The decorators at Nora's flat said it was a top-quality paint used for outside woodwork. Perhaps someone locally has had the front of their house painted recently.'

'In *lilac*?'

Ellie laughed. 'Yes, it does sound awful, doesn't it? But I can always ask around. Then there's the wax cat. I can visit that craft shop near the tube station and see if they stock a mould like that. Maybe someone bought them on an account and they'll be able to give me the names of all those they've sold them to over the last few years.'

'Let the police do that.'

'You're right, yes.'

Kate tapped her forehead. 'Maybe I can help, too. There's bound to be some information about the psychology of nasty letter-writers on the Internet. I'll see what I can find out and let you know — but I'm holding you to your promise to sort out our garden.'

'With the greatest of pleasure!' Ellie adopted a teasing, businesslike manner.

A plan of how the garden might be redone leaped into her mind. Something modern, using decking. No, not decking, because it tended to get slimy and slippery in wet weather, although there was something you could treat it with. She must do some research. 'What sort of budget are we talking about? Shall I draw you up a scheme, like the garden designers do?'

'Where can we find someone to heave rocks about and create a water feature?'

'Wouldn't it be easier to get the BBC in to do a makeover?'

They laughed. It was far better to talk about redesigning a garden than to think of poisonous missives winging their way around the parish.

* * *

When she got back home there was a message from an irritated daughter on the answerphone. Why couldn't Ellie have waited in till Diana got back? Where was she, anyway? Diana was feeling very depressed, because Stewart had been told he would not be considered for any more promotions in the near future, and they hadn't paid the mortgage for the last month . . .

Ellie felt guilty. She really must get on to Bill and see what could be done about bailing Diana out. Except that she had already told Diana what she thought she ought to do, and Diana didn't want to do it. It was all too difficult to think about.

* * *

The police station was a modern building, a short bus ride away near the tube station. Concrete, of course. Bullet-proof glass? An air of being slightly down-at-heel. A whiff of disinfectant, and dead air.

Ellie hadn't met this inspector before. A busy man, but courteous. He listened to her tale with eyes that wandered around the room, occasionally flashing a glance at her. She had brought along some of the letters Nora had received, and the wax cat with the sinister ligature around its neck. Then she placed on the desk the two letters she had received herself.

He opened a file, and with a shock Ellie recognized some more letters, each one bagged in plastic. She said, 'Nora refused to take hers to you for fear of harming the Reverend Gilbert Adams, but I see that other people have.'

He sighed. 'No fingerprints. All posted near the town hall. Received on different days of the week. We don't have anything much to go on, and frankly, with staffing levels the way they are, we can't afford to spend any more man hours on the matter. The organist committed suicide, didn't she? End of story.'

'It was murder, good as. She was hounded to her death.'

'Murder by suicide? A new one, that.'

'But you must want to stop the damage this woman is doing in the community. Who will she turn on next? I assume it *is* a woman?'

'Probably, yes. Who have you upset lately?'

'I wish I knew.'

'Well, if anything further occurs to you . . .'

And that was that. Most unsatisfactory. She took back Nora's letters, but left the wax cat with the police. She retained her own two letters, feeling obscurely that the fewer people who saw them, the better.

In something of a temper, Ellie took a taxi to Nora's flat, to check that everything was in order. The decorators had left. The rooms looked clean and spacious. It was only in her imagination that echoes of poor Nora's grey figure lingered.

Ellie thought of the new tenants who would be moving in within the next few days, and wished them well. Feeling rather self-conscious, she even said a small prayer, aloud, that Jesus would bless the flat and bless the tenants' lives there.

Absurd, of course, to think that a short prayer could have any such effect as she wished, but nevertheless it was done and no one had heard her.

She wondered how Mrs Bowles was enjoying her holiday in Australia. A kindly person, and a good neighbour, whatever you thought about her choice of make-up.

With a sigh Ellie left the flat for what she hoped was the last time, and made her way through the back streets to Aunt Drusilla's house. The shower of winter jasmine she had noticed on an earlier journey was fading. Soon the forsythia would be out and the kerria's golden balls, brightening these dark days.

Oh dear, Aunt Drusilla had got someone to cut her laurel bushes right back to their main stems. Ellie flinched, then reminded herself that she didn't like laurel, anyway.

The door was opened by the same glum-faced cleaner as before. It must be something of a record for Aunt Drusilla to have kept the same cleaner for more than a month. The old lady was sitting in her chair before the fire as usual, and as usual the cleaner brought in the tray of cups and cafetiere for Ellie to make the coffee.

'How are you today, Aunt Drusilla?'

'Never mind about me. What have you been up to, eh?'

Ellie almost spilt the coffee.

'Careful, girl!'

She's had a letter about me, thought Ellie. She said aloud, 'I've just been to the flat. The decorators have finished. They've done a good job, I think.'

'And the cleaners, have they done a good job, too?'

'I was not so impressed, but they did the job properly in the end.'

'They have complained to me about your attitude.'

Ellie set her cup down with a clatter. 'They disliked me pointing out that there were cockroaches in the kitchen. I believe the cleaners would have been happy to ignore their presence.'

'Cockroaches? Really?' Aunt Drusilla implied that she had difficulty believing Ellie. 'You think that we should employ another firm of cleaners in future? Well, if you wish, you may use another firm on the next flat. Number 18. The tenants leave at the end of next week, and the new people will arrive a fortnight after that, so you will have fourteen days to get it ready for them.'

Ellie told herself to take a deep breath or two. She pushed herself back in the uncomfortable chair that was always placed for her to sit on. She had never liked that armchair, but it was an antique, of course. Like everything else in the room, including Aunt Drusilla.

'I am not sure I understand you,' she said, as calmly as she could. 'I was prepared to clear out that one flat because I felt I owed Nora something.'

'Do you think you can exorcise ghosts so easily?'

Ellie remembered the prayer she had said in the empty flat and shook her head at herself. 'Perhaps that is what I was doing.'

'You think I was too hard on the woman? You know nothing about it.'

The sun came out and pierced the darkness of the big room, throwing colours onto the wall as it glanced off a cut-glass vase. Dust motes hung in the air. The shaft of light hit Aunt Drusilla, who put up a blue-veined hand to shield her eyes.

For the first time it occurred to Ellie that Aunt Drusilla might not be immortal. How old was she? Seventy?

Without being asked, Ellie stood up and drew one of the heavy velvet curtains across the big bay window. The old lady did not thank her, but then, she never thanked anybody.

Ellie returned to her chair and finished her coffee. 'You would like me to supervise the cleaning and redecoration of another of your flats? I understood that someone from the estate agency did that.'

'I am displeased with the young man who has been acting for me. My bills have of late been far higher than they ought to be, and the work inadequately done. I discovered recently that he is a director of the cleaning firm of which you have been complaining. At least you will not cheat me.'

'I have my own life to lead, now.'

'Nonsense. You need something to occupy yourself with. You know how to talk to people, you are conscientious and punctual. You were wasting your time working in the charity shop, as I frequently told my nephew. Of course, he never listened because he liked you to wait on him hand and foot . . .'

Ellie grew indignant. As if the old bat herself didn't require to be waited on hand and foot!

'. . . and it is time that you set about learning how to look after your inheritance.'

'Inheritance?' Ellie repeated.

'Don't gape, girl. Who else should I leave my estate to? Answer me that!'

The sun went behind a cloud, and the room lapsed into its usual semi-darkness.

The old woman smiled the nutcracker grin of the elderly. 'Don't think I am going to die yet, because I have no intention of doing so. I have a good many more years ahead of me. But Frank's death was a shock, and although I can make more money, having a flair for such things, it does not compensate for the fact that I now feel as if I am on, well, uncertain ground.'

Ellie groped around in her mind to make sense of this extraordinary turn of events. Aunt Drusilla was actually talking to her as if she were almost an equal. She said, 'You mean, because Frank left this house to me, and not to you?'

'Your mind is not quick, Ellie, but you do usually get there in the end. Yes. At first I considered making you an offer for this house, but then I had second thoughts. I have studied your character and though you are occasionally frivolous, you have a proper sense of family values. You would never dispossess me of the house in which I have lived all my life.'

Ellie bowed her head. She had thought of doing so, of course, particularly when she was in a rage with Aunt Drusilla. At the same time, she had always known she could never do it.

'As you have already discovered, I have been buying and managing property all my adult life. I started in a small way, leasing, clearing and redecorating a flat in which an old man had died. No one else would touch it because of the state it was in. I did all the work myself. I found a tenant and then looked around for a second flat.

'When my father died, he left the family firm to my unbusinesslike brother, but he left me the bulk of his money, guessing that I would look after it better. That was when I began to buy flats in the riverside building, and other houses around here. Of course, after a while I employed a firm to manage my properties for me.

'Now that you are at a loose end and I have discovered that the agents have been cheating me, I propose that you start to learn the business yourself.'

Ellie blinked. 'I'll have to think about it.'

'It will be a valuable apprenticeship for you. You don't need to earn any more money, and it will give you something to do.'

'I have other interests to follow, though. I've just been asked to landscape a neighbour's garden, and she will certainly pay me for my expertise and time.'

Aunt Drusilla gave a soundless laugh. 'I can't see you heaving rocks and paving stones around.'

'I shall employ a strong young man to do all that.' In fact, she had not realized the necessity until that moment.

'I see. Very well, then,' said Aunt Drusilla grudgingly, 'I agree. You will take over the management of the riverside flats for me, on the same terms as I paid the agency.'

Ellie put down her coffee cup with care not to shatter the delicate china. In some ways it was a tempting proposition, but she'd had years of running around after Aunt Drusilla because Frank had expected it of her. Now she was, more or less, free. As Aunt Drusilla's heir, she would be at the old woman's beck and call once more. She already had enough money to live very comfortably. She didn't need any more.

With a distinct feeling of relief, she came to the conclusion that this was one challenge which she could refuse. 'I think you should find someone better qualified than me to do the job.'

'Qualifications, fiddlesticks! Loyalty is what I need.' Aunt Drusilla coughed her neat, dry laugh. 'If you refuse to do what is obviously your duty, then I shall ask Diana to take over . . . and naturally, if she looks after my estate now, she will inherit it in due course.'

'You must do as you think best,' said Ellie, feeling rather dizzy. Did Diana know about this? Was she proposing to move down to London to take over the job? What about Stewart, and their house up north? Another nasty thought: had Diana asked Aunt Drusilla for a loan? And if so . . .

Before she could recover herself, Aunt Drusilla plucked an envelope from the side of her chair, and held it out. 'Now, Ellie, will you kindly explain this?'

Ellie took the envelope in a limp hand. It was an ordinary business envelope, containing one sheet of A4 paper. On that one sheet of paper someone had typed a damning message.

CHAPTER EIGHT

Ellie walked home, hardly noticing the traffic. She stepped onto the pedestrian crossing outside the library without looking in both directions, and had to draw back hastily, while enduring abuse from a white-van man.

'That will teach me,' she said to herself, waiting for a bus to decant its passengers. It was a school bus, full of chattering children returning from a swimming lesson, to judge by their damp hair and plastic bags. One of the boys called out and waved to her.

Ellie made an effort to smile and wave back. She liked Tod very much, but rather hoped he wasn't going to descend on her for tea that day. But no, of course he wouldn't if he was busy on his computer. Ellie was sure he had grown since she last saw him.

She hoped he would never get to hear what people were saying about her. It was a shock to realize that there was not one, but two letter-writers, both using the word 'slut' about her. The typist had used a top-quality printer for her message to Aunt Drusilla.

DID YOU KNOW YOUR SLUT OF A NIECE WAS SLEEPING AROUND?

Ellie felt herself flush, and then go pale. She wondered what would happen if she fainted right there in the middle of the zebra crossing opposite the church. No, she would not faint. She would continue to put one foot in front of the other until she got home, and then she would close the door behind her and SCREAM!

It was amazing that Aunt Drusilla had taken it so well. 'To whom does this anonymous letter-writer refer? I considered putting it in the wastepaper basket. A despicable habit, sending anonymous letters.'

'Someone seems to think that I'm having an affair with a newcomer to the parish, just because he's invited me out to lunch and supper a couple of times.'

'I would like to hear the details.'

Ellie sighed. 'I am not sleeping around. A newly retired architect called Roy Bartrick is staying in the area while looking around for a suitable property to develop. He met me at church and yes, he has been paying me a lot of attention. He's asked me out to lunch a couple of times, once to the theatre. He's lonely, divorced or about to be divorced. Big house down in Surrey somewhere. Pleasant company.'

'I despise these modern terms, but are you "in love" with him?'

'He is charming and attentive. That's all there is to it.'

'And what does he feel about you?'

Ellie shrugged. 'I really don't know. He likes me, I suppose.'

'Widows are often quick to seek consolation.'

'True.'

Ellie thought to herself: I resent her questioning me like this! Why don't I tell her to mind her own business? The truth is that I don't know how I feel. I miss Frank dreadfully, every day, every hour. Roy can't replace him. If I ever marry again, I suppose it might be to someone like Roy, who is very like Frank in some ways, but . . . not yet.

'Is there anyone else, apart from this architect?'

'Aunt Drusilla, you shock me!'

What if I told her that Archie the church warden has also been pressing me to go out with him? she wondered. Would the old lady throw a fit?

Aunt Drusilla surprised Ellie yet again. 'Well, girl, I am not responsible for your morals, but I do not care to have my family's affairs tittle-tattled all over the place. I advise you to take this letter to the police.'

She held it out and Ellie took it. 'I've had two such letters myself already, and I have taken them to the police. They don't seem able to do anything.'

'Ignore the matter, then. Take the coffee tray out with you when you go, will you? I am going to give you a few days to think over the question of managing the flats. Let me know after the weekend. After that, I shall talk to Diana about it. Shut the door behind you. There is a nasty draught coming from somewhere.'

Ellie wanted to slam the door but managed not to do so. Just.

If Diana knew how to blackmail, she had learned her trade in the family. Aunt Drusilla was the tops at it. Or the pits. Whichever. Ellie was so angry, she could have kicked something. Perhaps a small dog would run across her path, and give her an excuse to . . . no, no. How could she even think of it?

Whichever way you looked at it, Aunt Drusilla's plans opened another can of worms, and at some point would have to be dealt with.

Did Ellie want the old woman's money? No!

Did she want Diana to have it? Hm. Possibly not.

How mean could you get, begrudging your only child a chance of inheriting a fortune! Yes, but would it mean the end of Diana's marriage? Stewart had a good enough job up north, they had their house and circle of friends. Wasn't that worth more than a possible inheritance?

Ellie thought it was, but she had a horrid feeling that Diana might not agree.

As she plodded across the Green beside the church, Ellie noticed that there were lights on inside the building. What was the day? Friday. Was Timothy likely to be there now? If so, Ellie made up her mind to tell him to stuff his work. She had far too much to think about, without doing odd jobs for him, too. The side door into the church was open, and Ellie stepped inside.

Timothy was not there, but the flower ladies were, creating an enormous arrangement up by the altar, and hanging individual posies on the end of alternate pews. Of course, there was a wedding taking place tomorrow.

Mrs Dawes caught sight of Ellie, and called out, 'Come and hold this for me, will you, dear?' Well, at least she was still being friendly. 'Catch hold there, while I just cut this ribbon . . . there! What do you think of that?'

The profusion of yellow daffodils and tulips, mixed with lilac ribbon, was somewhat startling. 'Fantastic!' said Ellie. 'Are the bridesmaids wearing lilac, then?' There was a stifled giggle from one of the flower ladies, and Mrs Dawes directed a quelling look in that direction.

'Lilac trims on pale yellow dresses. The bride will be wearing white with gold trims, and her flowers will be purple orchids and yellow mimosa.' A shadow of anxiety crossed her face. 'You think the lilac ribbon too strong? It is the bride's favourite colour.'

And yours, too, thought Ellie, remembering many a violet and purple cardigan sported by Mrs Dawes in the past. 'I suppose white ribbon would be a little insipid.'

Mrs Dawes was relieved. 'My thinking exactly. Now girls, can I leave you to tidy up? I need a word with my friend here.'

Here it comes, thought Ellie, but she smiled and waited for Mrs Dawes to give a tweak here and a push there to each posy as they retraced their steps back down the aisle and up the path to Ellie's house. 'Coffee? Tea? Something a little stronger?'

It was a ritual, this. Mrs Dawes responded as usual. 'Perhaps a small glass, then.'

Seated in Ellie's living room, Mrs Dawes touched the petals of the newly opened iris, and for once forbore to criticize. Sherry poured out, Ellie waited for word of the letters, feeling it was a good omen that Mrs Dawes was still prepared to drink sherry with her.

'I hear you're planning to build a small conservatory out back.'

'That's right,' said Ellie, surprised. 'I've had a couple of quotes, but either they're hideously expensive or they want to put a version of the Crystal Palace on the back of my house.'

Mrs Dawes scrabbled in her carryall, discarding secateurs, twine, tissues, notepad, two pens, a pencil and a rubber, hairbrush and make-up bag, before triumphantly producing a bundle of crudely lettered advertisements for an odd-job man with the grandiose claim: 'NEIL CAN FIX IT.'

'My grandson Neil. He does all sorts of odd jobs — painting, decorating, gardening. You tell him what you want and he can put it up for you, half the price of the big firms.'

Ellie blinked. 'Is this the brother of Chloe, who works at the Sunflower Café?'

'Cousin. Chloe's my daughter's youngest. Neil's my son's eldest. Neil moved down here to live with me just before Christmas when my son got divorced and took up with a much younger girl who has two children of her own. Neil's done no end of jobs around the place for me, so I said I'd ask around among my friends, help get him started down here.'

'Building a conservatory is proper builder's work. Has he ever done anything like that before?'

Mrs Dawes waved a pudgy hand in dismissal. 'He's worked on building sites, done window-cleaning. You name it, he's done it.'

'Somehow I don't think building a conservatory is a job for a one-man operation, but it's possible I might have some work for a gardener.'

Mrs Dawes shifted in her seat. 'I don't say he really knows plants, not like we do. But you could trust him to cut hedges and mow lawns.'

Ellie leaned back in her chair. She was beginning to wonder about this handy young man. 'He's done some work for you, you say?'

'He decorated my back bedroom for me, put burglar locks on my downstairs windows, repainted the front door . . . My neighbour said I was daft to have the front door painted in this weather, but it was looking shabby and the weather was mild enough at the time.'

Suspicion hardened to near certainty in Ellie's mind. 'What colour did you have your door painted? Your favourite lilac?'

'I don't care what anyone says: it looks very nice.'

'Yes, I'm sure it does. I'd like to see it sometime.'

'Come back with me now and have a look. Neil might be there, too. He said he might pop back at lunchtime, because he's doing out the kitchen of a friend of mine round the corner.'

Mrs Dawes drained her glass, and set about buttoning herself into her layers of clothing. 'You did say you thought that lilac ribbon on the big display at church was all right, didn't you? Not too much of a good thing?'

Oops, thought Ellie. How do I get out of this one? 'If that's what the bride wants . . .'

Mrs Dawes concentrated on her buttons. 'Well, I've had my doubts, myself. Perhaps it is a little too strong. Perhaps I could pop back this afternoon and replace the big bows with some white ribbon, adding a couple of touches of lilac here and there, to give contrast.'

'What a lovely idea,' said Ellie truthfully.

The wind was getting up, blowing the branches of the trees around as they walked, heads bent, round to Mrs Dawes's house. There was no sign of young Neil, but the front door was indeed painted a most resplendent lilac. It looked to be the exact colour of the paint that had been thrown at Nora's door.

The tiny, over-furnished house was empty, but a snapshot on the mantelpiece showed a grinning young man with shaven head and earrings.

'Yes, that's Neil,' said Mrs Dawes. 'He must have been and gone again. I'll get him to call round and see you when he finishes, shall I? And if you happen to hear of anyone else who wants some work done, you'll be sure to recommend him, won't you?'

Ellie smiled, but did not reply.

Bingo! she thought. I've found the person who was persecuting Nora. He must be stopped from doing any more harm. What sort of twisted mind was capable of splashing paint on a defenceless woman's door? Presumably he had also written those awful letters. From the sound of it, young Neil was not highly educated, which would explain his choice of lurid paper, and the shaky capitals.

Poor Mrs Dawes! She had no idea what her grandson had been up to. How distressed she would be, to find that the lad she had taken under her wing was a bully and a sadist. It wasn't nice to think of her kindness being repaid in that way.

Yet the lad must be stopped. Perhaps Ellie should go to the police and tell them what she suspected? If the police were to haul Neil in for questioning and he admitted it, then the matter need never, perhaps, be taken to court. He could be cautioned or put under the supervision of a probation officer.

It would be a nine-day wonder in the parish, of course, and everyone would know. However would Mrs Dawes hold up her head again, once everyone knew that she had been sheltering a criminal? And punishing Neil wouldn't bring Nora back or salve the hurts of those he had written to or about. But was there any alternative to putting the matter in the hands of the police?

Ellie walked on to the park, noting where the daffodil spears were rising out of the ground, and the willows beginning to turn a pinkish green.

There was also the small matter of proof. Ellie could point to Mrs Dawes's front door and declare that this was the very same paint which had been thrown at Nora's door. 'Oh yeah?' Neil might say. 'Prove it.' She couldn't, because the door had now been cleaned and repainted a decent, boring, gingery brown. No proof existed now.

There were the letters, of course. They could take samples of his handwriting and compare them with the letters.

It would have been easy for Mrs Dawes to get hold of a pad of that brightly coloured paper, since she often popped into the charity shop.

Poor Mrs Dawes. A totally innocent accomplice, who had all unwittingly delivered her grandson into the hands of the police. Chloe's policeman boyfriend was away on a course. He might have helped.

What was needed was for Neil to be questioned by some authority figure, persuaded to admit his guilt, be brought to realize the harm he had done, and be made to promise not to do it again under threat of exposure to the police.

Yes, that might do. But who could play the part of Inquisitor General?

The obvious person was the Reverend Gilbert Adams. No, he was no longer part of the parish and it wouldn't be right to bring him back again for this, or any other matter. Also, he had been mentioned in the letters, and it would be best to have someone who was completely independent.

Timothy the curate? Ellie laughed aloud. No way, José.

Then who? Bill, her solicitor, would be perfect, but he was never available when she wanted him. Aunt Drusilla would be marvellous, if she could be persuaded to interfere. Which she would not. She was too old, anyway.

John at the charity shop? Mm, yes, possible.

Kate would be good, but would it be safe to have just two women alone confronting this Neil, who looked like a brawny six-footer with muscles out to here?

Armand, Kate's husband? He might do. Smart, sarcastic, head-of-department teacher. Yes, he might very well do.

Ellie turned her steps towards home. Problem solved. Perhaps.

* * *

She was eating her supper while reading the paper when she dropped her fork on the floor. Neil might well have created the handwritten notes. Yes. She thought he probably had.

But did he have the necessary background to produce the *typed* note that Aunt Drusilla had received?

She stared at the newspaper without seeing it. Then she did see it. The typeface used on that note was not at all like the typeface she was looking at in her newspaper. It was an unusual typeface, rather square and spiky. She had seen it somewhere before, but for the moment she couldn't place it.

Kate had said, 'Never assume anything.' It was one of Ellie's faults, and she knew it. She had assumed that there was only one letter-writer, and that it was the same person who had thrown the paint and killed the cat. But suppose there was more than one?

Of course there must be more than one.

Neil had thrown the paint and killed the cat. Probably. He had handwritten those brightly coloured letters of hate. But he wasn't computer literate, was he? His advertisements proved that.

She ought to have seen it before. There were two people writing those letters, one of whom was computer literate, the other not. The second one was Neil, yes. But the other . . . ? Was someone quite different. They must be working together, though, sharing information, getting inside knowledge about Nora's flat and habits. And Ellie's.

Two people happily playing the spy and the torturer. Murdering people by driving them to commit suicide.

Ellie pushed her almost empty plate aside. Real fish was tasty, but the bones were a pain.

Think, Ellie! Think!

CHAPTER NINE

The doorbell interrupted Ellie's thoughts. The hooting of a child's trumpet outside presaged not her neighbour Tod — whom Ellie would have been delighted to see — but the curate's pregnant wife and her six-year-old son. They had clearly just come from a children's party, for the boy was holding two inflated balloons, plus one that had been burst. On his head he wore a gilt paper mask, all the while blowing on a crude roll-out cardboard trumpet.

His mother looked frayed at the edges. Bottle-blonde, an uneasy compromise between out-worn girlish charm and worn-out motherhood.

The boy trumpeted into Ellie's face. Despite herself, she blenched.

'Stop it, there's a good boy,' said his mother, holding out an A4-sized envelope to Ellie. 'Timmy asked me to drop these in to you a couple of days ago, but they must have slipped under some other papers and I've only just found them. It's the notices for church this Sunday. He said you'd offered to do them. It'll be too late to have them run off in the parish office, so I suppose you'd better get them photocopied in the Avenue, ready for Sunday.'

Ellie blinked. She'd forgotten all about her promise to see what could be done about the weekly church notices. 'Heavens, I'll never be able to get them done in time! I suppose you don't know how to use a computer, do you?'

'Me? I wasn't a typist. I worked at the BBC before I got married.'

Which puts me neatly in my place, thought Ellie.

The boy's trumpet shot out and hit Ellie on the cheek as she took the envelope from his mother. He screeched with laughter, while his mother ineffectually pulled on his arm. 'Now, now! You know that's naughty!'

A bright green envelope was also handed over to Ellie. 'Found this on the doorstep. Looks like another of those poison-pen letters. Timmy had one this morning, too.'

Ellie's hand did not tremble as she took it. 'Yes, it does look like it, doesn't it? Will you come in for a minute?'

'No, thanks. Got to get back. My little lovey-boy's tired, aren't you, dear?'

'No, I'm not!' shouted lovey-boy, trying his best to kick Midge, who had appeared in the doorway to see what all the fuss was about. Midge doubled in size, his tail bristling like a lavatory brush. Ellie thought: I'd back Midge on this one.

'Come away, now!' the boy's mother pulled on his arm. Reluctantly giving way, he allowed himself to be drawn up the path to the main road.

I ought to be sorry for her, thought Ellie, but I'm not. That boy is a toad! I wonder what was in the poison-pen letter Timothy received this morning? It would have been about me, wouldn't it?

What will he do about it? Denounce me from the pulpit? Take it to the bishop? No, taking it to the bishop wouldn't get him anywhere, would it — not like when he was trying to get rid of Gilbert. Besides, Timothy needs my help with the church notices. Now, what on earth am I going to do about them?

Kate wasn't back from work yet. Ellie decided she must try to do something about the notices herself. Bother that girl for losing them all week. It was probably an unworthy thought, but if the curate's wife had heard the gossip about Ellie, she might subconsciously have 'forgotten' about handing over the notices, in order to put Ellie on the spot, make her look bad.

Ellie switched on Frank's computer and waited for it to settle down and let her into its works. Think clearly, girl. This is no time for panicking.

Timid Timothy had sent some handwritten notes about the Sunday services, which were reasonably easy to read. Then there were lists of people who needed to be prayed for and notices about events in the parish for the following week. He had included a couple of past weeks' notices as samples for Ellie to copy. These were decorated with flowery borders and looked as if they had been done in different typefaces.

Ellie had been attending the church ever since she was married and must have had hundreds of these notices pass through her hands, but never until that moment had she thought about the mechanics of how they were produced. Now she must. She pushed the green envelope to one side. She would deal with that later.

Manual in hand, she asked the mouse to oblige with a clean page. It did. Now the name of the church must go at the top, in large letters and a sort of Gothic-looking type.

Typefaces. Odd that she'd been thinking about typefaces earlier. Perhaps she could learn something while she tried to do Timothy's notices. Mouse on the tiny slot which said, 'Times Roman'. Click. Hmm. A lot of choices. Goodness, what on earth did they all look like?

She selected one called 'Century Gothic', just for fun. It came out as <ST SAVIOUR'S CHURCH>. This was a weird typeface, not at all Gothic, really, and quite unlike the typeface which was normally used for the notices. Suppose she made it larger — how did you make it larger? She used the mouse on the next slot along and got a baffling series of numbers. Presumably this was the size of the type to be used? She tried twenty-six, but for some reason she could not get the words she had typed to become larger.

Frustration!

Oh well. Try to put a border round the page. Borders, where are you? Ah, they're under 'Format'. Select and press 'OK'. Mm. A border had appeared, but it was not very interesting. Time being what it was, it would have to do. Now to put in the details of the Sunday service.

No, the date went first. What was the date? Somewhere in the computer there was a facility for putting in the date. But would that be today's date, or tomorrow's, or Sunday's? And what was the date today, anyway?

She pressed this and that, and the border went haywire.

More frustration and heavy breathing.

Stab, stab with the mouse, and . . . Ellie shrieked. The toolbar had completely disappeared. It simply was not there anymore. She stared at the screen, feeling half-guilty and half-angry.

She switched the thing off. Then she remembered that she ought to have gone through 'Start' before she switched off.

Hysteria.

What the heck! Why should she care what happened to the church notices? Timothy ought to have brought them round to her earlier if he wanted her to tackle them. The job was beyond her. The church would just have to do without notices this week. It wouldn't cause the spire to fall down. If people were cross, well, so be it. Amen and all that.

She picked up the green envelope, slit it open, and read without much surprise that her evil ways with her 'criminal lover' would soon be front-page news.

Anger carried you over such things nicely. It was only half-past three in the afternoon, but she tipped the note into the bin and went to find the sherry bottle.

Only after she had downed a large sherry did the message hit home. The writer was saying that Roy — presumably he or she meant Roy — had a criminal record.

The doorbell rang. What time was it? It wasn't dark yet, though beginning to gloam, and there she was, caught with an empty glass of sherry in her hand at half-past three of an afternoon. She hid the glass under her newspaper and peered out of the front window.

A young man in sweatshirt and jeans, with a baseball cap back to front, was just about to ring the bell again. Neil? Mrs Dawes's grandson?

Ellie's pulse rate accelerated. She hadn't envisaged facing him alone, but here he was. She could pretend she was not at home. No, that was silly. What could he do to her in daylight in this built-up neighbourhood? She stifled the thought that no one was in next door.

'Mrs Flick? Gran said you wanted some gardening done. I had a quick look around, back and front, and if you like I can start tomorrow.'

Ellie relaxed. 'It's Mrs Quicke, actually, not Flick. Quite a lot needs doing. Could you give me the name of someone you've worked for before?' It occurred to her to wonder if he had done the cutting-back of the laurel bushes at Aunt Drusilla's. But no, that was too far-fetched.

'I've only been down here six weeks, but I've been clearing gardens up north and I can see what needs doing. You want all that shrubby stuff clearing away, and make it all look neat, right?' He waved his hand towards the shrubs which bordered the front garden. The winter-flowering viburnum and the winter jasmine were just finishing, but the kerria and forsythia were about to burst into flower, and heavy buds were forming on the laburnum by the gate.

'You mean, cut down all the shrubs just as they're beginning to flower?'

'Cut down, dig out, take away. Make it all neat, innit?'

Ellie took a deep breath. 'No, it is not! Young man, I don't know where you've been trained, but it is clear you are no gardener.'

He shifted in his trainers. 'Odd jobs, that's me. Tell me what you want, and it's as good as done. Start tomorrow morning early. Finished by lunchtime out here, and then at the back, that might take longer' cause there's a lot of stuff there. And I'll take the stuff away and dump it, all in with the price, right?'

'Wrong! If I had the time — which I haven't — I'd give you a few lessons in gardening. You lay one finger on my garden, and I'll sue you.'

He drooped. 'Gran said you needed some gardening done . . .'

She saw he was very young still, possibly only just left school. Six foot tall and broad with it. Heavy eyebrows, big boned, awkward. Minimal education, couldn't possibly have worked a word processor.

'It's my neighbour who wants some gardening done.'

He looked where she pointed. Concrete slabs covered Kate's garden at the front, the only sign of plants being two wooden tubs containing dead conifers.

Sounding more confident, he said, 'Sweep it up, get rid of them tubs, right? Take me an hour only, maybe. Two to dump them tubs.'

'Come in, and we'll talk about it.'

She sat him down in the sitting room, where he looked around with frowning interest. His jeans were spotted with various shades of paint, lilac among them.

'Nice place,' he said, leaning back, trying to appear at ease.

'Lilac paint,' she said.

His eyes fixed themselves on a picture over her head.

'Doors,' said Ellie. 'Front doors. One for your Gran and one for . . . someone else. Right?'

He shrugged. Half-grinned. Stretched his legs out. He hadn't taken his cap off, of course. 'So?'

'You admit throwing lilac paint at the front door of our late organist?'

'So?'

Ellie sighed. This was hard going. 'You did the hand-written notes about her as well?'

He sat upright. 'No way!'

'But you do know about them.'

A grin. 'Sure. Gran talks about them all the time.'

'But you didn't write them, any of them?'

A twist of the lips. 'Why would I?'

Why indeed? He had a point there. 'But you did throw the paint.'

A wriggle. 'Weren't no harm in it. Stupid cow, ruining everything. Whyn't she just leave, like everyone said?'

'Like your Gran said?'

'Sure. And all her friends. They come round to Gran's and yak, yak, yak. Nora this and Nora that, and dear Gilbert this, and did he or didn't he. I seen some of the letters, too. A right old scrubber, that Nora. Time she took off.'

'So you thought you'd help frighten her away?'

Big shoulders shifted. 'Not frighten. Give her the word. A warning.'

'And if she hadn't gone?'

A shrug. He hadn't thought as far as that.

No, thought Ellie, he hasn't the brains for thinking things through. 'So how did you feel when she committed suicide? You were partly responsible for that, you know.'

Another wriggle. 'Not me. She did it to herself.'

'With a little help from her friends.'

'What friends?' He was perking up now. 'She din't have no friends. Everyone said she were rubbish.'

'I see it differently. I see a vulnerable, sensitive woman who was in great distress at losing her beloved father, who was in danger of losing her home, had no job and was in debt.'

'And she bonked the vicar, right?'

'No, she didn't. She loved him, that's all.'

Silence. He got to his feet. 'I'll go then, shall I? Seeing as you got me here under false pretences.'

'Sit down.' Ellie pressed her fingers to her forehead. She retrieved the last letter from the bin and held it out to him. 'Nora isn't the only one who gets letters.'

He read it, and whistled. Looked at her with assessing eyes in which there was now a hint of sexual speculation.

With heightened colour, Ellie said, 'Did you write that?'

He shook his head. 'I like capitals with curly bits. You seen my writing, on my adverts. Gran said she showed you one.'

He took a sheaf of them out of his back pocket, and handed one over. What he said was true. Bother!

'You got a boyfriend, then?' He was finding it hard to understand that oldies like her might still be capable of sex, but, on giving her the once-over, was generously prepared to admit that she might not be quite past it.

'There is someone who takes me out occasionally, yes.'

'Criminal type?' Now that he did find difficult to believe.

'No. Architect, retired.'

He frowned. 'Speeding fine, wouldn't you fink?'

'Yes, very possibly.' She laughed, easing the atmosphere. 'Thank you, Neil. I expect that's what it is. You see, the person — or persons — who writes these letters has a little knowledge about the victim, but twists things to make them seem worse. As they did with poor Nora, and as they are doing with me. This is the third handwritten letter I've had.'

'You been to the police?'

'Yes. They asked if I'd been annoying someone recently. Now you know what goes on at your Gran's, people dropping in, chatting all the time. Have you heard them talk about me?'

'Don't think so.' Frowning. 'I keep out of their way mostly. When it's fine, I'm out, working. Not enough room to swing a cat at Gran's. I only heard about that Nora 'cause I hadn't any work and the weather was so bad I was stuck indoors.'

'Do you remember who was saying the worst things about Nora?'

He shrugged. 'Don't know names. One's got a Zimmer, another's got two sticks. Zimmer-frame was saying someone ought to do something, get Nora to resign. Then my mobile went off and a job come up, so I got out. But I thought I might do my bit to help them, and there was this bit of paint left over, so . . . that was it, really.'

Old ladies gossiping. Young buck thinks it a lark to 'help'. End of trail.

'Here, kitty!' Neil flicked his fingers up towards the pelmet over the curtains. Midge had taken to climbing the curtains recently and sitting on top of the pelmet board where he could see everything that happened. The damage Midge was doing to the curtains gave Ellie another reason for having new ones.

She watched with some curiosity as Neil tried to entice the cat down. Midge, predictably, played hard to get.

Then he did his vanishing trick. One minute he was up on top of the pelmet, and the next he'd disappeared. He popped into sight again right by Neil's chair.

'Nice cat,' said Neil, rubbing behind Midge's ears. Ellie waited for Midge to do the bottle-brush act with his tail, but instead he sniffed all over Neil's trainers, taking his time about it. He then pounced on Neil's laces and tried to worry them loose. 'Gerroff, you!' said Neil, laughing. He picked the cat up and babied him.

To Ellie's amazement, Midge seemed to enjoy this. Perhaps Neil was to be trusted, after all. And maybe — if he were properly supervised — she could use him to help with Kate's garden.

'Coffee, or tea? And a biscuit?'

As she brought in a tray she noticed that her newspaper was now halfway across the floor, with Midge under it playing bears with Neil. Her sherry glass was in plain sight. He got back into his chair, trying to pretend that he hadn't just been tumbling around the floor with a cat. He watched as Ellie picked up her glass and set it on the table. Now it would be all round the neighbourhood that she was a secret afternoon drinker.

She said, 'You've noticed I had a sherry. I don't normally drink . . .' She could feel his scepticism. '. . . but that letter gave me a shock. I should have given myself a cup of sweet tea instead, shouldn't I?'

He grinned, not committing himself. Midge lost interest in the newspaper and wandered out into the kitchen.

Ellie said, 'Now tell me about yourself; what training you've had and what you've been accustomed to doing.'

He was very happy to talk and eat at the same time. It was as she had guessed. School, helping out with his friend's dad who did odd jobs in the building trade, aiming to take some carpentry course or other, but . . .

Fortunately she had put out the packet of Jaffa Cakes she had in the cupboard, because he ate through them as though he hadn't eaten for days. It did cross Ellie's mind to wonder if Mrs Dawes was feeding him properly, but she reflected that anyone of Mrs Dawes's ample girth would need three-course meals to maintain the status quo. It was more probable that this lad just had an appropriate appetite for his age and build.

He was just getting down to slagging off his dad's new girlfriend when there was a tap on the French windows leading to the back garden. Ellie gave a little scream, seeing what looked like an unrecognizable face pressed to the glass.

Neil swung to his feet, 'Wazzat?' Confiding in Ellie had somehow turned him into her champion and he appeared ready to tackle the newcomer with raised fists if necessary.

Ellie laughed. 'It's all right. It's only my respectable architect friend.'

'Ah.' Another assessing look. He was going to tell everyone that Ellie's friend had secretly turned up at the back window. 'I'd best be off, then. I'll let myself out and you'll give me a bell about the garden, right?'

Ellie wrestled the French windows open and in stepped Roy, cursing and holding onto the back of his right hand. 'Glad to find you in at last, Ellie. Thought I'd take a short cut this way, but some damn cat came streaking out of the bushes and slashed my hand . . .'

Midge?

Ellie took Roy into the kitchen, bathed the scratch and put a plaster on it. Men always made a fuss about such things and it was better to humour them — especially if it had been Midge who had inflicted the wound.

'Sorry if I interrupted something,' said Roy. 'You've been so elusive lately. Who was that young man, anyway? Have you been cradle-snatching?' He was only half joking. He continued, 'I phone you, and always get the answerphone. I drop in notes, and you don't reply. I wondered if I'd done anything to offend you.'

'Not you, Roy. Tea? Coffee? Something stronger?'

'Ouch, that hurt. Yes, a sherry would be good.'

She decided that another sherry would be one too many for her, but poured out a generous glass for Roy and a whisker for herself.

He drank deeply. 'Ah. So tell me, what has been keeping you so busy that you haven't time to see me?'

She had been perfectly all right up to that moment. She had dealt with poor Nora, the first two poisonous letters, the cleaners, the decorators, Diana, Aunt Drusilla and the typed letter, Timothy and the computer, and had retained her composure. It took Roy's kindly assumption of authority to break through her self-sufficiency. She began to tremble. She was going to cry. How embarrassing!

She felt for her hankie and as usual failed to find one. There was a box of tissues on the table. She mopped up and blew her nose. She was still shaking. She told herself not to be so stupid, she could manage perfectly well — but wouldn't it be a wonderful relief to tell someone like Roy all about it?

She fished out the poison-pen letters and handed them over to Roy. He put on his glasses to read them. Nice glasses, fashionable. They suited him, as did his smart but casual leather jacket and well-cut slacks.

He read them through and stilled. He didn't raise his eyes from them.

She thought, he's wondering how much of that is true, and yet he of all people ought to know that none of it is true. 'This is awful!'

Somehow she was sitting by his side on the settee, he had his arms around her and she was sobbing into his jacket. Oh, the relief to have someone kind and strong take over! Almost as good as having Frank back.

She sat upright and tried to push him away while reaching for the box of tissues yet again. She couldn't seem to stop talking — all about Aunt Drusilla, and Diana and the flat, and Timothy and the computer, and thinking that Neil had written the letters but of course he hadn't, and yes, that was Neil she'd been talking to, about gardening, although he really didn't have a clue . . .

'My poor dear love,' said Roy. This was exactly what she wanted to hear, wasn't it? 'There, there. Roy's here. Now, this has got to stop, do you hear me? I'm not going to have my little partner upset like this. Why didn't you tell me what was going on? I'd have been over like a shot. What are the police thinking of, to allow this to happen? It's outrageous. And you all alone, having to cope with all this . . . well, that's one thing you've got to get into your dear little head. You're not alone now. Understand?'

He kissed her cheek, and then made a dab at her lips too. She was still trembling, still weepy, and his kisses were very comforting, as was his arm around her shoulders. Even Frank hadn't been so loving. In fact, Frank would have been more likely to tell her to pull herself together. Roy kissed her again, his aim improving.

She liked it. She thought, Frank, I shouldn't, it's too early, but I've missed him so much, and does Roy want to go to bed with me? Because I would like it . . . yes, I would . . . or would I? Yes I would . . . no I wouldn't . . . what do I want? I don't know . . .

She needed to think . . . no she didn't . . . yes she did. She succeeded in drawing back a little. 'Sorry to be such a weepy-waily, but it's just been so awful!'

'There, there.' His fingers were at the zip of her skirt, and she didn't know whether she wanted him to go further or not. He put his hand inside her skirt and began to stroke her thigh, which was good, oh so good . . . She could feel that he was ready to unzip his slacks, and did she want that? She was going all soft and swoopy, but . . . no. He was going too fast for her.

She sat upright so that he had to withdraw his hand. She zipped up her skirt with one hand, while pushing his face away from hers with the other. Only her hand insisted on stroking his cheek, because really he was so nice, and very attractive, and it had been months since she'd felt a man's body wanting hers.

He smiled, taking the hint like the gentleman he was.

'Come away with me, Ellie. Let's take a little holiday. Get right away till everything's calmed down.'

'A holiday?' Her mind went to the travel brochures on the table. 'But . . .'

'Somewhere in the sun, a good hotel with a nightclub. I know one in Madeira which—'

'Roy, don't rush me.'

'Am I? I suppose I am. But I liked the look of you, the moment we met. I've been trying to hold off, telling myself it's too soon . . .'

'You call this holding off?'

'I was trying to.'

They both laughed. She got up and moved to her usual chair, away from temptation. It would have been so easy to give in, to let him do what he wanted, and she wasn't really entirely sure why she had withdrawn. It would be so easy to return to the warmth of his arms. Yet she didn't.

He went to stand by the window, looking out on the garden. Rain hit the glass. It had begun to rain quite hard, and she hadn't noticed it.

He said, 'So will you let me take you away from all this unpleasantness?'

'It's far too soon, Roy. People would talk.'

'Let them. What does it matter? What does matter is that against all the odds we've found one another. I care for you and you can't deny that you're beginning to care for me, too. We've both lost our partners. We're of age, independent. Why shouldn't we give this new relationship time to develop, away from the gossip?'

Put like that, it sounded all right. Didn't it? Then why wasn't she leaping into his arms again? He sat on the arm of her chair and took her hands in his.

'Ellie, my dear. You can't seriously mean to let a little gossip stand in the way of our happiness?'

'I've lived here all my married life. My friends are here. I care what they say about me.'

'Poor little dove.' He kissed her forehead. 'Has she been so damaged by life that she can't seize the chance for happiness when it comes along?'

She could feel herself turning soppy again. But calling her 'little dove' was a bit much, wasn't it?

'You and me,' he said, warm breath into her ear. 'Getting away from it all, away from this goddamn weather, somewhere warm in the sun, dancing in the moonlight on a beach. I know you! You're an independent woman. You think for yourself. I know you're brave enough to seize this opportunity . . .'

He began kissing her neck. She liked it . . . no she didn't . . . yes she did. But . . . She sighed, and he withdrew enough to look her in the eye. He smiled, lost the smile, regained it. Charm incarnate. But . . .

The doorbell rang. It would. Was she being saved by the bell, or was it sounding the knell of her happiness?

CHAPTER TEN

Running her fingers through her hair, Ellie checked in the hall mirror that her neck wasn't reddened with love bites before opening the door. It was Kate, in her long black coat, holding a laptop and a large pizza. Her wide smile turned to a frown as she saw Roy hovering in the doorway to the living room. 'Bad timing?'

Ellie hesitated, torn between 'yes' and 'no'.

Roy put his hands on her shoulders from behind. 'Kate, isn't it? Ellie and I have just been discussing when we can get away for a holiday together.'

A look of anxiety passed over Kate's face before she made herself smile and say, 'Oh, well in that case . . .'

Ellie didn't like Roy forcing her hand, so she disengaged herself and, knowing that she was being contrary, drew Kate into the hall out of the rain. 'Come on in. Filthy night. Lovely to see you. Roy's just leaving.'

Kate and Roy stretched their mouths into sort-of-smiles. Roy would perhaps have argued, but just then the doorbell rang again.

Dear Rose stood on the doorstep, trying to hold up her umbrella while clutching a box of cakes from the Sunflower Café. 'My, what weather! I remembered how much you liked chocolate éclairs, Ellie, so I thought I might just pop these in . . .' She took in the figure of Roy standing close behind Ellie. 'But . . . perhaps it isn't a convenient time to . . .'

'The more the merrier!' said Ellie. 'Come on in. Pizza and cakes for supper. Wonderful. Roy's just leaving.'

'Oh, this is Roy, is it? I've heard so much about you, Roy. I'm Rose, a very old friend of Ellie's.' She tried to shake hands with Roy while still holding the box of cakes and the umbrella. Kate dumped her stuff and helped Rose fold up the umbrella and take off her coat. Still Roy did not go.

He bent over Ellie to murmur in her ear, 'I'll ring to find out when you're free and come back later, shall I? We still have so much to discuss.'

The doorbell rang again. This time it was Tod from up the road. His hair was rumpled and wet, his clothes looked as if they had just been thrown on. As usual. Ellie hadn't seen Tod for some time. Not since his mother had bought him a computer, in fact. It was lovely to see him, but she wished he had chosen another evening to call.

'My computer's broke. I've just been swimming and Mum's not back till late today, so . . . party, is it?' he asked, dropping his school case and a plastic bag smelling of chlorine on the floor. 'Pizza, great!'

He had no qualms about walking right through them into the kitchen. 'Yes, do come in, Tod,' said Ellie, beginning to laugh.

'I'll phone for another couple of pizzas, shall I?' said Kate, dialling with the familiarity of an old friend.

'None of that salty fish on them for me,' said Rose, draping her coat over the newel post at the bottom of the stairs. 'Different kinds of cheese, that's what I like.'

'Pepperoni for me,' said Tod.

Roy raised his arms in defeat and left, banging the front door behind him.

'Well, isn't this nice!' said Rose, laying cakes out on a plate in the kitchen.

Tod was already picking knives and forks out of the drawer. They could eat in the kitchen, but it would be a squeeze. Ellie drew the curtains in the living room and laid out mats on the big table there. Returning to the kitchen, she noticed conversation among the other three had ceased.

'Talking about me?' she asked. 'Or about Roy?'

Kate gave a constrained smile and shook her head but Rose blundered in. 'Oh dear no, not really. Just to say how pretty you were looking tonight and how we hadn't seen you looking so well for ages.'

Tod despised women who prevaricated. 'They said he wasn't good enough for you, and I said, did you see what he was wearing? Nikes! At his age. That's sick!'

Everyone laughed and Kate changed the subject. The pizza man arrived with the order and they had an excellent supper. Kate retrieved the toolbar on the computer. Tod fiddled around with his homework, while casting sideways glances at what Kate was doing. Rose helped Ellie with the washing-up and brought her up to date on the latest impossible behaviour of Madam at the shop.

'. . . she only wants us to go through the stock and set aside everything that's been around for more than two weeks! Think how much extra time that's going to take!'

All the time Ellie was thinking: will Roy come back again tonight, and do I want him to? I wish my friends didn't dislike him so much. They're biased, of course. Used to having my undivided attention. Selfish of them. Why shouldn't I have a life of my own now?

Roy's a nice man, a good man, and an attractive one. I really don't see why, in this day and age, I shouldn't go away on holiday with him, separate rooms and each paying our own bills. I shall tell him so when next I see him. Though not perhaps tonight. It's late and I've had a long and tiring day.

Also, I must ask him about the letter saying he's got a criminal record. I'm sure it's nothing alarming.

'. . . and there I was, almost forgetting,' said Rose, helping herself to a dab of Ellie's hand cream. 'John and I put our heads together about the people we knew had bought those pads of paper, and then we asked the others too — though not Madam, of course; can you see her with that sort of paper in her house? More likely to have something handmade on vellum.

'She told us once that she had a stock of handmade paper she'd bought in a mill somewhere in the country, and then she had it embossed with their name and address, but of course the telephone numbers changing so often has made it very difficult for her, poor dear. I wish we were all so well off. Well, then John got a list together and I did, too, though we can't account for every single pad, but it's a start if you want to go around asking, isn't it? Oh, is that the time? Where did the evening go to, I wonder?'

Rose waited for Ellie to invite her to stay for the night, which she had done once or twice in the past. Ellie decided she wouldn't invite her, because she really did want to be alone to think. The rain had stopped, but it was still not a nice night to walk home in the dark. 'I'll ring for a taxi for you, my treat,' said Ellie.

Rose accepted the offer with many a twitter and fuss about getting her coat done up the right way, as she had lost a button, she thought, probably in the shop and goodness knows what would happen to it, but with a bit of luck it would still be there in the morning . . .

Putting her into the taxi, Ellie paid the driver in advance, but was called back by Rose waving some papers at her at the last minute. One sheet of paper torn from a writing block of ruled paper and one purple sheet, the two fastened together with a safety pin.

'Ellie, Ellie! I almost forgot your lists!'

'She don't half talk a lot,' said Tod, who had abandoned his homework to play on the computer in the study.

'Heart of gold,' was Kate's comment on Rose. 'With a nugget of common sense somewhere in there, if you can only find it.'

Ellie waved the papers in the air. 'It's her lists of who they think bought some of the multicoloured pads. Shall I bother to try to track these people down, Kate? Or shall I just give up and hope it all goes away?'

'Or lie back and think of England?'

Tod's head jerked up. 'What do you want to think of England for? You could think of Manchester United, or . . . Wow! Cool!' The game apparently reached a satisfactory conclusion, just as the doorbell went again.

This time it was Tod's mother, who had guessed that he'd be at Ellie's when she found her own house dark and empty. She was annoyed that Tod should have eaten at Ellie's when she had left some fish fingers in the fridge ready for him to cook.

'I hate fish fingers,' said Tod, slowly turning off the computer and packing his school books away. 'And my computer's packed up. Ellie's computer plays Minesweeper.'

Once he and his mother had disappeared into the night, Kate fidgeted around the room. 'Shall I go?'

'No, stay. It's been a long day; so much has happened. I found out who threw the paint at Nora's door. Goodness, that seems hours ago! It was a lad who ran with the gang, though this time the gang was a group of elderly gossips who ought to have known better. He's no threat to the community and I shan't tell the police about him. He's looking for gardening jobs. He doesn't really know much about it, but he's young and strong and if you tell him exactly what to do . . .'

'If *you* tell him what to do. I wouldn't know where to start.' Kate sat down. She was going to play by the rules. She wouldn't mention Roy if Ellie didn't. Ellie appreciated Kate's restraint, especially since she herself would have had difficulty in being so civilized if the positions had been reversed.

'Well, I did have some thoughts about your garden and started to jot them down, but maybe we should do this when Armand is around.'

'Oh, he never goes into the garden. Nor do I.'

'Maybe, but you have to look at it. If I agree to take it on, we'd need to work out whether you want to keep the hedge on this side and the fence on the other . . .'

'The fence is falling down and I hate cutting hedges.'

'Right. So perhaps we should have new fencing, both sides — I'll show you some samples. Or even a brick wall — but that would be hideously expensive.'

'I like the sound of a brick wall. It would give us privacy, wouldn't it? With a wrought-iron gate into the alley at the bottom? Expense?' A shrug. 'Well, we can afford it.'

'Water features?' said Ellie, as the idea of redesigning a garden with an unlimited budget went to her head. 'Rebuild the patio? A conservatory? Lawns? Ramps or terraces to deal with the slope? Paths, brick or stone? Trellising?'

'I see what you mean by needing a plan,' said Kate, laughing. 'Come to think of it, a better patio — large enough to eat out on — would be nice. And I do like the idea of a water feature. How about a series of terraces with steps between, to cope with the slope? No lawns. I can't bear mowing lawns. Can we have some beds with low-maintenance shrubs below the terrace? And yes, why not? More water. Can we have a water feature that drops down from one level to the next? And lights.'

'The cost!' Ellie tried to be sensible.

'I don't care! Why, a garden like that . . . we'd sit out in it and eat out when the weather permitted. Can we have some sort of awning over the top patio, which can be our new dining area in the summer — with outdoor heaters, perhaps? Or should we have a proper conservatory built on, which can double up as an extra room? How clever you are, Ellie! Draw us up some plans and I'll show them to Armand.'

'But will he want to spend all that much money on a garden? And what about the front garden, which you must admit is a disgrace at the moment?'

Kate's smile vanished, and anxiety took its place. 'We'll work something out. I earn enough to fund it, and . . . well, I'll talk it over with him. It's getting late. He'll be home by now. Parents' Evening at school, you know. You'll let me have something on paper soon, won't you? And — take care of yourself.'

'I will.' Ellie closed the door behind Kate and let herself relax. How exciting! What a wonderful, unexpected twist her life had taken. She must find a proper builder — not poor Neil, but someone who knew about costing for walls and diggers and drains and things.

There was so much to think about. Too many new developments to take in easily. Aunt Drusilla with her amazing offer of work, Diana in financial difficulties, the terrible onslaught of letters, Mrs Dawes and Neil, Kate and Rose and John and Tod . . . and Roy.

The phone began to ring. She thought it was probably Roy, ringing to see if the coast were clear for him to return to his courtship. There had been a couple of phone calls during the evening, but she had let the answerphone take the strain. She'd listen to the messages tomorrow.

She really didn't know what she wanted to do about Roy.

She was tired. She wouldn't answer the phone. She would go straight up to bed with a hot-water bottle because it was such a horrid night. Then she remembered the church notices and nearly missed her step on the stairs. Bother it! Oh well, she would worry about all that tomorrow.

* * *

Plump, capable hands laid out everything she needed. A block of wax, double boiler, thermometer, a mould, cotton wicks. Penknife to chip bits off wax crayons to colour the wax. A long steel pin and some scraps of blue and ivory material, a length of white nylon wool which looked silvery in the electric light.

This time it would have to be a proper woman's figure. Would it be better to model it out of an existing wax candle, a nice fat one? It wouldn't matter if there was a wick in it. In fact, the wick could be teased out to look like part of the hairdo. Fingers turned over the contents of the big cardboard box, where scraps of half-used candles discarded by the church had been thrown, for later use by her.

She would say a nice little prayer over the figure, to make sure.

* * *

Frank was talking to her, telling her something important. She was sitting in her chair in the living room and he was sitting in the big chair with his back to the window. He was drinking his after-supper cuppa, just about to go out for some meeting or other at the church. She could see his lips move, but she couldn't hear his voice. Strain as she might, she could not hear him. He was getting angry with her. It was all her fault because she never listened to what he said, never took his advice . . .

She reared up in bed, panting. So hot! She threw back the covers. Gradually her agitation subsided. She knew what he'd been trying to say to her. 'You just don't think before committing yourself! How many times have I told you? You're far too soft, and people take advantage of you.' Oh, Frank, you had such a clear mind, always knew what you wanted. You made all the decisions for both of us, and it's so hard now to know what to do for the best. Yet somehow I have to work things out for myself.

It was seven o'clock. She might as well get up. Saturday morning. She must do some shopping in the Avenue and try to think clearly.

Diana must be her first priority. She couldn't let her only daughter fall into debt, could she? No matter what it cost.

Bill would know how to arrange it, so somehow or other she must get in to see Bill. She didn't care how busy he was; he really must find time for her. She supposed she must do something about the church notices as well, though what, she couldn't for the life of her think.

Aunt Drusilla? Ellie supposed she ought to take that job. She couldn't leave her in suspense. She had to come to a decision about it. And Roy? Ellie didn't want to think about Roy for the time being. The phone rang as she was finishing her muesli and banana mix.

Diana. 'Mother? I'll be coming down to London tomorrow to see Aunt Drusilla—'

'Tomorrow? Sunday? Diana, you've never asked her for a loan, have you?'

'Of course I have. It was the obvious thing to do since you refused to help me. She says she wants to talk to me about it, so I can be with you for lunch and go to see her in the afternoon.'

'But Diana, even if she does agree to let you have some money . . .' Ellie's voice tailed off.

'You told me she was worth a mint, even though she'd always fooled us into thinking she was skint. She says there's a job going working for her, managing her properties. I like the sound of that. If she does own a lot of property, then who else would she want to invest in, if not her only great-niece?'

'Yes, but . . . she's a shrewd businesswoman. Diana, do be careful. She may agree to lend you the money, but my bet is she'll want an arm and a leg by way of interest.'

'Nonsense, mother. Trust me to know how to handle her. I haven't been PA to the MD of two different companies for nothing, you know.'

'I'd bet Aunt Drusilla against either of them.'

'Oh, mother, you're so out of date! What do you know about such things?'

Ellie sighed. 'Very little, I suppose. Well, it will be nice to see you. I'll be at church in the morning, so we'll have just a sandwich for lunch and I'll cook in the evening.'

'Can't you skip church for once? I was looking forward to a roast that I hadn't had to cook for myself.'

'No, dear. I can't skip church. I have commitments, you know.'

'But just for once . . .'

'I said "no", and I meant "no". Now, if it doesn't work out with Aunt Drusilla I'll see what I can do to help you myself. I was going to see Bill this morning, anyway, to ask his advice about giving you a loan to tide you over.'

'Don't bother. Your beloved Bill told me that Dad had tied up your money so tightly that I couldn't lay my fingers on it, so this way is much the best. Besides, I don't want a loan. I want enough to see us through without worrying.'

'I don't think Aunt Drusilla would agree to—'

'Don't fuss so, mother. Aunt Drusilla and I understand one another.'

Do you, now? thought Ellie. Oh well, perhaps I'm wrong. As she says, what do I know about such things?

'Very well, dear. I'd better clear out the little bedroom for baby Frank.'

'Yes, I suppose so. I wanted Stewart to look after him tomorrow and Monday, but he says he can't. Work, you know. Any excuse, if you ask me. Anyway, I thought I could stay a couple of days with you, see Aunt Drusilla and get that job fixed up, maybe take in a theatre, see some old friends, get myself a new winter coat while I'm at it. It's a whole different ball game now. And Stewart's at long last got an appointment with Human Resources down at their head-quarters in London on Tuesday or Wednesday.'

Ellie translated, 'That means Personnel, doesn't it?'

'He's been turned down for a promotion, but now this job has come up with Aunt Drusilla he'll have to try for a transfer to the London office. It's all working out perfectly.'

'Is that wise, Diana? I thought Stewart was happy where he was.'

'Oh, mother. Women have equal rights nowadays, you know. Of course Stewart wants me to have a good job, too. Anyway, I need to see you about another matter. Someone has been so kind as to let me know you're getting into dangerous waters with a con man. I assume it's that awful little church warden Archie Something you were seeing before Christmas? Really, mother, you ought to know better at your age. So I'll see you Sunday lunchtime. Oh, and remember I haven't got a key now, so be ready to let me in. Bye.'

Before Ellie could catch her breath from this broadside, the phone rang again, and this time she heard the imperial tones of Aunt Drusilla.

'Ellie, is that you? I left a message on your answerphone last night, but you haven't yet had the courtesy to reply. Your daughter Diana has approached me for money to bolster up her extravagant lifestyle. I have told her that I won't do business with her over the phone, but that if she cares to come down here, I will listen to what she has to say. I would have thought it was your duty to help her out, but I am a fair-minded person and I want to hear what you have to say about it, before I see Diana.'

Ellie explained the position, adding, 'Frank didn't want to give her any more money, since she used what we gave her to buy a totally unsuitable house, far beyond their means. I still think Frank was right, but I can't see Diana suffer for want of a loan to tide her over. I'm going this morning to see Bill, my solicitor, to see what can be done to help her.'

'I am not prepared to throw good money after bad. I formed the opinion that Stewart had reached the limit of his capabilities in his present firm. Am I right?'

'He's a lovely man and he loves her.'

'Hmph. In other words, he's incapable of earning enough to give her what she wants. In that case, I don't give much for his chances of hanging on to his marriage.'

Silently, Ellie agreed.

'And you, Ellie? Have you thought over my proposition? Or do I offer the job to Diana, who seems anxious for it?'

'Are you trying to blackmail me, Aunt Drusilla? I'm not prepared to play. Offer the job to Diana by all means, if you think it'll satisfy her and you're prepared to be responsible for the break-up of her marriage.'

'My offer to you remains open — until I have spoken to Diana. As for her, she is a responsible adult and will make her own decisions. Presumably Stewart can relocate if necessary.'

The phone went dead.

* * *

Think, Ellie, think! Make a list of urgent things to do. Lists provide a structure to life. Shopping in the Avenue. Call on Bill. Do something about the church notices . . . ah, there's some kind of secretarial services in the Avenue and they might be prepared to do them for me at a cost. Never mind the cost. The phone rang again. Was it going to be Roy? She let the answerphone take the message.

'. . . dear lady, how are you? Have you been avoiding me? It's your old friend Archie here, wondering if you might be free to take a little outing with me to see the snowdrops at Kew. Such a lovely blue sky, so tempting, don't you think? Ring me before twelve, and we'll make a day of it.'

Bother! said Ellie to herself. If Diana hears that message she'll think I'm collecting a harem, or whatever the men's version would be. Ellie wiped the tape. Then she remembered that there had been other messages that she hadn't listened to the previous night. Oops. Well, it couldn't be helped.

The weather had indeed improved. There were snowdrops out in the garden, and the Christmas roses looked fine. Ellie quickly made up the bed in the spare room at the back of the house, and made sure little Frank's cot in the tiny third bedroom was in working order.

She dusted around, checked the contents of fridge and freezer, picked up the pack of notes for the church, and braved the gusty, cold air outside. The people at the secretarial services were very helpful, and promised to have the notices ready in an hour. At a price.

Worth it at any price, almost, thought Ellie.

She did the food shopping, mindful that Diana expected a full roast dinner, and then walked to the end of the Avenue to see if Bill was in. His secretary looked down her nose at Ellie. Bill had a client with him, she said.

'I'll wait.'

Bill came out — big-boned, grey-haired, capable — noisily seeing a large, prosperous-looking businessman out. 'My dear Ellie! What a surprise!' He kissed her on both cheeks and held her arms to look her up and down. 'Where have you been? I thought you must have gone away on holiday or stayed on up north with your daughter. Come in, come in. My next client isn't due for ten minutes or so. Coffee? No?'

She followed him into his office. 'I've phoned ever so many times. I thought it was you who were away so much.'

'Me? I haven't been away at all. Oh, just the odd day here or there on business. I said to Harriet only the other day — you remember Harriet, don't you, my secretary? — that you must be still up north, and she said you were probably far too tied up with your new friends to think about us. An architect, is it?'

Ellie was conscious of rising colour. 'You shouldn't listen to gossip, Bill.'

'Is it only gossip? I hear talk of theatre outings, and candle-lit suppers.'

Ellie lost her temper. 'That's enough of that, Bill. It's no business of yours who I see and who I go out with.'

There was a short, super-charged silence. Bill was one of her oldest friends and Ellie knew he had always entertained a certain partiality for her, but he had overstepped the mark in a big way.

'I apologize,' he said, stiffly indicating that she be seated.

She remained standing. 'I had to come down to see you because I've tried and tried to speak to you on the phone, and you've never been available.'

'But that's . . .'

'If I can't rely on you to help me . . .'

'Of course you can!'

'. . . then I think I'd better find myself another solicitor.'

He sat down and folded his hands. 'That is your prerogative, of course.'

'Yes, it is. I wanted to ask your advice about giving Diana some more money, but . . .'

'Frank did not wish her to have—'

'Is the money mine to do as I wish with, or not?'

'Well, yours. Of course. But—'

'That's it!'

She wrestled the door open and swept past the startled receptionist into the Avenue. She wanted to hit something. To scream. To have hysterics.

Nicely brought-up women didn't do that sort of thing. Well, not in public, anyway. She considered going into the

Sunflower Café for a coffee, but thought she'd probably make a scene. Women like her didn't make scenes. They buttoned it up.

She had time to kill before collecting the church notices. She would go into the one expensive dress shop in the Avenue and spend a small fortune on some new clothes. Only, everything was in shades of mud or puce, neither of which did anything for her. And the largest size was sixteen, when she was really an eighteen nowadays. Here she was with money to spend, and nothing she liked to spend it on.

She came out of the shop and bumped into Roy.

He smiled down at her. 'We really must stop meeting like this.'

'People will gossip.'

'Let them. I've got an appointment soon with the estate agents, but I could kill for a coffee.'

'At the Sunflower Café? Why not?'

She pushed her rage into the back of her mind and smiled as Chloe came forward to serve them. Mrs Dawes would hear by nightfall that flighty little Ellie Quicke had been seen flirting in the café with a good-looking man. Who cared? Ellie didn't.

'You didn't ring me back last night,' said Roy, 'but then I remembered I hadn't given you my new address and phone number. I've rented a furnished flat nearby for a couple of months. Here's my card. I've put the details on the back.'

She took the card, and noted with a sense of shock that he'd moved into a flat in a road off the Avenue. Even closer to her than before.

'So have you thought any more about a holiday?'

She shook her head, trying and failing to put the row with Bill out of her mind.

He leaned over to take her hand. 'You've gone far away from me.'

She shook herself, dislodging his hand. 'Yes. I've just had a row with . . . oh, never mind. An old friend who thinks I don't know what I'm doing.'

'That's what I'm here for, to help you . . .'

'. . . to make decisions for me? No, Roy. You can't do that.'

He sat back in his chair, watching her as Chloe brought their coffees. 'What's up, Ellie? I thought we had an understanding. You weren't like this yesterday.'

Ellie flicked a glance at Chloe, whose bland expression belied the fact that she had certainly overheard what he said.

'I'm confused,' she said, knowing that this statement would go straight back to Mrs Dawes and into the gossip chain. Chloe left with a small but distinctive flounce. Black jeans today, black sweater with a lightning-strike logo on it.

Roy tried to take Ellie's hand again, but she removed it to pile sugar into her coffee. 'Now what's got into my little girl today?'

Hmph, thought Ellie. Don't try that 'little girl' line on me!

She said, 'You didn't tell me you had a criminal record.'

He drew back, eyelids fluttering. 'Well, it wasn't exactly . . .'

'Nor about the divorce. Messy, apparently.'

'That's all in the past.'

'Six months back? Three?'

He shifted in his seat. Grimacing, trying on the charm. 'Come on, Ellie, we're both old enough to know that a man can make a mistake . . .'

'So tell me about it.'

CHAPTER ELEVEN

Roy took out cigarettes and lit up without asking her if she minded. She was surprised. She hadn't smelled cigarettes on him, and his fingers were clean enough. Not those of a habitual smoker.

'Oh, sorry,' he said, catching her change of expression. 'I've really given them up, but every now and then I go back to my old habits. You don't mind, do you?'

Without pausing for her consent, he went on, 'What do you want to know? I married ten years ago, the daughter of the senior partner in the firm. I'd had several long-term relationships before, all very civilized, no commitment, no strings. But this was different. She was much younger than me, but she'd just been through a pretty bad experience with someone else and I thought — we both thought — that we'd be well suited. It did work for a while, but then . . . she wanted children and it didn't happen.

'We went for tests and it turned out she had some problem, might never conceive. I wanted to consider all the options, but she wouldn't discuss it. I didn't handle her well, I suppose. There were rows, and each time we rowed, we grew further apart. We stopped talking. She stopped cooking for me, not that she'd ever been that keen to spend time in the kitchen. Then she began to make eyes at a young architect in the office, just starting out, even younger than her.

'I got home one evening, found a message on the answerphone from him, for her, asking her to meet him at a local pub. I went there and confronted them. She said she was leaving me. I said the sooner the better, as it had only been a business arrangement between us, after all. I'm not proud of that. We all three got drunk and chased one another through the country lanes. Yes, I ought to have known better. He crashed his Mini into a tree and I ran into him. We all three ended up in Casualty being breathalysed. Cuts and bruises all round. Fines, suspensions. She left the hospital with him and that was that. It was two years ago.'

Ellie watched him as if she were looking at a soap opera on the television. 'Does it still hurt?'

'No, of course not. Well, perhaps a little.'

She thought: it was your pride that was hurt. And mine? What do I feel? No, don't probe, not just yet.

He said, 'I blame myself in a way. I was so much older, I ought to have managed it better. But she wanted to go and I couldn't stop her. I feared I might have to lose the house — our family house — at first, but then I managed to pay her off, so that was all right. They never married. What did hurt was seeing her toy boy doing so well in the business, favoured by her father. When he was promoted to partner, I decided to take early retirement. I arranged to continue to do some contract work for them, which worked out well enough but didn't keep me fully occupied.

'Last autumn I got restless. Not enough to do. I thought I'd look around, see if I could find a run-down property, drum up some business for myself. So I rented the house out for a year, put all my personal bits and pieces in store, and spent some time looking up old friends and relatives in different parts of the country. And found you.'

'And found me,' she repeated in a mechanical voice. His eyelids flickered and he blew smoke carefully away from her. Lying about something, she was sure. She replayed the scene in her mind and guessed: it was he who couldn't give her children, not the other way around. But what man would admit to failing in that department?

She said, 'Why do you think your marriage stopped working?'

He shrugged. 'We wanted different things in life. She really married not me, but my house. Georgian house, three floors, quite perfect in its way. When she tired of that period, she went ultra-modern, minimalist. Lives in a penthouse in a converted factory now. Not a comfortable chair in the place.'

Unlike me, she thought. I'm all cushy comfort and that's what he wants. Not a lover, but a mother. Do I want to be a mother to him? I don't think I do. Anyway, I'm not much cop as a mother. Look at Diana . . .

No, don't look at Diana.

'Which reminds me,' she said, gathering herself together. 'I have to pick up the church notices from the secretarial place and deliver them to one of the stewards, and this afternoon I'm having another driving lesson. Then my daughter Diana is coming down tomorrow, which means I have to do a bit of tidying up and cooking, so . . .'

He captured one of her hands and put it to his lips. The couple on the next table nudged one another and Chloe appeared at Ellie's elbow, pen poised to write out the bill.

He ignored them all. 'Give me the benefit of the doubt, Ellie?'

She smiled, constrained. 'Of course.' She removed her hand.

'Two coffees, that all?' said Chloe, meaning, 'I'm watching you!'

'Splendid, Chloe,' said Ellie. 'Will you pack me up one of your Victoria sponges to take away? Thank you, dear. Oh, and by the way, your cousin Neil has been round, asking if I had any gardening or odd jobs to do. Has he been working in that line for long?'

'Not really,' said Chloe, happy to break up the overcharged atmosphere at the table. 'He was doing A levels, but my uncle got himself a new girlfriend and she didn't like having him around, so he came down here to stay with Gran for a while. I'll put the sponge in a box for you, shall I?'

Roy realized this exchange had firmly replaced Ellie in her own world, which was what she had hoped it would do. He helped her back on with her coat and handed over her shopping bag, while ostentatiously paying for the two coffees. 'Dinner this evening?'

'I'll ring you if I can make the time.'

* * *

Clearing up before the arrival of guests is always tiresome. She found Frank's fountain pen under the settee. He had been fretting about it when he was in hospital and she hadn't been able to locate it anywhere. That nearly reduced her to tears.

She didn't allow herself to think about Roy at first, because she was afraid she might uncover feelings of hurt and dismay. When she did allow herself to think, she found to her surprise that, after allowing herself a little wince at the way she had been taken in, she was amused and a little touched by his story rather than distressed.

She told herself that she had been flattered by his attentions, had allowed him to get closer to her than she perhaps ought to have done, out of perversity, loneliness, what have you. She might easily have been drawn into having an affair with him. Yes, her body would have liked that. She sighed. But . . .

But she did not love him. No. And she was not the sort of woman who could take up with a man lightly, have a good time for a while and then move on. She was half-sorry about that. In a way, she wished she had more spirit of adventure. She thought she might well regret the passing of this opportunity to have a sexual relationship. Perhaps, when she was old and doddery, she would look back on the encounter with Roy and think fondly of What Might Have Been.

On the other hand, it was a lot safer keeping to the straight and narrow. A great deal safer. And calmer. If a little dull at times. A pity, in a way, because marrying him and moving away from the parish would have solved so many problems.

She picked up the two lists Rose had given her and put them down again in the same place. She wasn't going to do anything about them, anyway, so why keep them? She nearly dropped them in the wastepaper bin, but finally put them with other papers to be looked at — bills, National Trust magazines, an RAC membership renewal form. She must get round to writing to them.

Her driving instructor had left a message on the answerphone cancelling her lesson because he'd got bronchitis. It was a nuisance, just as she'd got herself all psyched up. Now she'd have to wait for weeks, maybe, until he could fit her in again.

She picked up the pile of papers which needed attention and took them through to the study. Frank's computer sat on its mat, daring her to approach it. Nasty, sneery, smug machine. She thought she would rather like to turn this room into a proper dining room again, like Kate's. Then she would have the perfect excuse to get rid of the computer and go back to her old electric typewriter.

She dropped the papers on the flap of the desk. Rose's two lists floated out and parachuted to the floor. Again, she nearly disposed of them. Instead, she decided that, as they had taken so much trouble to make the lists, the least she could do was to look at them.

John and Rose had each made up their own list, Rose in pencil on lined paper, John on a piece of coloured paper from the pad he'd bought himself. The two lists overlapped, of course. All the people they'd mentioned at lunch were there. Rose had added, 'Working in the back room, I don't see many customers, but I think the thin woman who works in the library bought one.'

Ellie lifted Rose's note to read John's. The same names at the top, followed by a note saying, '*Very fat woman, Thurs pms, buys good china. A dealer?* and also, '*Teenaged girl, v. short hair, dark blue school uniform.*'

That was it. Nothing much to go on. Ellie supposed she could always drop in at the library and ask the thin woman there whether she had bought one of the pads. Or hang around on a Thursday to see if the woman who bought china might drop in.

No. She dropped the lists into the wastepaper bin.

She bent down to retrieve them. Lilac paper. Ellie had had a lilac letter, and so had Nora. Ellie unpinned Rose's note and set it aside. She stared at John's note. There was something about it . . .

The phone rang. Automatically she answered it, then wished she hadn't, because it was Archie.

'Gracious lady, I hear you have been a perfect saint and produced the notices for the church this week. I was ringing our beloved curate to ask who was doing them — a catastrophe with our dear secretary in the parish office, I hear — and he said you had kindly undertaken the job. I'm just about to go out, so I'll come round to pick them up from you, shall I? Save you from coming out in the cold.'

'That's very kind of you, Archie. I did mean to drop them in to you this morning, but I got diverted and found them still in my basket when I got back. Don't bother yourself. I'll bring them straight over to you.'

'No bother, dear lady. None at all. In five minutes, then. And perhaps, if you're not doing anything for lunch, you might care to join me at the carvery?'

The phone went dead. Archie was not risking a refusal on the phone. Now she would have to decline his invitation face to face, and he really did have the most beseeching eyes. Rather like a poodle. No, not a poodle. A soppy black retriever.

Yet there was a brain there. Frank and Archie had always been meeting about church affairs, and Archie was supposed to be something pretty bright in the financial world. She could ask him to help her with her finances . . . no, she couldn't. He would use any such invitation as licence to take over her life. Archie was also looking for a cosy little wife. Yuck.

She returned to her scrutiny of John's note. The doorbell rang. Blast! The man must have sprinted over the Green to get here so quickly.

It wasn't Archie. It was young Neil, dusting off his hands. 'I finished that, missis. Anything else?'

Ellie blinked, then looked where he indicated. The tubs containing the dead conifers had been removed. The concrete slabs covering Kate's front garden had been swilled over and scrubbed clean. The slabs looked even worse now than when the eye had been led to the decaying wooden tubs and their contents, but that wasn't Neil's fault.

'She said she was out today, but that if I cleared all this stuff away, no messing, you'd tell me what else she wanted doing. She said you'd pay me and she'd pay you later.'

Ellie blinked. 'She didn't tell me this.'

'I saw her early this morning, when she was on her way out. She said she'd phone on her mobile to you and tell you it was all right.'

'Are you so short of cash that you can't wait till Monday?'

He shuffled around in his shabby trainers and she thought that, yes, he probably was. Mrs Dawes would be happy to house him, but living on a widow's pension, she would expect him to pay for his keep. Then he would need to go out of an evening, chat up the girls, sink a few pints. He had done a good job.

What could she find for him to do for her? She couldn't ask him to tackle any other jobs for Kate until the new garden design was agreed. It was too early in the year for him to mow her lawn, but there was some tidying up he could do for her on the herbaceous border — that is, if he knew the difference between a camellia and a forsythia, which she suspected he didn't.

'My garden shed needs a good tidy out, if you'd like to do that? Take everything out onto the lawn, sweep out the floor and — yes, there's a fraying cable that needs mending. If you like, you can wash out the plant pots I used for bedding plants last summer, which I put away all dirty. When you've got everything out and clean, I'll show you what to put back, and what to throw. Right?'

'Right.'

'Well met, my dear lady! Surveying the domain, are we? Have we time for a spot of nosh at the carvery today?'

It was Archie, puffing a bit from a short journey taken without the benefit of his car, which he'd parked a little way up the road. He was genteelly overlooking Neil's presence. Ellie saw the boy take in the details of the newcomer's appearance, and knew it would be all round the parish by nightfall that Archie had wanted to take Mrs Quicke out for lunch.

'Thank you, Archie, but I'm attending to the garden today. I'll fetch the notices for you, shall I? Neil, come through the house and I'll show you what I want done.'

* * *

It was another quarter of an hour before she could get back to John's note. She took it to the window and slanted it this way and that. Then she scrabbled around in Frank's desk until she found the magnifying glass he had used now and then to help him mend his glasses.

She found the colourful handwritten poison-pen notes she had received, and the last letters sent to Nora. She laid them side by side on the table. After a while she put all but one of Nora's letters to one side and studied that one, comparing it with John's note, and the letters she had received.

She rubbed her eyes. She simply could not be seeing what was right before them.

She switched on Frank's desk lamp and pulled it towards her. Now the evidence was even clearer.

The last letter Nora had received and the ones Ellie herself had been sent had a very slight stain down the right-hand side. The edges of the paper were ruffled, as if they had come into contact with water, or perhaps tea. Someone had quickly mopped up the liquid but had left traces behind if you knew where to look.

You wouldn't really see it if you just looked at one piece of paper in isolation, but when you had several before you the sequence of events was clear.

Ellie placed John's note under the others, and the stains matched perfectly. There was no doubt about it: the letters had come from the pad John had purchased and which he was still using for notes.

It couldn't be.

But it was.

No. John could not possibly, could never have written those notes! But suppose he had?

Why should he do such a thing? There wasn't a mean thought in his head. He's retired, his wife's always ill, never enough money for travel and good holidays, which is what he wanted to do when he retired. That doesn't make him the sort of person who writes those horrible letters. He would never have persecuted poor Nora like that, or sent her a wax cat and killed a real one, or thrown paint at Nora's door, or worked a computer.

Hold on. Neil threw the paint. You've already worked it out that there was more than one person involved — the paint-thrower, the one who writes handprinted letters, and the one who uses a computer. Plus a fourth, perhaps, who killed the cat.

Look at John's handwriting: neat, square letters. Now look at the wavering capitals used by whoever wrote on the same pad as John.

His wife? What was her name? Sue? She was hardly ever seen out of the house. Nerves, poor thing — or so people said.

Ellie could hardly remember what she looked like. Had they ever met? Oh, she must have met her sometime in the past, at a church do or something. An out-of-focus picture of a droopy, washed-out, greyish woman floated into Ellie's mind and crystallized. A permanent sniffer? Liked wearing sandals in winter. Bunions? A stiff face without much expression. On medication?

Almost a recluse. Children grown up and gone away. John out at the charity shop most days. A car? Yes, but nothing splashy. Sue didn't drive. 'Too nervy, you know, for London traffic.'

Holidays? 'No, Sue can't face it this year.'

Birthdays? Anniversaries? 'I wish I could take her out to a show, but she gets palpitations; the crowds, you know.'

Gilbert had visited her, Ellie knew.

Ellie picked up the phone and dialled St Thomas's Rectory on the other side of London. Gilbert wasn't in — surprise, surprise — but his wife Liz was.

'Ellie, lovely to hear from you . . . Sue? Yes, I remember her. Gilbert used to visit. He doesn't now, of course. Why do you ask?'

'These poison-pen letters. I've come across something that points in her direction. What do you think?'

A long silence.

'Liz?'

'You've thrown me, Ellie. I hardly knew the woman. I'm trying to remember what Gilbert said about her. Agoraphobic? Couldn't leave the house by herself, except perhaps at night. That's it. Couldn't stand crowds. On medication for it. Quite bad, I think. Very supportive husband, who spent a lot of time at the charity shop. Is that the right person?'

'I think so. Could she have written the poison-pen letters?'

'I'm no expert. Someone whose life was very circumscribed and who had come to depend on Gilbert's visits might perhaps resent it if he wasn't able to give her as much time as he had been doing.'

'Such as when Nora flipped after her father's death, and mopped up all his free time?'

'Do you think that's what it was?'

'I don't know. It looks rather like it. The last letter written to Nora and the ones written to me come from the same pad of paper, which was quite innocently taken home by John, Sue's husband.'

'That's horrible.'

'No, it isn't. It makes it much easier to deal with if you know who sent the letters, and you can get some understanding of why they should have done such a thing.'

'What are you going to do about it? Go to the police?'

Ellie sighed. 'Would you? Knowing what a poor sort of creature she is?'

'But the damage she's done! Not to you, perhaps, because you're so strong, but what about the harm done to Nora? You could say that Sue murdered Nora. Oh, perhaps she didn't mean to, but that's what happened.'

'I have to think about it. I've met another couple who were targeted by the poison-pen letters before Christmas. I have no idea why Sue should have picked on them. Then paint was thrown at Nora's door. I found out who that was, but it was reasonably harmless and I don't want to set the police on him . . . Liz, are you still there?'

'Yes, but the front doorbell's just rung, and I'll have to . . . can I ring you back later? Oh, bother. No, I can't. We're going out tonight to the theatre. I'll ring you tomorrow or Monday, right? Bye.'

Ellie cradled the phone, and it rang again immediately.

'Ellie, this is Kate. Listen, I'm on my mobile at the conference, can't stop for long. Brilliant sessions, and I've actually been asked to speak at the next one, would you believe! What I wanted to say was, that young man Neil Something was outside the house this morning when I left and . . .'

'We've met. He's cleaned up your front garden and is turning out my garden shed at the moment. You want me to pay him, and you'll reimburse me.'

'Oh, that's all right, then. I got so caught up with things here, I only just remembered . . .'

'Before you go, Kate, did you manage to get anything about poison-pen letter-writers on the Internet?'

'Yes, sorry, forgot to give it to you last night. Usually female of a certain age, frustrated in some way. Typically a spinster, though not always. Very rarely found out because they have a certain low cunning. Quite often uses capital letters cut from newspapers, or writes with the left hand to disguise the handwriting. Takes pleasure in hearing the victim's name dragged in the mud, but rarely makes personal contact. A watcher, not a doer.'

'Writing with the left hand. That makes sense. Kate, I think I know who wrote the letters on coloured paper, though I can't say at the moment. Have to check it out. But would such a person also use a word processor?'

'I wouldn't have thought so, would you? I mean, why bother to write if you can type? Typing's even more anonymous than writing with your left hand. Are we perhaps talking about two different people here?'

'Possibly three. Kate—'

'Sorry, got to go. I'll try to ring you later. If not, I'll be back tomorrow afternoon and we can talk then. See you!'

The phone went dead.

Ellie put the stained letters into the middle drawer of the desk and locked it. She trusted both Liz and Kate, but perhaps not all her friends had such clean hands. Mrs Dawes, for instance, must know more than she had said. Neil had admitted throwing the paint. Mrs Dawes must have known that, or at least have suspected it.

Ellie sighed. No, Mrs Dawes would never have countenanced any such activity, if she had known about it. Gossip was her forte, but there was no malice in her. At some point Ellie would fill her in on what had happened, and Mrs Dawes would be shocked, really upset that her careless words might have had such a dreadful result. But even if she got a bad fright, it wouldn't still her restless tongue for ever. That was the way she was.

Now Kate had confirmed that it was probably a third person who had used a computer for the typed letter. The thought pounding through Ellie's head was that there must be a connection between the letter-writers, the paint-thrower and whoever had made the wax model and killed the cat.

She considered the women likely to have gossiped with Mrs Dawes. She knew both by sight. Elderly widows, arthritic, short-sighted. There was something she knew about one of them . . . if only she could remember. But neither of them could have operated a word processor, or stalked a cat. What was more, John's wife would never drop into Mrs Dawes's house for a coffee and a chat. The connection must be elsewhere.

Should Ellie go to the police with what she knew? No. No, because Neil didn't deserve that, and Sue — if it was Sue — was not mentally strong enough to cope.

So what should Ellie do? She could go round to John's with the evidence and confront Sue. But this would probably drive poor Sue even further into her problem. She could take John aside and show him the proof and leave him to decide what to do about his wife. He would know how to stop her. That might be best. Or would it be too awful for John to cope with?

Perhaps it would be best to leave it. Now that Ellie knew the identity of the person concerned — or guessed it, rather — she could cope with it. Couldn't she? The damage was done and poor Nora was dead. Ellie herself would survive any gossip stirred up by Sue's letters. In fact, they might have done her a good turn by making her question Roy's attentions to her.

Or perhaps Kate and Liz had got it all wrong, and it had been John himself who had . . . ? No, ridiculous!

But, said a voice in her head, it's only instinct that tells you so, and instinct can lead you astray.

There was something happening in the garden. A man was laughing, a full-bellied laugh — that was Neil, chasing something or somebody with a besom. Young Tod, dressed in sweater and jeans, was also leaping about and laughing.

Streaking in and out of the shed, crouching low and then bounding high into the air, tail wagging furiously, was Midge.

What had he found? Spiders? Mice? Rats?

Ellie found herself smiling as she pulled on an anorak and went out to join them.

Tod saw her and ran up the garden. 'It's your cat! He thinks the end of the hosepipe is a mouse or something! He's crazy!'

Midge suddenly lost interest in the hosepipe, scratched his left ear with a hind paw and walked sedately up the garden path, erect tail gently waving. He purred around Ellie's legs as she bent to tickle him. This is happiness, she thought. For the first time since Frank died, I can feel happy. People laughing, a cat purring, the garden being attended to.

Tod hopped over on one leg, just to show he could. 'I was supposed to go straight home and do my homework after swimming, but Mum's out and the computer's still broken and I saw Neil working in the shed, and I thought maybe I could help and stay for tea.'

'Of course you can,' said Ellie, consigning thoughts of Roy to the dustbin. 'Show me what you've done, you two.'

* * *

Over a substantial fry-up-cum-high-tea in the kitchen, Neil asked about clearing Kate's garden. He was a good worker, he said. Always stuck at a job till it was finished.

'Half-term soon,' said Tod, eyeing the last two biscuits. 'Nothing happens, holidays. Mum's working. The computer she got me was second-hand. Well, passed on from someone at work, actually. She says she can't afford to get another, but I could play on yours, Mrs Quicke, couldn't I? After swimming I could come round and help Neil, and then perhaps I could play on the computer here for a while, couldn't I?'

'Can you mix concrete?' asked Neil.

'Can *you*?' said Ellie, amused. 'At least Tod knows what a weed looks like — most of the time, anyway.'

'Only 'cause you taught me.'

Neil concentrated on wetting his finger and collecting the last of the cake crumbs on his plate.

Tod said, with the crashing truthfulness of the very young, 'Neil doesn't know much about gardening, he says. But you could teach him, couldn't you, Mrs Quicke?'

Neil reddened. 'I can mow lawns a treat. Cut hedges. Dig. Dad had an allotment when I was a kid. I used to help him on that. Sometimes.' He met Ellie's sceptical eye and fidgeted, dropping his knife on the floor. 'Well, there was football, like.'

Ellie understood how it had been. It occurred to her that it would be pleasant to teach young Neil how to look after plants. Perhaps she could lend him some of her gardening magazines for a start? But she needed to know more about him first. 'Your cousin Chloe tells me you started A levels?'

'Thought I might as well. But then, well, things went pear-shaped.'

Both glanced at Tod, rummaging in the freezer for ice cream. Ellie liked Neil all the better for not going into the sordid details of his home life in front of the boy, although she reflected that Tod's own father had walked out on his mother when she became pregnant. Tod had never seen him, wouldn't have recognized him if he saw him in the street. Maybe their single-parent background was another bond between the two boys.

She said, 'It's true that next door are thinking of having their garden redesigned, and they've asked me to produce a scheme for it.'

'They could have a heated outdoor swimming pool, wow!' said Tod.

'A really fine lawn,' said Neil.

Ellie laughed. 'Can you see them using an outdoor swimming pool? And Neil, they're not the sort to spend time keeping a lawn under control.'

Neil leaned back to allow Tod to give him a plateful of ice cream. 'Suppose I offered to mow the lawns for them and cut the hedges on a regular basis?'

'A contract gardener?'

'Why not? I really like the work, helping people, making things tidy. I've been studying the neighbourhood, going round doing odd jobs. There are lots of people here who go out to work all day, let their gardens go. And even more old people who can't manage their hedges or cope with their mowers anymore. You can see it everywhere, if you look.'

'That's brilliant!' said Tod, shovelling in the last mouthful and eyeing the carton for seconds. 'You could do ours, for a start. Mum's put it all under concrete, but if we had some big tubs and stuff, you could come along and fill them with plants and then look after them for us. That would be brill!'

Ellie was amused, even intrigued. 'Mm, it's an idea. But Neil, wouldn't you need to buy all the equipment — a new mower and a strimmer, for a start? And I suppose you could store them in a van, but it wouldn't be really safe, would it? You'd need somewhere to work from, rent a garage or something.'

'I could get a start-up loan from the government.'

'What about keeping the books? VAT and all that?'

Neil looked stricken. 'I don't think I could manage that.'

'No. Well,' briskly, 'let's deal with one thing at a time. It's getting dark, and we need to get those things back into the shed.'

Working half by torchlight — Tod's own big torch — and the light from the lamps around the Green, they sorted out what needed to be kept and what needed to be thrown.

'Hang about!' said Neil, bringing out a clean white shoebox from the shed. 'I don't remember this being here before. It's addressed to you, Mrs Quicke.'

'Is it a bomb?' cried Tod, leaping up and down.

'Don't be silly!' Ellie laughed, but her heartbeat went into double-time. The box was identical to the one delivered to Nora with the strangled cat figure inside it. She looked around for Midge, but he had disappeared. Probably sleeping off his tea on her bed.

'Let me see!' said Tod. 'Someone must have put it in the shed while we were having tea.'

Ellie looked both ways along the alley, which was now shadowy and looked threatening instead of picturesque. She slid the box lid up and saw, not a wax cat, but the wax effigy of a woman clad in blue with a silvery thatch on her head. A long pin secured a drawing of a crab onto its torso.

A crab meant cancer, didn't it? Someone hated her enough to wish her dead of cancer.

'Oh, it's only a doll,' said Tod, disappointed.

Ellie looked at Neil. He, too, had seen what the box contained. 'That's sick,' he said.

Ellie put the lid back on the box with shaking fingers. Well, she thought, at least I know now that Neil had nothing to do with it.

CHAPTER TWELVE

Ellie didn't sleep well that night. She had taken the box inside and hidden it in the drawer in Frank's big desk. She kept telling herself not to panic. She couldn't think straight. For the first time she understood that this affair didn't just threaten her reputation, but also her life.

Neil knew nothing about it, that was plain. He had never seen the doll before. She'd asked him outright, and he'd shaken his head, frowning. She'd believed him.

She was too hot. She threw off the bedclothes.

She got a drink of water, pummelled the pillows. Got indigestion. Took a tablet. Was too cold. She thought, it's late. Diana is coming tomorrow, and if I don't get to sleep soon I'll be good for nothing. And if she starts trying to boss me about, I won't be able to cope . . . and woke up shivering.

She went downstairs and made a cup of tea, walking about the house in the dark, with only the light from the kitchen to guide her. She pulled back the curtains in the sitting room, and looked out at the moon dodging in and out of clouds above the church.

She went back to bed. Slept. Woke. Did a crossword, listened to the early dawn chorus of birds, and finally drifted off.

She woke to the consciousness that Diana was coming and she must hurry or she would be late for church. Again. She always seemed to be last arriving, even though she lived nearest.

As she was about to leave, the phone rang. Aunt Drusilla.

'Well, girl? Have you decided to accept my offer?'

'No, Aunt Drusilla. I can't work for you. Anyway, I thought you had made up your mind to give the job to Diana. She'll be here at lunchtime.'

A long pause. Ellie fidgeted.

'I would prefer to work with you.'

Ellie was surprised, and rather touched. 'Well, I'm sure Diana will be very efficient.'

Another silence. Then the phone was put down. Was the old girl losing her marbles?

Ellie shot out of the house, trying to calm her thoughts. Poison-pen letters, wax figurines . . . how did they know she had always been afraid of getting cancer? Her mother had died of cancer. Suppose she did have it? Or the stress of the letters was giving it to her? No. Use your common sense. Of course you can't get cancer just because someone wishes it on you.

She tried to still her thoughts, to prepare for the morning service. She was overtired. Images whirled around in her mind. Diana, Aunt Drusilla; John and Sue; young Neil, the letters, the quarrel with Bill — oh dear, what was she going to do without him? She'd relied on him for so long. Then Roy and his tempting offer; but really it would be cowardice to leave all her troubles behind by going away on holiday just now. In any case, she was not one hundred per cent easy in her mind about him.

She tried to stop worrying. Tried deep breathing. She must put all these things aside. She knew He was aware of all her problems. She must pray a little. Try to concentrate on Him. 'Centring down', they called it. Or some such expression. If only Timothy would preach an inspiring sermon today. There was little hope of that. If only Timothy had been the kind of man you could take your troubles to! But he wasn't, and that was that.

Praying helped. Offering up her voice in the choir helped, too. She would survive.

* * *

Diana unloaded three suitcases, a baby buggy and a fretful toddler from her car. The car really belonged to Ellie. Diana had co-opted it for her own use, sharing her father's opinion that Ellie would never learn to drive. Handing the sodden child to her mother, Diana said, 'What a journey! What's for lunch? I'm starving. Are there any messages for me?'

Wrong-footed by her daughter's neediness, Ellie became flustered. Besides, Frank was both heavy and unhappy. 'Were you expecting any messages? Aunt Drusilla is expecting you this afternoon, I know, but . . .'

'I told some of my old friends that I'd be down this week. Do be careful with that buggy, one of the wheels is loose.'

Ellie had already discovered this, and that baby Frank was wet and smelly. At Christmas he had been a loving, cuddly child, but he seemed to have suffered a sea change since then, and was now a roaring, struggling bundle of hate.

Diana began to take the suitcases upstairs, ignoring her son.

'Oh, have you put me in the back bedroom? It's very small, isn't it? Much smaller than I remembered it. Of course, we have such a nice-sized master bedroom in our house.'

It was annoying how quickly Diana could make Ellie feel inadequate. She could hear herself being placatory.

'I put little Frank in the small bedroom. Is that all right?'

'Oh yes, I suppose that will do. The journey down was terrible. He cried most of the way. Teething, I suppose. Stewart didn't want me to bring him, but I know Aunt Drusilla will want to see him.'

Ellie was not convinced about that but set about changing the little boy and soothing him. His dark eyes looked up at her with an expression she had often surprised on Diana's face. It was not a loving look. She smiled at him, clucking away, trying to reach him with her love, but his expression did not change.

Oh dear, were there going to be two tyrants in the house? 'When's lunch?'

'I've just got soup and sandwiches for now. We'll have roast beef with all the trimmings tonight.'

'Roast beef? Mother, I did think you'd remember that roast chicken is my favourite.'

'But you always used to want—'

'That was when I was young. Beef is so bad for you. You don't know where it's been.' Diana snorted with laughter at her own joke, but Ellie was perturbed.

'Honestly, darling. The butcher gets all his beef from Ireland, and . . .'

'Oh well, never mind. Shall I wear this suit . . . or this one . . . this afternoon? I need to impress the old bat with my executive abilities, don't I? Either way, the blouse will need ironing. Perhaps you can do that while I snatch a bite and ring Stewart to tell him I've arrived. He does fuss so.'

Ellie pressed the blouse and fed baby Frank — who was growing fast and, yes, definitely teething. She listened to Diana talking on the phone, and over lunch while she coaxed baby Frank to eat, she listened to Diana explaining her plans. Ellie kept her mouth shut. Come to think of it, that had been her role in the past, before Diana got married and moved away, and before Frank died. Oh well. Only once did she venture to raise a query during Diana's monologue.

'You've actually given up your job? But . . .'

'Yes, of course I have. This job with Aunt Drusilla solves all our problems. I'll make her give me a whacking big salary, and who knows what other opportunities there'll be for making money when I'm working for her.'

'Are you so sure she will give you the job? And what about Stewart, and your house and his job?'

Diana waved all this aside. 'We couldn't afford to keep the house, as you very well know. If you hadn't been so miserly, if you'd bailed us out, then perhaps it might have been all right and I might have found another good job up there eventually. But with me working down here — and of course I'll move back in with you for the time being so that you can look after Frank while I'm working — it's a perfect excuse to put the house on the market without losing face. Stewart is going to ask Head Office if he can transfer down here, and if not, he can get some sort of flat up there and join me down here at the weekends.'

'But . . .'

'I've got it all worked out. The old bat's getting on, and will be only too happy to leave the management of the flats in my hands. I expect some of the people who have been working for her are not very good, and it'll be a doddle to get her to change to others . . . and that's where those handy introductory fees come in . . .'

'That's corruption!'

'Oh, mother. You're so old fashioned. It's sound business sense. I'll be making double what I made up north, and I'll be my own boss, too. What's more, she's not going to last for ever, and she's bound to leave me her house and all her flats, and then . . . you won't see me for dust!'

Ellie saw that Frank had opened his mouth to yell, and automatically shoved another spoonful into the gap. She thought: Diana's fooling herself, isn't she? Aunt Drusilla may be old, but she's as sharp as a tack. Besides, Diana has had a copy of Frank's will. She must have seen that I inherited Aunt Drusilla's house. Do I remind her, when she's so happy and excited about the future? No, I don't. Aunt Drusilla will live for years, with care. Besides, perhaps Diana is right, and she does deserve some of the family money. But I really don't like the thought of her moving back in with me.

Diana swept out to have her interview with her great-aunt, leaving Ellie to put a fractious Frank to bed. He resisted with all his might. She had only just got him settled, done the washing-up from lunch and started the preparations for supper, when Diana returned. She slammed the front door so hard that Ellie was afraid little Frank would be woken again. Ellie took off her apron and stepped into the hall, only to see Diana lifting the phone with the squinty-eyed air of one doing mental arithmetic.

'Stewart? Yes, of course I got the job. I beat her up on terms, too. It's going to be even better than I thought. I start tomorrow. Mother will look after baby Frank, get him into a crèche or something. Did you get an appointment to see about transferring down to London? Oh. Well, that will do, won't it? Now, put the house on the market first thing tomorrow . . .'

Ellie went back into the kitchen, redonned her apron and put the kettle on for a cup of tea. Diana only drank Earl Grey. Or perhaps she was into one of the herbal infusions nowadays? Anyway, it was time to put the beef on for supper, and make the Yorkshire pudding. She could hear Frank wailing upstairs, but she closed her ears to the noise. Let Diana deal with her son. There was a limit!

The front doorbell rang. Diana sang out, 'Mother, doorbell!' She had finished her conversation with Stewart but was now on to one of her old friends. Ellie finished putting the joint in the oven, poked an onion under the foil covering the beef and, still with her apron on, stepped past Diana to the door.

It was Archie, wearing an orchid in his buttonhole and carrying a bottle of wine. He looked taken aback to see Diana, with whom he'd had harsh words when she'd last descended on Ellie. Diana scowled and turned her shoulder on him, still talking on the phone. Frank was making an appalling noise upstairs.

Ellie hesitated. 'Oh, do come in Archie. I wanted a word, anyway. You remember my daughter Diana, don't you? That's my grandson making all that noise upstairs. Diana, what about little Frank?'

'Oh, leave him. He'll tire himself out presently. No, not you . . .' and she returned to her phone conversation.

Ellie gestured Archie into the hall, her mind on the timing for supper. She really ought to be making the batter for the Yorkshire pudding at that very moment. Archie's timing was way off, if he'd planned a romantic tête-à-tête. She invited him to come into the kitchen if he wanted to talk to her. Diana's eyes swivelled in annoyance as Archie tiptoed past her and went into the kitchen after Ellie.

He said, 'I wouldn't have thought you were old enough to have a grandson.'

Even he recognized the falsity in his tone. He reddened. Ellie sighed, and resumed weighing out the ingredients for the Yorkshire pudding. She wondered if he expected to be asked to join them for supper. She decided that the invitation would not be given.

He flicked on a gold-glinting smile. 'I thought you might like a quiet supper out somewhere.'

She shook her head, breaking an egg into the seasoned flour in the bowl. 'As you can see . . .'

'Is your daughter planning to stay long?' That didn't come out very smoothly, either.

'I'm really not sure.' Ellie whisked in milk. 'Half a tick, and we can go in the other room and have a cuppa or a sherry.'

He looked totally out of place in the kitchen. He tried to perch on the edge of the kitchen table but was not tall enough and slid off. There was an indignant squawk from Midge, who had been sleeping on one of the chairs, and then a clatter as he exited through the cat flap. 'Gracious, what an enormous cat! Is he yours?'

'He is,' said Ellie, throwing the tea things onto a tray. 'Would you carry this into the living room while I fetch baby Frank down? I can't let him cry himself sick.'

'Ah, suffer little children.' Archie tried to be understanding. 'We never had any, the wife and I.'

Ellie gave him a social smile, recalling that, according to gossip, his ex-wife had had cause for complaint in the bed department. She whisked upstairs, retrieved a red-faced and soaking toddler from his cot, soothed and changed him and bore him back downstairs, to find Archie and Diana sitting at opposite ends of the room, with Diana pouring out the tea. Archie was eyeing Diana as if she were a time bomb.

Diana pulled a face. 'Mother, you've made this tea far too strong.'

'Have I, dear? Do give Archie a cup, won't you?' She put little Frank on the floor on a blanket and placed his box of toys within reach.

Diana produced a business envelope from her handbag, unfolded a single sheet of A4 with a word-processed message on it, and waved it in Archie's direction. 'I presume this piece of filth refers to you, Mr Whatever-your-name-is . . .'

'Mr Benjamin,' said Ellie, taking a seat and a cup of tea. 'And no, if that letter says what I think it does, then Mr Benjamin is not involved. Archie, would you like a biscuit?'

'What? What?' Archie went a dull purple. 'Is that another of those poison-pen letters? But . . . about *me*?' His voice went up an octave.

Diana read it out. '"Did you know your saintly mother was consorting with a con man, whose only interest is in her money?"'

'What?' Archie tried to laugh. 'How absurd! Me? After Ellie's money?'

But the glint in his eyes as he sought and then avoided Ellie's gaze told her that he had known she'd been left very comfortably off. Frank must have told him. Oh.

'You deny it?' Diana was well into her best tragedy queen mode.

'Of course I do. It's absurd . . . known Ellie for years . . . best friends with Frank . . . always working together . . . want to help the little lady all I can . . .'

'You can't deny you've been courting her!'

'No, no. I mean, yes. That is, I would have if . . . a few invitations, nothing to make a fuss about, really. That's true, isn't it, Ellie?'

'Yes,' said Ellie. 'Really, Diana, you're barking up the wrong tree. Archie has been very kind and helpful, but . . .'

'And he didn't come round specifically to ask you out this evening? I heard him ask you out, remember.'

Archie gobbled. 'Yes, of course I did, but no harm intended, I assure you, and then there was the question of the church notices which your dear mother kindly produced for us this week, the details not quite right, and our dear curate's name misspelt, such a small thing, but you know people do notice, and I thought I could just mention it, make sure it didn't happen again . . .'

'Faugh!' said Diana, smacking her hand down on the arm of her chair.

Archie hesitated, mouth open. His eyes sought Ellie's. Young Frank started bawling. Ellie picked him up, one eye on the clock. Such sound and fury, she thought. And all about nothing.

She said, 'Diana, you are quite wrong. Archie is innocent and so am I. Oh, and by the way, Archie, I meant to have a word with you about the church notices. I was not experienced enough on the word processor to produce them properly, so I had them done at the secretarial place in the Avenue. I'm sorry about the misspelling. I'll have another go this week and see if I can do better.'

Diana was not to be deflected. 'Mr — er . . .'

'Benjamin.'

'Whatever. Can you truthfully say that you have no designs on my mother?'

Ellie cringed. 'Oh really, Diana. This is too much — and none of your business, anyway.'

The doorbell rang again. Everyone froze. Then Ellie put Frank back on the floor and went to answer it.

This time it was Roy, bearing a bunch of carnations and a bottle of wine. Ellie wondered who else was going to call. Bill, perhaps? Kate and Armand? Young Neil? She had a schoolgirl-ish impulse to giggle as she ushered Roy into the sitting room.

'Join the party. Shall I make some fresh tea, or is it time for a sherry? Do you know Archie Benjamin? Yes, of course. You've met at church. This is my daughter Diana, and my grandson on the rug. Diana, this is Roy Bartrick, an architect prospecting for development work in the area.'

Roy, like Archie, was dismayed to find Ellie in a family situation but pulled his mouth into a superficial smile and held out his hand to Diana. She ignored his hand, so he gave a sort of welcoming wave and took a seat near Archie with a smooth comment about the weather forecast being stormy. Archie looked at his bottle of wine, and then at Roy's offerings. Roy looked at Archie's bottle and set his bunch of flowers and his own bottle down on the floor in front of him.

Ellie thought, Archie made a bid of one bottle, Roy upped the ante with a bottle plus some flowers. What is Diana going to make of that? Diana looked down at the letter in her hand, and up at Roy. Ellie could see her reassessing the potential of the newcomer. Before she could start cross-questioning him, Ellie rushed out of the room, calling back that she had to put the potatoes on, and would Diana get the sherry out?

The potatoes had already been peeled and cut lengthways. Ellie put them on to boil, checking that she'd salted them already. The carrots were also already peeled and diced.

Roy appeared in the kitchen, ostensibly to ask if there was any more Amontillado sherry, as the bottle was almost empty.

Actually he came to ask, 'How long is your daughter going to be around? Could we get away for a quiet dinner somewhere?'

'Can't you see I'm cooking supper?'

He sniffed the air. 'Ah, home cooking!'

She aimed the tea towel at him, half-amused and half-annoyed. 'You're not getting an invitation, no matter how much you beg. Now get out of here.'

He didn't move. 'Look, Ellie. We really do need to talk. Can't you get rid of the others and—'

'Get rid of who?' Diana appeared, looking thunderous.

Ellie rescued the pot of potatoes which had come to the boil, drained it, emptied some flour into the pan, and shook it till all the potatoes were covered with flour. 'Out of my way everyone, please!' She took the roasting tin out of the oven, emptied the potatoes into it, turned them over till they were basted, and returned the tin to the oven.

Diana said, in an unpleasant tone, 'What I want to know, Mr Arctic . . .'

'Bartrick.' Roy was keeping his temper beautifully.

'Bar-tick,' said Diana, deliberately misunderstanding. Roy's mouth tightened.

'Back in the other room.' Ellie swept them before her. 'Sherry, everyone?'

'What I want to know,' repeated Diana in a louder voice, 'is which of you two is the fortune-hunter? Who has been turning my mother's head with flattery?'

Roy's eyebrows did their juggling act. 'Are we talking about the same woman?'

Archie heaved himself to his feet. 'This is outrageous!'

Ellie intervened. 'I quite agree. Diana, this is none of your business.'

'Of course it is. Someone has been kind enough to inform me that you are being conned by a man who is only after your money. Well, whichever of you it is, perhaps you'd better understand that my mother is not the sole owner of this house, because I am the legal owner of half of it. So put that in your pipe and smoke it! Perhaps that will make you think again!'

Ellie caught a fleeting look of amusement on Roy's face as Archie bent over and took her hand in his. 'My dear Ellie, I was not going to say anything yet. Far too early, I know. But this has forced my hand. I'm not interested in your money. I'm very comfortably off, as you know. But I've often wondered, hoped . . . dreamed even, of the day when perhaps you and I . . .'

Roy held up his hand. 'I don't believe this! The man is actually going to propose! Go on, Archie. Do it properly, if you're going to do it at all. Get down on your knees and . . .'

To Ellie's horror, Archie felt for the arm of the nearest chair and prepared to go down on one knee. She jumped to her feet, muttering that they must excuse her, they really must, the parsnips, you know. She ran for the kitchen, where she buried her face in some tissues and bent over the kitchen sink, trying not to make too much noise. She laughed until she felt weak and had to hold on to the nearest chair for support. There was pain in the laughter, too, for that nasty little scene had shown her that not only Archie but also Roy knew more about her finances than she had realized.

It had been sweet to be courted again, even if she had never had any intention of marrying Archie. As for Roy, well, she had to admit that a daydream or two had featured a future with him at the beginning, but the notion had floated away — not, perhaps, without a twinge of regret. No, it would never had done. He was too like Frank in many ways, and . . .

Oh, she missed Frank dreadfully.

She put the parsnips on to boil and removed the foil from the joint, basting it at the same time. She wished the men away from the house. Diana had succeeded in devaluing her relationship with both of them. Made her feel dirty. She could hear raised voices from the sitting room.

'. . . do you really think I couldn't afford to look after your mother . . . ?'

'Who knows what you'd try to get away with!'

'Your mother has a great deal more sense than you give her credit for.' That was Roy's deeper voice. 'It's true there has been some malicious gossip . . .'

'Well, that will all stop how I'm back!'

'You're moving back down here?' Archie, sounding appalled.

'I am to manage my great-aunt's properties, and I can't do that from the Midlands, can I? My husband is arranging to transfer down here, so that we can all be together and I can protect my mother from unsuitable friends.'

'Really . . . !' That was Archie again, spluttering in shock.

There was a movement in the kitchen doorway. Roy was standing there, leaning against the lintel. He looked sombre.

'Why do you let her make a slave of you?'

In that moment Ellie saw that Roy really did care for her. He might or might not be interested in her money. He probably was. All that talk about her being his partner in a business venture had probably been leading up to a request for investment. But he did care for her, too.

She said, 'Habit, I suppose. Both she and Frank are — were — so dominant that I'm used to keeping the peace.'

'She's jealous of you, you realize that, don't you?'

Ellie considered that, head on one side. Yes, it might be. Diana was tall, dark, handsome and bossy. Men didn't usually like bossy women. Diana had never had a boyfriend until she'd brought Stewart back one day. Stewart thought she was wonderful. Diana agreed with him. A marriage made in heaven, but possibly not one destined to last.

She said, 'Thanks for the wine and the flowers, but I think it might be best if you went now.'

'Bad timing.' He smiled crookedly. 'Tomorrow, perhaps?'

'Ring me.'

'Yes. Your daughter said something about staying here, taking a job with Miss Quicke.'

'I apologize for her behaviour.'

He shrugged. 'Well, I daresay Miss Quicke can look after herself.'

Now that was an odd remark to make, thought Ellie, as she showed him out. Diana hadn't mentioned that her great-aunt was called Miss Quicke. So how did Roy know? In fact, it would be interesting to find out exactly what Roy did know and how he had come by the knowledge. Of course, he'd probably heard the valuers at the flat refer to Miss Quicke as the owner. Yes, that would have been it.

A storm was brewing outside. And inside.

She must rescue Archie, put the Yorkshire pudding on, then the carrots . . . and have a good think about everything. Housework was a marvellous invention. It almost stopped you thinking, if you concentrated on it hard enough.

CHAPTER THIRTEEN

Ellie went down the stairs as quietly as she could. She had only just got little Frank off to sleep. He was fretful, poor thing, sleeping in a strange cot in a strange room. At eleven months old, it wasn't surprising if he was reacting badly to this sudden change from everything that was normal.

Ellie found herself wishing that Diana had not brought him. It wasn't that she didn't love him. Of course she did. She was just ashamed of herself for not loving him so wholeheartedly that whatever he did, and however crossly he looked at her, she would always feel warmly towards him.

She wondered, slightly hysterically — but then, she must remember that shortage of sleep could distort the way you looked at things — whether she was perhaps not as maternal as she had thought. Perhaps it was all her fault that Diana was as she was. A depressing thought.

Diana was on the phone again, laughing like a mad-woman at something one of her friends had said.

Ellie surveyed the mess from their roast dinner. She hadn't had to face so much mess from a meal for months. When her friends came round, they always helped her clear up. Diana, of course, wouldn't do that. It was going to be difficult to lead her own life with Diana and little Frank in the house.

Ellie tackled the clearing away and the washing-up. Diana finished one phone call and started another. Ellie went through into the living room, switched on the television for the news and put her feet up. Diana came in, walking on springs. On top of the world. And why wouldn't she be, with her mother to slave for her? Roy was right, and Ellie ought to do something about it.

'A night at home for a change,' said Diana, throwing herself full length onto the settee and reaching for the remote to change television channels. She didn't ask if Ellie minded. Ellie thought of going to bed. She thought of hitting Diana over the head with the nearest heavy object.

She swallowed all that and said instead, 'Diana, I'm worried about your job. You said you've given in your notice, but won't they expect you to work out a month?'

'Sh! I've been looking forward to this all week. I didn't have to work out my notice. I was due some holiday and then, well, we had a row. He was way out of order. So I don't have to go back.'

Sacked, thought Ellie. Now, did Diana provoke it, or had she been just her usual difficult self? In her head, she rehearsed what she must say. 'Well, Diana, if you're going to be staying here for a while, there's something I think you ought to know.' Then she would get out the colourful handwritten poison-pen letters, the word-processed one that Aunt Drusilla had given her, which matched the one Diana herself had received, and the wax figure.

She would say, 'They come at all hours, some left in the shed, some delivered through the front door by hand. Aunt Drusilla's is one like yours. But I think I may know who is responsible for the handwritten notes. The problem is what to do about it. I think I ought to confront the woman — if it is who I think it is. Would you come with me?'

Diana would be horrified. She would say, 'Oh, poor mother! Yes, of course. Let me help you get to the bottom of this.'

No, she wouldn't. Diana would say that this confirmed her worst fears, that Ellie was incapable of managing life on her own, that it was a blessing in disguise that she, Diana, had to move back in with her mother, and that now she was back nothing more would happen. Let the police deal with it, she would say.

Then she would go on about 'those awful men who've been smarming around you'. She would call Roy 'the Bar-tick' and make snide remarks about 'the fat little church warden'.

Ellie would be unable to deny that both men knew she was very comfortably off.

Fatigue damped down her indignation. She looked across at Diana, animated, absorbed in her programme. Do you honestly think I could forget your father so quickly? asked Ellie silently. If she said it aloud, Diana might say something about never knowing what stupidity would strike her mother next. In an uncanny echo of her father.

Ellie said, 'What was that?'

'Shhh!'

The letterbox on the front door had plopped open, and something had fallen through onto the mat in the hall. Diana didn't move, so Ellie went to investigate. It was yet another anonymous typed letter in a business-style envelope. She read:

YOUR SINS HAVE FOUND YOU OUT,
AND AN HONEST MAN IS FREED FROM
HIS CHAINS.

What on earth did that mean? Good quality paper, just like the other ones. It occurred to Ellie to check for a water-mark, something she had not done before. Yes, there was one: 'Zeta'. The paper was of such high quality that you could almost see the weave. Would there be lots of that paper around?

She checked on the headed notepaper in Frank's bureau. That had a different feel to it, and a watermark of a knight in armour, with the word 'Conqueror'. Frank's letterheads had been done by the local printing press in the Avenue. Would it be worth checking if they stocked the Zeta paper? It might. On the other hand . . . oh, everything seemed so hopeless!

The grandmother clock in the hall chimed ten o'clock.

'I have to be up early tomorrow,' said Diana, turning off the television and yawning. 'I promised Aunt Drusilla I'd be at the estate agents to pick up their keys at nine. You'll look after baby Frank tomorrow for me, won't you? Oh, heavens! I have to wash out my best blouse and I'll have to buy some new tights on the way in tomorrow.'

'Give me your blouse and I'll do it,' said Ellie, knowing that she was dropping back into slavery, but too tired to stop herself. 'Go on. Get a good night's sleep.' It was more than she would do, she knew.

Somehow or other, she seemed to have come to the conclusion that tomorrow — when John would probably be at the charity shop — she must tackle Sue about the poison-pen letters. Alone. Without Diana, and without the police. Although what she would do with young Frank she hadn't the slightest idea. Someone bent on solving mysteries didn't visit suspects pushing a baby in a buggy, did they?

* * *

Monday morning, and Ellie had overslept. Little Frank had been restless in the night, and she had got up to see to him twice. Diana had also got up, once. Now his left cheek was bright red. Very obviously teething.

Diana was fratchy, finding fault with the breakfast Ellie provided, borrowing her last good pair of tights, and kissing Frank hastily before dashing off to her new job.

The post contained two nasty surprises for Ellie. One was a bill from her solicitor, word-processed as immaculately as usual, with a covering letter confirming that their long-standing agreement was at an end and he would be grateful if Mrs Quicke would inform him who was to act for her in future, so that all relevant documents could be handed over.

Well, he hadn't wasted much time, had he?

Automatically she checked the watermark. The same, Zeta. Just as she'd thought. There must be a lot of firms using it. The typed letters must have come from someone local, perhaps someone who also bought paper at the printing press in the Avenue. No use asking who.

There was also another handwritten, hand-delivered letter, on violent green paper this time.

CANCEROUS BITCH!

Ellie struggled between terror and anger. The threat, the wax image . . . all would be enough to defeat a woman who wasn't having to look after a fractious toddler for the day.

But baby Frank brought everything back to reality with a bump. Ellie held him on her hip while she phoned the doctor's surgery for an appointment. She would show the doctor the messages, and ask for a scan or whatever it was you had these days to determine whether or not you had cancer.

The doctor was busy. Of course. A popular woman. An appointment was made for a week's time with the promise that if a slot became vacant before, the receptionist would let Ellie know.

Ellie soothed Frank's swollen gums and with relief felt the tip of a new tooth breaking through. He would soon feel better. Until the next tooth started. Calpol might help. Was there any in Diana's luggage? Luckily there was.

Ellie struggled to get Frank and herself dressed. By the time she had got him strapped into his pushchair, he was sleepy and she was exhausted. Had she given him too much Calpol? She checked the bottle. No, the dose had been correct.

Trying to jar him as little as possible, she negotiated the front door and step and then the gate onto the road. He stirred, but did not wake. Hallelujah. And spring was on the way, wasn't it? The early *Kaufmannia* tulips were opening out flat. Great colour, that scarlet. It lifted the spirits.

They passed a garden which was brilliantly yellow with miniature daffodils. When depressed, buy a bunch of daffodils. She would do just that at the greengrocers.

She stopped at the church hall to ask if the playgroup had a vacancy for Frank. The organizer reacted in surprised amusement. Didn't Ellie know they had a waiting list? He was too young, anyway. They never took toddlers who were still in nappies. Ellie might try the toddlers' group which met in the afternoon, but they didn't take unaccompanied children, so she would have to stay with him. Ah. There were day nurseries, of course, but — sniff — she didn't know anything about them.

The walk through the Avenue was held up several times as various people Ellie knew wanted to exclaim over her being in charge of little Frank. Luckily he slept through it all, one hand still clutching the ear of an indescribable animal which might have been a dog, or possibly a rabbit. Whatever it was, it was known as 'Gog'.

Ellie checked the window of the closed charity shop as she passed. Yes, John was there, hauling books around. Good. That meant Sue would be alone.

Ellie did some shopping and then continued down the Avenue to Bill's office. She felt sore about Bill. They'd been such good friends for so long — but his behaviour had been inexcusable. At one point during the night she had wondered if she ought to apologize and try to make it up with him, but she'd thought better of it in the morning. Best to pay the bill and look for someone else. Perhaps Kate could help.

Bill's secretary, as neat and well groomed as ever, was parking what looked like a brand-new red car in front of the office as Ellie arrived. 'What do you want?' she said, not bothering to look directly at Ellie.

Very rude, thought Ellie, handing over an envelope with the bill and cheque inside. 'Just tidying up the odd loose end,' she replied, and turned the pushchair round to get on with the rest of her life.

Ellie negotiated the pedestrian crossing, frowning at the secretary's lack of courtesy. That nice waitress Chloe was cleaning the window inside the Sunflower Café. She waved to Ellie, who waved back. She was tempted to stop off and have a cuppa . . . but no, she must not be diverted. John's wife was at home alone and the opportunity must not be missed.

John and his wife lived in a large semi-detached house behind the library. The garden was trim enough, but the paintwork could do with renewing. Ellie remembered John saying that he didn't know what to do about repainting the house, because his wife couldn't stand having workmen about the place.

Little Frank still slept — making up for his lost sleep the previous night. Ellie rang the doorbell and waited.

She knew that Sue would check on a visitor by looking through the front window before she let anyone in. Often, John said, she simply refused to open the door, even to the officials who came to read the meters.

There was a sign up by the door: 'No free newspapers, no junk mail.' Ellie wondered if such signs worked. If so, she might try one herself.

The door opened to reveal Sue, wearing a plastic apron and yellow Marigold gloves. A droopy black top over a sagging skirt. Bare feet in sandals. Her hair was pulled back into an elastic band. She had her finger on the nozzle of an aerosol spray and was pointing it at Ellie.

Ellie recoiled. Was the woman going to attack her with that spray? And what on earth was in it? Did she always greet people at the door like this? Her recoil seemed to please Sue, who put the can away and held the door wide open. She said in a disagreeable tone, 'I'm in the middle of my spring-cleaning, but come in, if you're coming.'

Ellie hesitated. What was she letting herself in for? Then she manoeuvred the pushchair into the hall. It smelt clean. A mop and bucket stood nearby. Sue gestured that Ellie should follow her past closed doors, down the hall and into the kitchen.

It was a large kitchen with old-fashioned fitments — an old pine table with a newish working surface applied to the top of it; an old-fashioned Belfast sink and stainless-steel draining board; ranks of cupboards painted dark green. Everything was thoroughly clean, and there were no signs of any cooking in progress. The blinds were drawn and the overhead light on, so that the room swam in a false, unhealthy light.

'Don't stand in the hall. I've just done the floor. I lock the other rooms as I finish them, of course.'

Is she barking mad? thought Ellie. Oh dear, I ought not to have come.

Sue switched on an electric kettle and Ellie relaxed. At least she'd get that much needed cup of coffee. On a small shelf by the door was a telephone, a biro, a ruler and a pad of gaily coloured paper.

'So what brings you here, Mrs Quicke? It's the first time you've bothered to visit me, isn't it?'

'This.' Ellie took out the handwritten letters she had received and laid them on the table, together with the pad from beside the telephone. The stain down the side of the pad matched that on the later letters. 'I got a note from John which showed the same staining as on the letters I received recently, and you can see that the stains match the remains of your pad.'

Sue hissed through her teeth. Startled, Ellie retreated a step.

'It was John, not me.'

'No,' said Ellie heavily. 'It was you.'

'Prove it!' Sue made a lunge for the letters and tore them into small pieces, wrenching through the layers. She threw them into the bin and closed the lid with a snap. Then she laughed, and there was a wild note in her laugh which caused Ellie's shoulder blades to stiffen. The woman was definitely barking. And the house was very quiet. A large house in a quiet back street. No one would hear Ellie if Sue became violent and attacked her.

'It was you, all right,' Ellie said, as steadily as she could manage. 'You don't have many visitors and you appreciated Gilbert taking the trouble to spend time with you. Then Nora's father died. Gilbert had less time to spend with you, because Nora needed him. You were angry with Nora, so you started sending her letters anonymously.

'I expect you thought the letters would stop Gilbert trying to help her, but of course the reverse was the case. So you began to hate Gilbert, too. You could have lost him his job, but luckily his bishop removed him from your orbit. So that just left poor, helpless Nora, whose head you filled with such terrible ideas that without Gilbert's support she had nothing to live for. Were you pleased when she committed suicide?'

Sue laughed again. 'You have no idea!'

The kettle was boiling, but Sue ignored it. She had not asked Ellie to sit down, so they stood one on either side of the wide table, with Frank snuffling in his pushchair beside the door.

'Nora wasn't the first person you wrote letters to, either, was she?'

'What makes you think that?'

'People talk. I listen. You go out walking at night and early in the morning, don't you? And post the letters then, or slip them under doors? I suppose you thought no one would ever find you out and that, if they did, they would be unable to prove anything.'

'Neither can you.'

'Oh, I could make a fuss about it, I suppose. Go to the police, make life difficult for you.'

'I don't think you will. I'm not the only one who . . .'

'Ah. I thought so. Who is the other person? The one who types her letters?'

Sue laughed again. 'Torture me, if you like. I shan't tell you. So you'll have to behave properly, or I'll tell on you and then you'll be sorry.'

'Tell what?' said Ellie, feeling rather tired. 'There's nothing to tell, except in your overactive imagination.'

Sue leaned forward over the table, hissing. 'She says there's nothing to know, does she? What about the men visiting her at all hours? And the rich aunt disinheriting her? And the daughter having to come down to look after her stupid mother, who doesn't even know when the wool's being pulled over her eyes because she's too busy fancying all the men in sight, with her husband not yet cold in his grave!'

Ellie took a step back, but Sue advanced around the table, picking up the boiling kettle as she went. 'Who's a stupid little woman then, coming here with her pretty face and her pretty clothes, with a lovely sleeping little toddler, walking into the spider's den without a thought for what boiling water can do? So which of you shall have it in the face, then, the little boy or his whore of a granny?'

Ellie screamed, looking round for something — anything — to use to protect herself. An apron, a towel, anything . . . She lunged for the pushchair and thrust it forward as Sue flung the contents of the kettle at little Frank.

The pushchair skidded along the floor and Frank woke up with a whimper as the first drops of scalding water hit Ellie. By this time Sue was both screeching and laughing.

Ellie grabbed the pushchair with one hand and the kitchen door handle with the other, just as John pushed open the door from the hall.

'What's going on?'

Sue, still screaming, got hold of Ellie's coat and, with amazing strength, flung her round and away from the pushchair. The chair tipped over and Frank roared in shock and anger. Ellie's shopping tumbled out all over the floor. John, bewildered, tried ineffectually to stop his wife kicking and clawing at Ellie, who was doing her best to protect the toddler with her own body.

'They'll kill you!' screeched Sue. 'I'll tell them and they'll come after you and they won't rest . . . you don't know them, but they'll not rest till they kill you, just as they killed Nora!'

John managed to get his arms round Sue from behind, and shouted at Ellie to get the pills, quick, upstairs in the bathroom cabinet!

Ellie righted Frank's pushchair, unstrapped him and carried him with her in a rush up the unfamiliar stairs, opening doors at random till she found the bathroom and the cabinet. Frank bawled all the time, but she couldn't stop to calm him. She found the bottle and took it back down with her.

On John's instructions, she poured out a glass of water and tried not to be intimidated by the foul language Sue was directing at her. Luckily John was very strong, and could restrain his wife even when she tried to break his grip by lunging suddenly at Ellie. Ellie looked away as John forced Sue to take a couple of tablets with the glass of water.

She rescued Gog from the floor, and sat down to cuddle and quieten Frank. After a few minutes, John got Sue to sit down in a chair while he collapsed in another beside her. Sue's head drooped. She began to cry.

'What happened?' said John.

'I showed her the poison-pen letters I'd received, because there was a stain on one side matching the stain on the note you sent me about who had bought the pads. The letters came from your pad.'

John rubbed his face with both hands. 'Sue did that? No, she couldn't have. Sue? Sue, tell me you didn't.'

Sue looked up at him. 'No, of course I didn't. She's making it up, just like she makes lots of things up. She's evil, John. You really shouldn't go to lunch with her, or accept presents from her, or run her errands. You really shouldn't.'

'Is that what this is all about?' said Ellie, who felt very much like crying herself. 'Did you send me those letters just because I gave John a Christmas present, and invited him to lunch with Rose and me? I invited you as well, Sue.'

'But you didn't mean it, did you? You didn't really want me.'

This was so true that Ellie did not reply.

John said, 'Sue, let's get you up to bed, so that you can have a nice rest. You could do with a lie down now, couldn't you? And I'll bring you up a cup of tea in a little while. You'd like that, wouldn't you?'

Sue smiled up at him. 'Oh yes, John. That would be lovely.'

John helped his wife to her feet and half-carried her limp form to the door. Looking back, he said to Ellie, 'Don't go away, will you?'

Ellie had no intention of going away, or even of moving from her chair. Except that young Frank was getting restless. He was also smelly and wet. It was more than time for his lunch, too. She rescued the Pampers which had got wedged in the shopping tray of the pushchair, and changed him. Then she strapped him securely back into his pushchair, despite his forcible objections.

Before popping the dirty nappy in the bin, she remembered to rescue the fragments of torn-up letters, and the telltale original pad. These she put in her handbag before washing her hands and feeding Frank a soft bun she had bought that morning. Luckily she had thought to bring a bottle of milk for him. More or less content now, he began to kick rhythmically as he sucked.

Frank was getting over his fright quicker than Ellie was. What a narrow escape she'd had. How appalling of her to have put little Frank into danger! She ought never to have brought him out with her. Suppose he had been scarred for life? She discovered that she was trembling. One side of her face and one of her hands were stinging. Scalding water can do a lot of damage. She ran her hand under the cold tap and bathed her face.

Her coat felt uncomfortable, although she couldn't see why. Taking it off, she found the lining had been torn from nape to hem. 'My coat!' she said, on the verge of tears. 'I'll never be able to repair that.'

'You can afford to buy yourself another one,' said John, returning with a grim face.

'Who says?'

'Sue says it's common knowledge that you've been left a million. I must say, I do think you might have told your old friends. But perhaps you don't consider us old friends anymore.'

'The amount Frank left me was supposed to be a secret. Perhaps it was rather a childish attitude, but I was warned by my solicitor not to let anyone know that I'd been left well off, in case I was targeted by con men and fortune-hunters.' Which, she thought, is exactly what has been happening. So who leaked the good news?

'How did Sue hear of it? From someone in the charity shop?'

'No, I don't think so. Ellie, sit down. We must talk. You realize Sue is a very, very sick woman. She has been saying terrible things about you. I can't think they're true, but . . .'

'Your wife isn't just sick, but dangerous! She attacked Frank with boiling water!'

'I realize she's not herself at the moment. The least little thing seems to upset her.'

'Is it all right for her to upset me with her poisonous letters? And drive Nora to her death? There was somebody else, too. A woman who married her first cousin and . . . you know about that.'

'Now look, Ellie. I just don't believe this.'

'Let me show you.' Ellie placed the torn pieces of letter on the table, next to the pad. Piecing together a couple of pages, she pushed them at John. He pushed them back.

'No, no. That's not her handwriting.'

'Perhaps she did them with her left hand, or wearing gloves. She admitted to me that she had written them. See where your pad is stained down one side? The same stain is down the side of these letters. Therefore, they came from your pad, and she wrote them. You didn't suspect her at all?'

'No, of course not.'

'She hasn't talked to you about me? Or about Nora? Or about the woman who married her first cousin and now has cancer?'

'She did mention that she'd given some neighbours a piece of her mind when they got married, but that was months ago. You see, Sue's parents were first cousins, and Sue always thought that was why she's had these bad times.'

185

'Bad times! Lasting for months? She deeply distressed her first victims, drove Nora to suicide . . .'

'No, no!' John shifted on his chair. 'You're exaggerating!'

'I can show you some of her letters to Nora, if you wish. They destroyed her. Then Sue started on me. If you hadn't tried to help me by making a list of those people who had bought the pads through the shop, I probably would never have realized it was Sue behind them.

'It's horrible, John. She made up the most dreadful allegations, about sex and . . . oh, everything. Twisting everything till I can hardly look anyone in the face anymore. You didn't suspect her at all?'

He looked stricken. 'No, I didn't. I thought she'd been so much better lately, more cheerful, even getting out and about a couple of times a week in the daytime. She's on medication permanently, of course, but the doctor was very pleased with her. We talked about going away on holiday for a few days. Oh, God. This is terrible.'

He went over to the sink and washed his face. Little Frank starting bawling. He'd lost his bottle and his Gog. Ellie replaced both.

John dried his face and his hands, taking his time. 'What are you going to do, Ellie? About Sue, I mean. You won't go to the police, will you? She'd be sectioned again and pumped full of drugs till she's a zombie. Then they'll send her home and I'd have to get someone to sit with her whenever I went out to the charity shop or did the shopping. I have to have that outlet, or I'll go mad too.'

'She ought to have some sort of treatment.'

'I'll see to it,' he said, eagerly. 'I'll ring the doctor this afternoon, and get something underway. There's no great harm been done, is there?'

Frank threw his bottle across the floor and tried to burst out of the straps containing him. 'I must go,' said Ellie. 'I wouldn't agree that no great harm has been done, John, but I do agree about not going to the police, at least for the time being. On one condition: somehow or other Sue must be stopped from making other people's lives a misery. Can you get her to sign some sort of confession, which we can lodge at the bank together with the evidence, the letters she sent me, and the pad of paper she used? Then, if she gets some more treatment . . . dear John, I can see that it would just make life more hellish than ever for you, if I did anything else.'

'Bless you, Ellie. I'm often at my wits' end . . .'

'Yes, yes. But I forgot — do keep still for a moment, Frank; yes, we're going, we really are, back to see Mummy — John, there is one other thing. Sue hasn't been doing this all by herself. There's at least one other person involved, someone who types letters. I've also been sent a wax image of myself with a pin through it.'

'What? You're not serious? In this day and age?'

'In this day and age. Yes, I'm very serious. I asked Sue who else was involved and she refused to tell me. She also threatened me, saying that the others would kill me when she told them. It's absurd to think that anyone would actually want to harm me, but then Sue did try to pour boiling water over Frank. So I don't quite know what to do — yes, in a minute, Frank — but John, perhaps you could find out who else has got it in for me? Does anybody spring to mind?'

'No. No! She hardly goes out in the daytime, except to her exercise class once a week, and a creative writing class that meets in the library, which they thought might do her good.'

Ellie struggled into her torn coat, reflecting that Sue's efforts at creative writing had been very effective, if not precisely what the course tutor might have had in mind.

John held the front door open so that Ellie could manoeuvre the pushchair outside. The house lay quiet around them. Dead quiet. Ellie shivered, and set off at a brisk pace back home.

CHAPTER FOURTEEN

By the time Ellie reached home again, Frank was kicking and screaming fit to burst. Hungry, of course. Tired of being cooped up in the pushchair, and probably dirty again as well. He was like that. Above the clamour that he was making, Ellie could hear someone leaving a message on the answerphone, but she was too distracted to attend to it.

As she was settling Frank into the baby seat that fitted over one of the kitchen chairs, Diana swept in, demanding lunch.

'What's the time? I have to be at the flats by two. Those wretched decorators want to do the whole place out in magnolia paint; definitely too boring for words, and when I said — isn't lunch ready yet? — I said to them that I thought we could do better than that, and where were their shade cards, they had the nerve to tell me that Miss Quicke always has everything done out in magnolia. So I have to go back to the old trout and get her signature on a letter saying that I'm managing the flats in future . . . and what is my baby crying for, then?'

'Hungry,' said Ellie, throwing bread, cheese, butter and some salad stuffs onto the table. 'Would you sort out something for him to eat? For yourself as well, of course.'

'Give him anything he likes. Cheese on toast, some homemade soup, something like that. I'll make myself a sandwich quickly. Have you managed to get him into a nursery yet?'

'No.' Anger welled up in Ellie. She wanted to throw something at Diana, scream, lie on the floor and have hysterics.

She did none of those things, of course. She began to put out the ingredients to make some soup while passing a biscuit to young Frank, who swept it off his tray onto the floor. The cat flap flipped, as Midge made a hasty exit.

'What was that?' said Diana. 'Don't tell me you've got a stray cat coming in. Really, mother. You must know that cats give diseases to young children. You've been feeding it on the floor, I see. Well . . .' as she picked up Midge's plates and threw them into the sink, '. . . we can't have that with little Frank around, can we? Your stray will have to find himself another home.'

It was too much. Ellie banged an onion down on the table so hard that Frank gave a great start and stopped yelling — for a moment. 'Midge is my cat,' said Ellie, controlling herself with an effort. 'He lives here.'

'Oh really, mother! You're so comical. A cat, indeed! Whatever next? Oh, must dash. I've got to see Aunt Drusilla and get on top of those decorators, or they'll think they can rule the roost. I told them, "I'm in charge now, and what I say goes!" They wanted to argue, talked about ringing up Aunt Drusilla to check on me — what a nerve! I told them the old bat's not up to much these days, and they'd better mind their manners because it's me who's going to pay the bills in future.'

Ellie sat down, trembling at the knees. 'Aunt Drusilla has used those same decorators for ever. They do a good job and she's satisfied with them. What do you mean about her not being up to much nowadays? When I saw her the other day, she was fine.'

'Oh, she's going downhill fast, I reckon. She said she wanted to see you urgently, but I told her you were busy baby-sitting and couldn't spare the time. I'll have to see about getting her into an old people's home.'

Ellie said, 'But . . .'

She spoke to the air, for Diana had scooped up her keys, kissed the top of Frank's head and disappeared. Ellie whizzed up the vegetables she had been sautéing, dunked some bread in it, and started to feed Frank. He fell asleep halfway through. Ellie took Frank upstairs for his nap and finished the bowl off herself.

Midge came back through the cat flap and yowled for his dishes, which were in the sink. When he'd been fed, too, Ellie sat with him on her lap, trying to work out what she ought to do next. It was a temptation to fall asleep, but she resisted it.

She was worried about Aunt Drusilla. Diana meant well, of course, but she was a bit of a steamroller and it sounded as if Aunt Drusilla had come off worst in their morning's encounter. Perhaps it would be a good idea to give her a ring later.

Sue's threats of retribution worried her. Perhaps she should get what evidence she had to the bank, without waiting for Sue's confession, which could be added later. Yes, she would feel a lot safer if she did that, even though she balked at pushing Frank along the Avenue twice in one day.

She picked up the post, which had arrived after she'd left, and found another missive from Sue. That went, unread, into her handbag with the rest of them. Someone had also pushed an envelope containing notes for the church notices next Sunday through the door.

On the answerphone was a message from Roy, asking her to call him. And one from Kate explaining that she'd only got back very late on Sunday evening, but she and Armand were very keen on Ellie doing something with the garden, and they'd be in touch as soon as either of them had a free moment, possibly Tuesday morning when Armand had a couple of free periods.

With Frank still peacefully sleeping, Ellie went into the study to phone around the agencies for a baby-sitter or day nanny. They all seemed expensive to her. The two local council day nurseries were both full. Eventually one of the organizers of a day nursery recommended her younger sister, who perhaps wouldn't mind looking after Frank during the day, since her two were now both settled at school. She would, of course, have to meet Frank and his mother first.

Ellie recognized the girl's name — Betty's grandmother was a regular at church and the girl had been in Sunday school there some years ago. A nice child, Ellie remembered. So she got Betty's telephone number and had a long chat — yes, her granny was well enough, except for her asthma; Betty had married young, two boys now at school, waiting to go to college in the autumn and at a loose end.

Being extra careful, Ellie took up her references and was satisfied that she had discovered a treasure. Phoning Betty back, Ellie invited her round to meet Diana and Frank that evening. Only after Ellie had put the phone down did she remember that she herself would be out at choir practice. She didn't alter the arrangement. Let Diana cope.

With some trepidation, she switched on her husband's word processor. Manual in hand, she opened a new document and typed in everything she knew about Sue and the handwritten poison-pen letters. She was a fast and accurate typist on an electric machine, and in some ways this was even better, although it did throw up a great many wavy green lines because it took exception to her grammar. A nasty little cartoon figure kept bobbing up, saying, 'It looks as if you are writing a letter. Would you like some help?' She wasn't and she didn't.

Ignoring the fact that the typeface was too small and the margins seemed to go in and out at will, Ellie managed to print off the document. Stuffing it into an envelope with the evidence she had gathered so far, she addressed it to herself at the bank and stuck some stamps on it. She would post it in the letterbox on the Green as she went off for choir practice.

She continued to worry about Aunt Drusilla. Why had the old lady allowed Diana to walk all over her? Perhaps she was going down with something? No. Aunt Drusilla was never unwell. She was legendary for never getting a cold, or flu, or rheumatism, like other people. True, she walked with a stick, but Ellie had always thought that was for effect rather than necessity.

The phone rang. Ellie fell on it before it wakened Frank. It was Aunt Drusilla at her most imperious.

'Ellie, is that you? I need to see you. At once.'

'I'm looking after little Frank for the day . . .'

'Get that daughter of yours to look after him. Take a cab over.'

Well, why not? thought Ellie.

Diana had a mobile phone. Ellie found the number and keyed it in. No reply, except for an anonymous voice saying that the mobile was switched off. Ellie glanced at the clock. It was getting late. Frank would be waking up soon and needed to have a good roll and crawl around to burn off some energy. Then he'd need his tea. Who did she know who could look after him at such short notice?

Rose! Of course. If she were only in . . . Dear Rose was in, and happy to help out, provided that Ellie paid for the minicab to fetch her. Ellie rushed the dishes into the sink, set out everything for Frank's tea, plus plenty of biscuits for Rose, left a note for Diana and scrambled into her old winter coat by the time Rose arrived in her minicab — which Ellie took on to Aunt Drusilla's house.

The tall Victorian house looked threatening in the dusk, and no lights had yet been switched on inside. Aunt Drusilla let her in, wearing a fur coat, with an unexpectedly chic turban on her head.

'Really, Ellie! I thought you'd have put that old coat in the bin before now. Come on. I want you to go round the garden with me before it gets quite dark.'

Was that what the old bat had summoned her for so urgently? Mm. No, probably not. So what was she up to?

'My old handyman and gardener has retired, giving up at the tender age of sixty-five, if you please. I had this lad come to the door, asking if I needed any work done. I thought I'd give him a try. He cut back the shrubs round the front for me and did a good enough job, but then he suggested he replaced the trellis round the back. I was doubtful, but he said he'd worked for you and that you could give him a reference. I always take up references, you know.'

Neil, of course. So he'd taken her name in vain, had he?

'I know him, yes. His grandmother's a friend of mine. Neil's strong, has had some experience and is anxious to please. I really don't know yet whether he can tell a rare plant from a weed.'

Together they looked at the trellis, which topped the ancient brick wall running round three sides of the large garden. In some parts the trellis had disintegrated, overcome by rampant honeysuckle and the too-close proximity of some aged shrubbery. Anyone who tackled the job would need enthusiasm and a strong back.

Aunt Drusilla poked and prodded at the wall, which seemed sound enough. 'This boy Neil told me he wanted to set up locally as a contract gardener and was hoping a cousin of his might do the book-keeping for him. He said he was thinking of applying for a start-up grant. I was impressed, but your daughter gave him short shrift. She said she could find me a gardener at a cut-price rate. What do you think?'

'I was thinking I might invest in Neil myself, and if his cousin — she's called Chloe, a bright girl working at the Sunflower Café at the moment — well, if she took on the responsibility for doing the books and he got a grant, then I think he might do well.'

'Your daughter doesn't think so.'

There was no reply to that.

'Your dear husband used to attend to all the major repairs for me. I really do not know how I am to manage without him.'

Aha, thought Ellie, as enlightenment struck. 'You want me to pay the bill, since he left the place to me rather than you?'

'Naturally. By the way, I'm told the wiring needs renewing throughout the house and the boiler also needs replacing.'

'Let me think about it. I expect the rent you pay will cover everything you've mentioned.'

A short silence ensued. 'My dear nephew would never have dreamed of asking me for rent, after all I did for him.'

'It's different now, isn't it?' said Ellie calmly. 'You're quite right in thinking I won't turn you out of the house unless you wish to go. But perhaps it might be a good idea to have a repairing lease drawn up? You continue to live here rent free, but do all the repairs that my surveyor thinks necessary. My surveyor, not yours.'

Aunt Drusilla gave a soundless laugh, and patted Ellie on the arm. 'You learn quickly. I daresay we can come to an agreement along those lines. Now, what about young Neil? Shall I use him, or shall I allow Diana to get a cut-price contractor in?'

'A cautious "yes" to using Neil. Just keep an eye on him, that's all.'

'My feelings precisely,' said Aunt Drusilla.

They went back indoors, where the daily help had already laid the tea tray in the drawing room. Ellie turned on lights, drew curtains and switched the kettle on.

'What have you done with my great-nephew?'

'Diana was not available, so I found an old friend to baby-sit. Let's hope he doesn't wear her out entirely.'

'Diana was sacked from her last job. I checked. She demanded more money than she was worth and became abusive when it was denied her.'

Ouch, thought Ellie, making the tea. Would Diana have been driven to such extremes if I'd given her the money she wanted? Oh dear.

'She has been living beyond her means, I gather,' said Aunt Drusilla. 'Well, selling that expensive house and moving down here might solve her problems, and it might not. I'm prepared to wait and see how she behaves. I have given her a letter of employment with one or two clauses she would have been wiser to read rather than rush over. For one thing, either of us can give a month's notice to the other without giving a reason, and for another, I employ and pay the contractors and not her.'

'I see,' said Ellie, thinking that Aunt Drusilla was uncomfortably prescient.

'That girl,' said the old lady, 'was foolish enough to say that I was past it and ought to retire to a nursing home.'

'I trust you disillusioned her.'

'Not I.' Aunt Drusilla's nutcracker face split in a wide grin. 'Let her go on thinking it, for the time being at any rate. She's cheaper than the estate agents who were managing the property before. But I won't stand for any nonsense. I've had the decorators on to me already. That stupid girl thinks my tenants would like bright, modern colours. Well, they wouldn't. I should know. They want something clean and bland that they can redecorate to their own taste. I told Diana that if she wishes to become an interior decorator, she must find her own clients. What do you say to that?'

Ellie cleared her plate of the last biscuit. She'd been hungry. 'I think that's a matter between you and Diana.'

'Opting out?'

Ellie laughed, refusing to be drawn.

'You've changed, Ellie Quicke. When my dear nephew died and you went to pieces, I thought Diana was right wanting you to sell up and go to live near her. But you came through very well . . . until this recent problem with the anonymous letters. Diana sees them as a perfect excuse to move into your life. What do you think about that?'

Ellie thought: we're actually talking adult to adult for a change. Shall I tell her what I've found out? Yes, why not?

'It's a wretched business. I found out today who has been sending the handwritten letters, but I'm not going to the police because . . .'

Aunt Drusilla listened, head slightly inclined to one side. Once or twice she moved her lips, but did not interrupt.

'. . . so I still have to find out who wrote the typed letters. Perhaps someone with connections to the church or my solicitor. You and Diana both received typed letters. How did they know about you, and where to send the letters? Sue won't tell, but until I find that out and deal with it, I suppose the letters will continue to arrive.'

'Fascinating! You have all the evidence in a safe place, I assume?'

'Waiting to be posted off to myself at the bank, yes.'

Aunt Drusilla scrabbled in her enormous crocodile-skin handbag. 'I had another letter myself today. Scurrilous!' She snorted. 'No, I remember now. I didn't keep it. I tore it up and threw the pieces away. You have done well, Ellie. I am very agreeably surprised. I suppose I owe you an apology, too. I sided with Diana over her wanting you to sell up and move north. I was wrong.'

Ellie blushed. Praise from such a quarter was praise indeed. A little voice at the back of her head said, Now that Aunt Drusilla herself feels threatened by Diana, she wants you to fight on her side, doesn't she?

Perhaps so, thought Ellie. And I will.

She glanced at the clock. 'I must go. Choir practice tonight, and I have to feed the family first. Also I've arranged for a prospective day nanny to call later.'

'With your usual efficiency, my dear.'

Ellie blinked. She couldn't remember Aunt Drusilla using a term of endearment before.

'One thing before you go. This Roy Bartrick. I know him slightly. He was enquiring about one of my flats. How do you feel about him?'

So that was the connection. It explained a lot.

'He's very charming; a trifle pushy. I've enjoyed going out with him and I think he likes me, but I don't imagine it will go any further. My friend Kate says he's got a hidden agenda, and I'm beginning to agree with her.'

'And the other, the man from church?'

Ellie laughed. 'No, really! Aunt Drusilla, if you could meet him, you'd realize how impossible that would be. No. I still miss Frank terribly, you know.'

'Yes, so do I. Well, that is very level-headed of you, Ellie. Keep me informed.'

* * *

Ellie glanced at her watch as she scurried home. On balance it would have taken longer to call a minicab than to walk, but if only she'd learned to drive in her younger days! London traffic got worse every year and there was no denying she was a little frightened of it, even when sitting beside a big, calm driving instructor. When she would get back into the swing of having lessons again, she didn't know.

She must get that envelope in the post straightaway, see to supper, pay Rose and . . . She opened the front door to the sound of young Frank bawling his head off while Diana was calmly working on the computer in the study. Something was amiss. No Rose, for a start.

'Mother, what on earth are you wearing? That coat's a disgrace. I got back — you'll have to give me a set of front-door keys again — and this strange woman let me in, gibbering something about your having an urgent meeting out and wanting me to pay her cab fare home. I told her I didn't know her from Adam, and what's more she'd got little Frank in a sort of cage made of chairs and the poor dear couldn't get out . . .'

'Sounds sensible to me, and yes, you do know her, dear. Rose McNally from the charity shop, an old friend of mine. Aunt Drusilla summoned me urgently and I was at my wits' end what to do with little Frank . . .'

'She's going ga-ga, you know.'

'That wasn't the impression she gave me.' Ellie rushed into the kitchen and started getting things out of the fridge for supper.

Diana followed, looking thunderous. 'I suppose she wanted to complain about me. I gave her some excellent advice, but she's too stupid to take it. She ought to go upmarket with the decorations and put up the rents at the flats. I'll have to work on her, make her see sense. Oh, by the way, I've cleared all the old files off the computer, because I shall have to use it in future . . .'

'What?' Ellie suspended operations on a tomato. Had her notes on the anonymous letters been deleted?

'. . . and I hope supper won't be late. I'm due out at half-seven.'

Ellie stirred rice into a little oil in a saucepan. 'Diana, I have choir practice at eight, and besides, I've got a possible day nanny coming round for you to interview.'

'A day nanny? Do you think I'm made of money?'

'Let me remind you, dear, that I make you an allowance for someone to look after Frank.' She switched the kettle on to boil.

'Oh, that. Well, I expect I can find a day nursery somewhere, much cheaper.'

'If you can, fine. I couldn't. So until you do find something suitable, we will use this woman, who comes highly recommended.'

'You found her, so you can be responsible for hiring her. I have to go out, as I said.'

'Not until nine, when I get back.' She poured the boiling water onto the rice, and turned the heat down.

'Don't be absurd. I can't ring up my friend and tell her I can't meet her just because you've got choir practice.'

Ellie considered weakening, but didn't. Instead she said nothing at all, which seemed to disconcert Diana. Pushing past her daughter, Ellie picked up an onion and looked for the chopping board, which she kept behind the taps on the sink. It wasn't there. Come to think of it, the bin had been moved to the other side of the stove, and Midge's dishes had disappeared again.

Ellie counted to three. 'Diana. You've been moving things around. I do wish you wouldn't.'

'Oh, that little toady of a handyman came around wanting you, asking for work. So I cleared away some of the clutter, old papers and sacks from the garden and stuff. He took it to the dump. I said you'd pay him tomorrow.'

'You threw away my chopping board? And Midge's dishes?'

'That chopping board was a disgrace. You ought to have one of the new plastic ones.'

'They scratch, and you can't clean them as well as the old wooden ones. Mine may be old, but it's scrubbed clean. And Midge's dishes?'

'I told you, you can't possibly encourage a stray cat with baby Frank around. I told the lad to screw the cat flap shut. He said he couldn't because it was plastic, but I made him lock it. He can take it out and board it up tomorrow.'

Ellie had a nasty thought. She dashed back into the hall. The notepad beside the phone had been stripped clean of messages. All the old newspapers had gone, as had her carefully collected gardening magazines and, worst of all, the envelope with the poison-pen letter evidence in it.

She gasped, struggling for control. It was too much! She ought to love her daughter. Well, she did. But like her? No.

The immediate future looked bleak. And what was more, young Frank had managed to crawl to the living room door, clutching his grandfather Frank's silver christening cup which had been on the coffee table. Ellie saw that everything that had been on the coffee table was now on the floor. Little Frank had left a broken vase and a trail of water behind him, plus shredded irises. Now he was screwing his face up, ready to bawl his head off.

For the first time in her life Ellie seriously considered the benefits to be gained from murdering her daughter. She had a sharp kitchen knife in her hand already. She could make a half-turn, and stab . . .

Frank opened his mouth and yelled.

Diana said, 'Well, who's a clever boy, then? If granny won't pick him up, then his mumsy will, won't she! Oh, look what the little darling's been playing with. Have his toothy pegs been hurting? That nice cold silver must have helped. How clever of him to think of it! Look, granny! See the marks of his dear little teeth on the silver?'

Ellie breathed out slowly, counting to twelve this time. She went back into the kitchen, got out a heavy Denby plate and started chopping the onion on it. 'Diana, we must sit down and have a talk. If you're going to move back in with me for the time being — and of course you're very welcome — then we must come to some agreement about certain house rules.'

Diana reddened. 'Stewart said you'd want us to pay rent.'

'No, I don't want rent. I want you to respect my way of life.'

Diana laughed as if Ellie had said something amusing. She put the toddler down and picked up her mobile phone. 'Which reminds me, I must ring Stewart. You haven't forgotten he's coming down tomorrow for his interview, have you? And since you have made such a fuss about going to your highly important choir practice, I suppose I shall have to cancel my date tonight.'

Halfway through making the chicken curry, Ellie remembered that Diana didn't like it strong. Ellie did. She put a trifle more than the usual amount of curry powder in.

Supper was interrupted by telephone calls for Diana, and only after the second interruption, while Diana was fetching herself another glass of water, did she remember to tell her mother that her stupid old vicar friend had phoned, and would Ellie get back to him soonest. 'Anything else you've forgotten to tell me, Diana?'

Diana laughed that one off, too.

* * *

It was a rush to get to choir practice in time. Ellie had hoped for a quiet word with her old friend Mrs Dawes, but instead everyone was crowding around Rose's daughter Joyce, as she formally announced her engagement to the scoutmaster, who was also their replacement organist. Ellie had never liked Joyce much, but was sincere in her congratulations since the girl looked almost happy for once. It must be a handicap to be born with a sharp nose and down-turned mouth.

Everyone wanted to hear when the wedding was to be, and there was much speculation as to who would play the organ when the organist was getting married himself. Then Archie came in to hand out typed notices about the Spring

Craft Fair, reminding everyone that they needed to make even more money this year towards the building fund for the new church hall.

'Ellie, could you manage some posters for us to put up in the parish?' He thrust one of the typed notices at her and, still holding her hand, asked in a conspiratorial whisper if she'd have time for a little drinkies with him afterwards. She shook her head, suppressing an impulse to tear the piece of paper into tiny pieces and throw them back into his face. She would very much enjoy a good scream. She sat down in her pew to quieten her pulse.

'Are you all right, dear?' Mrs Dawes, looking anxious.

Someone said, from behind Ellie, 'She can't bear to have the attention off her for once!'

Someone else giggled.

Ellie mumbled, 'Sorry.' She stood up and tried to thrust all her worries out of her mind as the choir started rehearsing an anthem. I'll faint, or burst, or something, she thought. But she knew she wouldn't, because people like her didn't make a fuss in public, no matter what that sour-faced would-be solo soprano Gwyneth might think.

She was still hoping for a quiet word with Mrs Dawes after the practice: she really must confide in someone or explode. But Mrs Dawes wanted to buttonhole various people about manning her Country Gardens stall at the Fair. So Ellie walked quickly back across the Green by herself, hoping to avoid Archie.

'Hsst!'

As she reached her garden gate, Tod erupted from the garden shed, closing the door firmly behind him.

'I was watching for you. Neil couldn't wait. He's got a gig on tonight. Or an audition for one, anyway. Did you know he played in a band? Anyway, he said to tell you that he's kept all your gardening magazines, he thought you wouldn't mind, and we got Midge in the shed here with all his food and he's happy as anything, mousing or ratting or something.'

201

'You clever boy! You didn't rescue an envelope which I left all ready to post, did you?'

'Nah. I stopped on my way home from school when I saw Neil carrying Midge down the garden and I thought that was odd, and then I remembered seeing Diana arrive and I thought maybe the baby would frighten Midge and when Neil put him in the shed, I said I'd stay till I could see you and tell you where Midge was. Only then I had to go back home for tea, and forgot for a bit. Just now I remembered again, and came out to see if Midge is all right and he is, and then I saw you.'

'Bless you, my dear.'

'I asked my mum if we could have Midge if you didn't want him anymore, but she said no. You know how she is.'

Ellie did indeed know how his frantically busy mum was. 'I'll sort something out with Diana.'

'I thought there might be another surprise present left in the shed for you, so I searched, but there wasn't. I said to Mum, our house is dead boring. People never leave us surprise presents and it's only the postman who puts letters through our front door, and they're mostly bills and not what I call proper letters at all.'

'You mean, you've seen someone apart from the postman put letters through my front door?' Tod's bedroom overlooked the road and he did make use of binoculars to scrutinize passers-by. His favourite fantasy was of catching a burglar at work, and in his mind even the most respectable of citizens might suddenly produce a jemmy from their brief-case or shopping bag.

'Only the woman in the poo-coloured mac. I've seen her a coupla times. Drives a brand-new red Fiesta.'

Ellie felt a shock right down to her heels. The only person she could think of who answered to that description was . . . no. Impossible.

She tried a laugh on for size. Failed. Recapped her reasoning and found holes in it. Suppose . . . ? Would that account for the inside knowledge of the typed letters? Thinking fast, she said, 'That's very interesting, Tod. You don't have the registration number of her car, by any chance?'

'Of course I do. In my notebook back home. Shall I fetch it? Is she a terrorist?'

You might well say so, thought Ellie. But she shook her head. 'No, but that's another little mystery on its way to being solved. Thank you, Tod. Extra chocolate biscuits for tea next time you come round.'

He kicked at the ground. 'I thought you might let me play on your computer for a while, but I suppose you can't if Diana's staying. Is she going to stay for long?'

'I hope not,' said Ellie, thinking to herself: she'd better not. Something had to be done about Diana.

Short of murder, that is.

CHAPTER FIFTEEN

Tuesday morning, and little Frank was already wailing. Ellie had gone to bed worrying about Diana and the missing packet of evidence, the woman who had delivered the word-processed letters, the quarrel with Bill, Roy, etc., etc., ad infinitum. And Midge. Poor Midge was presumably still shut in the shed. What on earth was she going to do about him? Give him up? Never!

She had slept badly, waking to tend to Frank at two o'clock. So she didn't exactly spring out of bed in the morning with a cry of 'All's right with the world!' No. More a groan, and a 'Please, Lord, show me the right thing to do, because I haven't a clue.'

As she disentangled a wet and dirty Frank from his bedclothes, she heard Diana brushing her hair behind her. Diana's hair was wiry, full of electricity.

'That woman, the day nanny, she asked if she should take him back home with her and I said certainly not, that she was to stay here with him where you could keep an eye on her.'

Ellie sighed. 'No, dear. I have things to do as well, and Betty is perfectly capable of looking after him.'

'Well, I expect you can rearrange, can't you? Oh, and I still don't have a key, remember. Do you still keep them on a hook in the kitchen? If so I'll help myself. And Stewart likes fish for supper if you can find some. He seems to be developing a weak stomach.' This was said with the callousness of one who had never suffered indigestion in her life.

'Hold it!' said Ellie. 'There's a label dangling from the back of your jacket. Let me take it off for you.'

Diana did a twirl. 'Do you like it? I got it yesterday at Harvey Nick's.'

Ellie liked the price tag, too. Ouch. The suit had cost more than Ellie had ever paid for a piece of clothing in her life. Diana had bought it yesterday, had she? When she had turned her mobile off, and Ellie had been unable to find her to look after Frank?

Ellie was slow. Diana had pounded down the stairs before she had thought of a reply which wasn't composed of words beginning with the letter 'f'. And she had always prided herself on never swearing!

'Bye, mother! I've taken a front-door key, so I can let myself in this afternoon. Bye, Frankie! Kiss, kiss!'

The front door banged shut as Ellie carried Frank down the stairs. Blessed silence descended as the little boy had Weetabix and milk inserted into his mouth. Fingers of toast and a bottle of milk followed. After dealing with the bottle and eating the first few toast fingers, he began to throw the rest around. Ellie didn't notice as she stared out of the window, nursing a cup of coffee. She had so many things to do, she didn't know where to start.

First, she must rescue Midge. Only, Midge seemed to have rescued himself, for he wasn't in the shed anymore, but sitting on top of the roof ridge. He turned his head aside and refused to come down when she called him, so she had to leave food out for him and rush back to deal with Frank. By the time she got back to the kitchen, Frank was screaming to get out of his chair.

Having cleaned him up and changed him yet again, Ellie created a cage out of chairs in the sitting room, and coaxed him into it with his box of toys. How on earth did Diana manage to keep him occupied all the time? Answer: she dumped him in the day nursery on her way to work. Diana was a very part-time mother. But was she, Ellie, any better as a granny? She had thought she would love to have the time to look after her grandson, but here she was, planning to get rid of him as quickly as possible. She felt guilty about that. But not too much.

Ellie managed to get up speed. She cleaned up in the kitchen, sorted out what to have for supper, picked up Diana's and Frank's dirty clothing and shoved it in the washing machine. Dusted. Put the television on for Frank, to keep him company. Then, thank the Lord, Betty arrived.

As a day nanny, Betty was everything the younger generation of mothers liked: plump and hippy, no make-up, jeans and boots, heavy sweater, fair hair pulled back in a ponytail with a long fringe that drifted around her face. An open, almost childlike expression, but with the firm chin of one who would stand no nonsense.

Frank took to her immediately. Yes, Betty could take the little boy from nine o'clock after she'd dropped her own two children off at school. She would bring him back at five every day, after she had given him and her own children their tea. She certainly did not want to spend the time in Ellie's house, and said she had everything set up to look after children in her own place, if Ellie agreed. A front-door key was handed over, Frank was bundled into his outer clothing, and off they both went.

As they went out of the front door, Midge plopped in through the cat flap at the back. He inspected the sitting room for alien scents, then settled down for a good wash and a sleep.

Peace, perfect peace. Ellie righted the room, forming a list in her head of the phone calls she needed to make. The phone rang as she reached it.

It was a voice unknown to her. Heavy, cracked. A man's voice?

'You're dead, Ellie Quicke.'

The connection was broken at the other end.

Ellie sat down, breathing fast. Sue had said her friends would come after Ellie, and they had.

It must be a joke. No. No joke. She must act fast.

First she rang Gilbert. He was concerned for her, and though he tried to make light of her fears, it was clear that he shared them.

'. . . but what about the police?'

'Would it be right to set them onto poor Sue?'

'John might confirm . . .'

'. . . and again, he might not. He's very protective of her.'

'You say the boy Tod gave you a lead to the second woman? I don't know her. What's she like?'

'I'm not really sure. I mean, I know what she looks like and I've spoken to her in passing for years, but I don't know where she lives or what she does outside work hours. I don't know why she started writing those letters to me, and I don't know how she connects with Sue. I assume it was she who threatened me on the phone this morning, but I can't swear to it.'

'Do you think it's wise to confront her by yourself? If I hadn't got this meeting this morning, I'd . . .'

'No, I'll be quite all right. I mean, what can she do to me in broad daylight in the Avenue?'

Gilbert was worried and asked her to ring him later. She promised to do so.

There was a ring at the front door. It was foxy-faced Armand, Kate's husband, from next door. Ellie took a deep breath. She'd always been slightly wary of him.

He was equally wary, but willing to be friendly. 'Hope it's not inconvenient. I've got a couple of free periods, so I thought I'd take the opportunity to have a chat with you. Kate's been talking me into having the back garden redone and said you'd lots of ideas. Do you want to come round and show me? I mean, I'm not against the idea in principle, but I can't see myself having one of those television makeover gardens with bright blue concrete and black flowers and decking and such.'

Ellie was more than ready for distraction. She abandoned all the nasty jobs she had been intending to do, fetched her notepad, locked up and went next door. An hour went by very pleasantly in discussion of how the garden might be transformed.

Basically, Armand and Kate knew they wanted a low-maintenance garden with shrubs and tubs around a stream which would trickle this way and that down the garden, but hadn't a clue how to achieve it. Now they had thought about having a conservatory, they were dead keen on building as big a one as the garden and their incomes would permit. Ellie sketched a possible layout and borrowed Armand's tape to measure the site.

Eventually Armand sighed, looking at his watch. 'I'll have to go. Form U2 awaits. Ugh! You'll let us have some sort of plan and an idea of costs?'

'As soon as possible. Best of luck,' she said, waving him off.

She went back to the phone. Squaring her shoulders, she rang Bill's office and asked his secretary if he were able to see her.

'No,' she said. 'I'm afraid he's out for the rest of the day.'

Fine. Ellie pulled on her old coat, sighed over its tatty state and wondered if she had time to pop into the charity shop to buy another one on her way. She'd feel more in control if she were wearing something smarter. Besides, she needed to pay Rose her cab fare back, and give her something for looking after Frank yesterday. She'd probably need to apologize for Diana's behaviour as well.

What was she going to do about Diana?

She waved at Chloe as she walked past the café. Chloe waved back. Chloe had discarded her usual black and was wearing string-coloured everything today. Nice.

* * *

208

The charity shop was almost empty for once. John was not there and neither was Madam, but dear Rose came out from the back and twittered about her daughter's engagement and plans for the wedding. Ellie tried on three coats and eventually settled for a rather pretty off-white camel-hair coat, with an enormous collar. Light, warm, and becoming. It certainly made Ellie feel better able to cope with the forthcoming interview.

Rose twinkled, 'That was a coat one of our most fashionable customers brought in. Madam was dying to buy it herself, but the sleeves were far too short for her. It looks lovely on you!'

'Dear Rose, you always say the right thing. And by the way, about yesterday . . .' Ellie pressed some money into Rose's hand.

It disappeared with, 'Oh, you don't have to, you know. I enjoyed looking after the dear little fellow and really, he did seem perfectly happy in the funny little house that I made for him until Diana came back and he started to cry. Besides, I have a confession to make.' Rose turned an unbecoming pink. 'I forgot to post your letter, and I've still got it in my bag.'

'What letter?'

'The one you left in the hall to post. I saw it there and realized you had forgotten to take it with you, so I popped it in my pocket to post on the way home, but then I forgot, you know the way it is, and I'm so sorry, dear. I do hope it wasn't anything important. I'll fetch it for you now, shall I?'

She returned with that all-important envelope. Ellie felt like a criminal reprieved on the scaffold. 'Bless you, dear Rose. I was worrying about it. See you for lunch later this week, perhaps?'

The next stop she visited was the Printing Press, where they were only too happy to show Mrs Quicke the various types of paper she might like to use when ordering printed or embossed letterheads for herself. Then on to the offices of Bill Weatherspoon and his junior partner, whose name Ellie was always forgetting.

She hesitated on the doorstep. This was going to be a difficult interview. The red Fiesta was parked three doors up the street. 'Ring and enter,' said a note on the door. She rang and entered.

The mud-coloured mackintosh hung on the hat stand just inside the door. The reception room was large and square, painted magnolia, with two bland desks with computers and phones on them, and plenty of seating for clients. Doors led off to Bill's office on the right and to his partner's room at the back. It was the kind of office where you were surprised not to see hunting scenes or Spy cartoons on the walls.

'Good morning, Harriet,' said Ellie. 'Is there anywhere we can talk in private?'

Bill's secretary was a well-turned-out Margaret Thatcher lookalike. Discreetly suited, spit and polished, the very model of what a personal assistant should be. She had been with Bill for as long as Ellie could remember, and Bill had always said he didn't know what he'd do without her.

Harriet's eyebrows went up. 'He's out, I'm afraid.'

A woman with reddened nose and eyes was snuffling into a handkerchief on one of the visitors' chairs in reception. Hay fever, or going through a divorce? A wide-awake-looking office junior had followed Ellie in from the street, carrying a bag of doughnuts and a takeaway coffee. Lunch hour.

Ellie seated herself, unasked. 'I hope you're telling the truth for once, as it's really you I came to see. I don't think Bill has always been out when I've rung these last few weeks, has he?'

The office junior looked startled, but the tearful visitor merely sought for another tissue in her pockets.

Harriet bridled. 'Why would I say he was out, if he wasn't? Unless, of course, he'd asked me to do so. Which he did.'

Ellie fished out the typed anonymous notes and held them up for Harriet to see. Harriet stared at them, drumming her fingers on her desk. Her face was mask-like beneath the carefully applied make-up. The office junior thoughtfully chewed her way through a doughnut, taking everything in.

The inner door opened and Bill's junior partner — a youngish, darkish, competent-looking man — ushered out a man in a blue suit while beckoning the tearful woman into his office. Harriet spoke to the junior. 'Melanie, perhaps you'd like to eat your lunch outside in the fresh air today?'

It was clear that Melanie would have preferred to stay, but she dutifully gathered her things together and made a slow exit.

'Perhaps you told me Bill was out when I phoned,' said Ellie, 'because you were afraid he'd find out about these anonymous letters. As you can see, they have been sent to me, to my aunt — Miss Drusilla Quicke — and to my daughter Diana. They refer to matters which are not common knowledge but which you would certainly know about. Also, how many other people would know their addresses?'

'Me, send anonymous letters? Oh, really!'

'Perhaps I should rephrase that. You hand-delivered at least some of the letters. You were seen, and your car registration number noted down.'

'Nonsense. Now, if you'll excuse me, I have work to do.' She tapped a number into the telephone and turned away, examining perfect, pink-polished fingernails. Ellie waited. The conversation was short. Mr Weatherspoon wished to remind the client that he had not yet received certain papers. Oh, they were in the post, were they? Splendid.

Harriet replaced the phone, and tried to stare Ellie down. 'Still here? I can't think why. You have no further connection with this firm and no right to be here. If you don't leave, I shall be forced to take measures.'

'Such as?' Ellie helped herself to a sheet of A4 from a stack on top of the filing cabinet and held it up to the light. 'Ah, here we go. Excellent quality paper, with the watermark 'Zeta'. See? A perfect match. Also the font you use on your correspondence is the same as on these anonymous letters.'

'A common enough watermark for a common type of paper. We get it from the Printing Press here in the Avenue, as do dozens of other businesses.'

'I checked. This is very expensive, heavy paper, and only two of their customers use it. One is a retired doctor I've never heard of and you are the other.'

'You have absolutely no proof . . .'

'I have enough to take to the police, unless we can sort this out between us. How do you know Sue?'

There was a sudden flash of awareness in Harriet's eyes. 'I don't know any Sue.'

'Her husband John works at the charity shop, and I happen to know that he's also a client of Bill's.'

'Oh, that John. Why didn't you say? I don't think I've ever seen his wife.'

Ellie put the envelope containing the evidence of Sue's involvement on Harriet's desk. The phone rang and Harriet answered it but kept her eyes on the envelope. This time she informed the caller that Bill was with a client, but she would ask him to ring back as soon as he was free. Harriet flicked at the envelope. 'I see an envelope addressed to you. So?'

'This envelope contains some very nasty poison-pen letters, together with proof that the letters came from a pad which John took home.'

Harriet's hands stilled, then she made a grab for the envelope. Ellie held on to it. Harriet let go, and slowly and deliberately leaned back in her chair.

Ellie said, 'Your reaction proves you knew all about the letters Sue was writing.'

With startling suddenness, Harriet lunged for the envelope again and whisked it out from under Ellie's hand. Harriet rushed across the room to the office shredder and switched it on as Ellie tried to stop her.

'Don't do that!'

'Get off me!'

Harriet blocked the way to the shredder with her body while Ellie tried to wrestle her away. Harriet's elbow caught Ellie in the stomach just as the door to the street opened and Melanie returned. At the same time Bill opened his door to show a client out.

'What the . . . !' That was Bill.

'Effing' ell!' said Melanie.

'Get . . . her . . . off . . . me!' Gritting her teeth, Harriet tried to jam the whole envelope into the shredder, which refused to take such a bulky package.

'Ellie, what is this?'

From the floor Ellie gasped, 'Stop her! She's trying to destroy evidence!'

'Harriet? What's going on?'

Harriet snarled as Bill laid his hand on her arm. Melanie revealed her quality by leaning past Harriet to switch off the shredder.

'You . . . !' Harriet tore the much-abused envelope open, releasing the scraps of gaily coloured paper and throwing them into the air. The remains of the pad slipped to the floor as Harriet tried to catch the torn-up scraps and jam them into the shredder. Her hair had fallen over her forehead and she looked demented, a domestic pussy cat turned feral.

Bill shouted, 'Harriet! Calm down!' in a parade-ground voice.

Everyone froze — Ellie bent over on the floor, Melanie with her hand on the shredder switch, Harriet holding a double fistful of coloured paper, Bill with his mouth agape, his client wide-eyed behind him. All Ellie could hear was the sound of people breathing hard. And brains whirling.

'Well!' said Bill's client, amused. 'How the other half lives, what?'

'Yes,' said Bill, in a restricted voice. 'Let me show you out. A storm in a teacup, an office spat, merely. I'll ring you later today . . .'

'Next week, you said.'

'Yes, of course. Next week.' He showed his client out.

The phone rang and Melanie leaped to answer it. Harriet slowly put down the fistfuls of paper and returned to her seat. She looked both shaken and stirred. Ellie got to her feet, dusting down her no-longer-pristine white coat.

'Well, Harriet?' asked Bill.

Harriet's voice cracked. 'Sorry, Mr Weatherspoon. I ought not to have let her in. She's made up the most awful story about me. She needs a doctor, I think.'

Ellie bent down to retrieve the evidence. She also rescued the typed letters, which had drifted to the floor in the mêlée. Melanie was answering both phones at once. A capable girl. Harriet picked up her notebook and stared at it. Then she began to cry in great, gasping sobs.

Bill gazed at her and then said, 'Melanie, will you make us all a cup of coffee when you get off the phone? Ellie, Harriet, shall we all go into my office and get this cleared up?'

Wearily, Ellie followed him into the well-known room. There was a bunch of carnations on the windowsill and a brightly coloured landscape calendar on the wall. Fine china cups and saucers advertised the fact that the last client had been treated to coffee. Harriet came in, still crying, keeping her eyes down.

It was about the best thing she could do, thought Ellie. Men like Bill always feel protective about women who cry. I can't do that. She shoved the torn-up pieces of paper and the typed letters onto Bill's desk and flopped into the chair just vacated by his client. Bill seated himself and stared at the two women, without touching the papers. Harriet continued to weep. Noisily. Annoyingly.

Bill pushed a box of tissues at Harriet, and said, 'There, there. Calm yourself, Harriet. There's nothing to cry about. Mrs Quicke will apologize for upsetting you, and leave.'

So I'm 'Mrs Quicke' now, am I? thought Ellie. She leaned forward and began to sort out the torn letters, forcing herself to speak in a matter-of-fact tone. 'What we have here are pieces of some rather horrible poison-pen letters, written in biro by someone literate. Also the pad from which they came. You see the stain down the side of the pad matches a stain down the side of some of the letters. Here is a list of names on a piece of paper which has come from the same pad. The list is signed with the name "John", but it is in a different handwriting from the letters. This is John who helps at the charity shop, whom you've known for ages. I expect you've got samples of his handwriting in your files.'

Harriet said, in a strangled voice, 'I've never seen them before in my life.'

'I expect that's true,' said Ellie. 'But you knew about them, all the same. Bill, I traced the handwritten letters back to John's wife Sue and went to see her about them yesterday. Sue admitted writing them and then tried to attack me. Luckily, John came back at that moment and he's taking her to the doctor for treatment. Sue threatened me, saying that "the others" would get me. This morning I had a telephone call confirming this, from someone who spoke in a disguised voice.'

'Indeed!' said Bill, still hostile. 'Well, that's all very sad, but I don't see why you should upset Harriet by accusing her of having anything to do with it.'

'Of course I didn't!' said Harriet in a muffled voice. 'The woman is deranged.'

'Then why did you try to destroy the evidence?' asked Ellie.

Bill winced. 'Ah. Harriet?'

'She's mad. You can see what sort of woman she is, from the letters.'

Bill leaned over to study the coloured scraps of paper. Silently, Ellie handed him the typed letters.

'You see, Bill, that the writer of these typed letters is familiar with my legal affairs. Also, the paper is unusual. Only one other person in this area uses it, apart from you. The typeface is the same as the one you use. Also, Harriet has been seen delivering letters to my house. I came here hoping to have a quiet word with her about it. I can't think why she should have sent me these letters, though I'm sure she did and that she has some connection with Sue . . . otherwise, why would she try to destroy the evidence?'

Silence. Bill might have been carved out of rock. Harriet watched him over her tissue.

Ellie thought: I've lost. She felt worn out, but continued, 'I'm not going to go to the police about it. I don't think there will be any more letters from Sue, who is a very sick woman. In coming to see Harriet, I just wanted to ensure that this whole nasty business stops here. I don't like being threatened, or being sent wax dolls that look like me, with pins through them. I don't like being rung up by people threatening to get me. I don't like my friends being persecuted, and my reputation attacked. I just want it to stop, Harriet. OK? I'd be satisfied with a letter of apology from you, admitting your guilt. I intend to put everything in the bank as a guarantee that it will never happen again, to me or to anyone else.'

Bill was in shock. 'Harriet? You didn't, did you? No, no. You couldn't . . .'

The door opened to reveal that very intelligent girl Melanie, carrying a tray of coffee cups.

Ellie had an idea. 'Melanie, can you confirm that Harriet has been fobbing me off whenever I've rung Bill in recent months? I've rung so many times, only to be told he's out or away.'

Melanie looked for guidance to Harriet.

'Tell us, Melanie. We need to know,' said her boss.

Melanie looked as if she might burst into tears, too. She struggled with herself for a moment, then decided to tell the truth. 'Yes, Mr Weatherspoon. She did block Mrs Quicke's calls. And sometimes when you asked her to get Mrs Quicke on the phone, Harriet didn't even try to get through, but told you Mrs Quicke was out or away. Sorry, Harriet, so sorry.'

'Harriet? Why?' A very puzzled and distressed Bill.

Harriet shot Ellie a vicious look. 'Well, if you must know, it's all her own fault. She waltzes in here playing Lady Muck and you'd do anything to help her, even if it means setting aside other people's work. Her, with her pretty clothes and big blue eyes and all that money that she doesn't deserve and hasn't worked for, and all the men flocking around her, and everyone knows she's no better than she ought to be and I can't think why they don't see what a little whore she is, and I hate it when you look at her like that and you never look at me like that and I shall die if you give me the sack . . .'

216

Bill looked shaken. 'Harriet, I would have gone on oath to swear to your integrity. I can't believe that you . . . but this betrayal of trust! Harriet, how could you?'

'You say you trusted me, but you refused to see me as a woman! I was just your secretary, someone to look after you, but never to be looked after! Can't you see how I feel about you? Are you so blind, you can't see?'

The words sank into the plush green carpet and died away.

Melanie noiselessly removed herself. As she opened the door to the outer office, Ellie could hear both phones ringing. The door shut. Ellie wondered what Melanie would say to those who rang, asking for Bill. There was another client sitting on a chair outside, too. Ellie got to her feet. Some fresh bruises seemed to have joined the ones she'd collected at Sue's house.

Bill also stood up. 'Ellie, I don't know what to say. May I ring you later? You can trust me to deal with Harriet. As for the evidence that you've gathered, if you don't wish to take it to the police — and I think we'd all be grateful if you didn't — then I'll have Harriet add her bit and see that the whole packet is locked up here for the time being. Do you agree that's best?'

Ellie nodded.

Bill came with her to the outer door, with a pleasant handshake for his next client, and a promise to be with him shortly. 'Supper tonight, Ellie? Pick you up at half-seven?'

Ellie nodded again. She needed a long sit down and a large pot of tea before facing anybody else. Come to think of it, she might feel better if she ate a good meal. What with the strain of having Diana around and the hustle and bustle of the last few days, Ellie couldn't remember when she had last had a good meal. Sunday night, probably. Was that only two days ago? So much had happened since.

She wouldn't mind a short talk with Chloe about her cousin Neil, either. And perhaps she would go and buy herself a new dress or something. Another coat? It was best not to think in detail about what had just happened. Too alarming. She made for the Sunflower Café.

CHAPTER SIXTEEN

The busiest part of the lunch hour was over and Ellie managed to get a table by herself at the back.

'Nice coat,' said Chloe as she materialized with the menu. 'But did you know you had a black streak down the back? Sausages is off. Best is liver and bacon, freshly cooked.'

'Thanks, Chloe. I'll have to get the coat cleaned. Liver and bacon would be lovely, with a large pot of tea straightaway.'

Ellie leaned back in her chair, pushing away thoughts of the poison that had spewed out of both Sue and Harriet. Ellie had always thought of herself as a well-meaning, likeable sort of woman, the sort who helped out in emergencies. She shuddered. She could make allowances for Sue because she was obviously a couple of pies short of a baker's dozen, but Harriet . . . !

Perhaps the worst of it all was that she'd had absolutely no idea that she had aroused such hatred in someone. It was a shock to realize that in her ignorance — or perhaps the right word was pride? — she hadn't even noticed how she'd been hated. Ellie was ashamed of herself. How could she have been so blind?

After she'd eaten some of the excellent meal, she went on to wonder how *Bill* could have been so blind. The answer to that produced a sour face. Bill had always had a soft spot for Ellie and perhaps, if she had encouraged him after Frank had died, he might well have wanted to deepen their friendship. Oh dear. Perhaps Harriet had been right all along and Ellie had been toying with men without realizing the harm she had been doing.

Without meaning it, certainly.

She sighed. Put her knife and fork down. Poured another cup of tea. Grinned a little.

What would her dear old Frank have said, if he knew that his pliant little wifey had become a sex object? Well, not precisely a sex object. Too old and too rounded for that. Except that Roy had seemed to think . . . feel . . . and she had felt it, too.

Roy. Another sigh.

Diana and Stewart. A bigger sigh. Ellie faced the fact that she dreaded going back to her house to find it taken over by Diana. She had an idea about that which might work, but it would cost a lot of money to carry out and anyway, would Aunt Drusilla play ball? She must think about it.

Chloe removed dirty plates. By now the café was almost empty.

'That was lovely, Chloe. Just what I needed.'

'Make the most of it. I've got my ticket for Australia, leaving on the first of March.'

'What does your boyfriend say about that?'

'Bob's sulking, doesn't want me to go. I said I'll be back in six months. I'm starting uni in the autumn, got my place in the halls of residence and all. He doesn't like that idea any better. I told him, "You're a dinosaur, Bob."'

Amused, Ellie said, 'You've got him wrapped round your little finger.'

Chloe laughed. 'He wants to buy me a ring to wear while I'm away in Australia. I said, "What, and get mugged for its value?" No, there'll be no ring. It's best for us to have some time apart, see how we go. He thinks he loves me. I think I'm comfortable with him, and maybe we will end up together.

But how do I know what he'll get up to while I'm away? There's a couple of very pretty girls in the house where I live, you know.

'Oh, by the way. Message from Neil. He's going to move into my room when I go, get away from Gran. Don't blame him. It'd drive me round the bend living in that titchy house — and the meals she serves, you can hardly see the meat for chips. Not that I'm against chips in general, but greens and salads ought to get a look-in as well.'

'Tell me, Chloe. Neil has been talking about setting up as a jobbing gardener, getting someone to do the books . . .'

'Not me. Hopeless at it. One of the girls in the house is thinking about it, yes. Business degree, cool head. Yes, I think he might do all right. He said you'd given him some work and he's picked up a few other customers as well. He's honest, if that's what you're wondering.'

'I was wondering how much he knew about gardening.'

'Some. He'll learn. He's bright enough — should have gone to college, but for that bitch my uncle married. You should see her, bottle-blonde and itsy little voice. Barbie doll, you know? Or perhaps I'm being hard on Barbie.'

Ellie laughed, paid the bill and left. She always felt better after a chat with Chloe. She looked in the windows of the dress shop in the Avenue. Everything seemed to be size twelve and under, in black or grey. Ellie went in anyway.

She came out without buying anything. Then she remembered there was a seconds boutique just opened at the other end of the Avenue. Nice manageress, six foot tall with a cleavage to marvel at. There wasn't much in a size sixteen but you could browse at your leisure without having the shop girl turn up her nose and say, 'I'm afraid we don't stock clothes in your size, madam.'

* * *

An hour later Ellie dropped the dirty white coat and the dress she had been wearing at the cleaners and made her way home via the fish shop. She had found a lightweight, pale blue wraparound coat and under it was wearing a new cream dress with matching jacket. She needed the jacket on that blustery day. She also treated herself to a sheaf of brilliant yellow mimosa at the florist's. When the sun wasn't out, it was good to have lots of yellow flowers around the house.

Returning across the Green, she saw with alarm that the back bedroom windows were wide open. In that cold weather!

Midge met her as she opened the gate from the lane into her garden. She picked him up to give him a cuddle, but he leaped from her arms onto the fence and from there to the roof of the shed. Ellie dished him out some more cat food and left the door of the shed open a little way, so that he could take shelter there if he felt so inclined.

Inside the house, she confronted a hot and sweaty Stewart, who was trying to heave one of her precious antique side tables up the stairs.

'Stewart! What on earth are you doing?'

Stewart lost his grip and the table slid back down the stairs, with Ellie lunging forward to break its fall.

Diana appeared at the top of the stairs, also looking flushed. 'Mother, I didn't expect you back so early. Stewart's interview isn't till tomorrow morning, so he's just moving some furniture round for me.'

Stewart stood aside as Ellie marched up the stairs. 'Don't you think you should have asked me first?'

She stood on the landing and nearly died. Her bedroom, her own particular refuge, the one in which she had slept nearly all her married life, had been turned upside down. The double bed from the back bedroom was now standing in place of her own bed. The dressing table was halfway through the door into the back bedroom, and as her fitted wardrobe doors stood open, Ellie could see that her own clothes had been removed and Diana's put there instead.

'You see, mother, how much better it is this way. Stewart and I will have so much more space in the front room, especially with your big old dressing table out and the smaller table in the window instead. You'll be much cosier in the smaller room at the back . . .'

Ellie found she was shaking with rage. She took a deep breath. 'Diana, I have never struck you in my life. Believe me, you are within an inch of it now. You will return everything to the way it was, and you will do it right now. Stewart, see to it, will you?'

'Mother, you can't . . .'

'I will leave the fish for Stewart's supper in the fridge. Don't expect me to cook it for you, because I have been invited out for supper myself.'

'Mother, you can't be serious!'

'Oh, I am. Believe me, I am deadly serious. Stewart, if I don't see you before your interview tomorrow, then I wish you the best of luck.'

Ellie banged the front door shut behind her, and thought: that's torn it. Now she can tell all her friends how unreasonable I am. I know, of course I know, that my bedroom is old fashioned, but Frank liked it like that and . . .

She stopped to blow her nose. How forceful she had been! Had she actually threatened to strike her own daughter? She was halfway between a giggle and a scream. I'm going to be labelled the Wicked Witch of the West, she thought. And I don't care. So, what do I do till it's time for Bill to pick me up?

Her feet were already taking her across the Green. She sighed. She had not particularly wanted to ask Aunt Drusilla to help her out with accommodation for Diana. In fact, she had fought against it. But this was the last straw.

Turning into the driveway of the big house, Ellie slowed. Ought she to recognize the car that was parked there? It had a familiar look to it. She examined it for clues. A Jaguar. Oh. Roy had a Jaguar. Yes, it might be his. Aunt Drusilla had mentioned that she knew him.

Roy opened the door to let himself out as she mounted the steps. He looked surprised, almost shocked. Then he shrugged, smiled and stood aside for Ellie to enter the house. 'We must talk. May I ring you later?'

She nodded and he drove away without saying anything else.

With a feeling of uneasiness amounting to panic, Ellie thought up a wild and fanciful explanation for his presence. Was it possible that . . . ? No. No, of course not. But she reminded herself that when she had got up that morning, she had believed black to be black and white to be white. Now she was not so sure.

Aunt Drusilla was sitting in her big chair before the fire. All the lights had been turned on, and on the table beside the old lady stood a selection of brightly polished, silver-framed photographs.

'It's only me, Aunt Drusilla.' Ellie bent to kiss the old lady's cheek, with her eyes on the photographs. She knew those photographs. She had seen them before in Nora's flat. Roy had taken them to sell for Aunt Drusilla. Or so he had said.

Aunt Drusilla was clutching a large man's handkerchief. It looked as if it had been made much use of.

'Sit, girl. Have you worked it out, then?'

'I'm not sure. Roy is . . .'

'. . . my illegitimate son, yes.'

Ellie sat down with a bump. The old lady wasn't one to beat about the bush.

Aunt Drusilla tried on a smile. It looked grotesque, but then, there were tears in the folds of her cheeks and beneath her eyes.

She said, 'I suppose I'd better explain. I fell in love with his father when he came to teach at the school I attended. I was in my last year there, a lanky, ugly girl. I couldn't believe it when this charming, handsome young teacher singled me out for attention. Naturally I fell for him. My father disapproved, saying he was a fortune-hunter.

'I didn't believe him. What teenager in love ever does? When I left school we became secretly engaged and I got pregnant. Percy had vowed we would be married the moment I was old enough to marry without my father's consent. My father made it clear that there would be no money if we married, and Percy cooled off. In those days you didn't keep illegitimate babies. My father arranged for me to stay with a distant cousin in the country and the baby was adopted at birth. Luckily he went to a professional family who doted on him, gave him a good education and left him a small fortune.'

'Roy. He was fortunate in his adoptive parents.'

'Yes. As for me, I returned home and learned how to make myself useful to my father. Over the next few years, he proved my business abilities and discovered that my younger brother — his only son and Frank's father — was lacking in that respect. When he died, he left me the bulk of his money. I enjoyed making money. It became my one aim in life. I did have one or two men hanging around after me over the years, but I never encouraged them. I'd had enough of that.

'Percy married his headmaster's daughter, sired the unprepossessing Nora, and eventually took over the school. It amused me to give him a lease on one of my flats and to see what a pig's ear he made of marriage to his whining wife. As for the child, she turned out about as badly as could be expected of such a union. When I heard that he'd died, I laughed. Certain people thought I ought to help Nora out of her difficulties, but I didn't see it like that. He ruined me, and he ruined his daughter. So be it.'

Ellie was reassessing everything she'd known about the family. 'And then Roy found out that you were his mother, and came looking for you?'

'He found out that his mother was a wealthy woman, and came looking for a handout to finance a development scheme. I would have sent him away with a flea in his ear, but for some reason he reminded me of my own dear nephew Frank . . .'

'. . . and so you pointed him in my direction, thinking that if he married me, he would get the finance he required and you'd be shot of him.'

'Something like that, yes. But you didn't want him.'

'No. Like you, I was reminded of Frank at first. I was attracted to him, yes, and he tried hard enough. But, no. It wouldn't do for me, or for him.'

'He expects me to act like his mother! Now, after all these years!' Aunt Drusilla laughed, a high, almost mad sound. Then she sobered. 'Make a pot of tea, will you, Ellie? I asked Roy to do it, but he couldn't even find the kitchen. And talk about ham-fisted! I don't know where he gets his clumsiness from. His father, I presume.'

Ellie made the tea, and they sat in companionable silence until the old woman said, 'Get rid of those photographs for me, will you, Ellie? I don't want them.'

'Perhaps Roy will. He's polished them up beautifully.'

'Got someone else to do it, more like. Put them in the top drawer of the armoire. I'll give them back to him next time I see him. He wants to develop that big house on the Green. What do you think? Is it a good proposition?'

'I really don't know enough about finance to say. I like his ideas, yes, and I think they'd pass the planning committee.'

'Hm. Then I might take it further. Unless, of course, you want him out of your life, in which case I'll tell him I can't help.'

'I don't want him in my life particularly. I get angry when I think how he tried to bamboozle me, but no . . . on the whole, I think I feel sorry for him. As to developing that site, I don't want to come between a friend and a good business deal.'

'You think of him as a friend? No more than that?'

'No more than that,' said Ellie firmly. 'He amuses me, but it won't go any further. Tell me, do we recognize the relationship now?'

'Yes, I suppose so. I leave it to you to tell Diana. Turn the central heating up, will you, dear? I'm feeling the cold.'

Ellie put the silver frames in the drawer the old lady indicated and turned up the heating at the thermostat in the hall. On her return Aunt Drusilla said, with a return to her imperious manner, 'And now, to what do I owe the pleasure of this visit?'

Change of subject, thought Ellie. 'Well, the truth is that Diana is driving me mad, and I have to get her out of my house or I shall do something I shall regret. Can you find some suitable accommodation for her elsewhere? Until they manage to sell the house up north, she won't have enough to pay rent on anything decent down here, so I thought I might offer to pay the rent for her on a two-bedroomed flat, possibly furnished, for anything up to six months.'

'You are no businesswoman, Ellie. You ought to start by asking me to give her free housing, since, as you very well know, I am getting her services cheap.'

'I thought we'd got past that stage. I suspect that Diana may not be as . . .' she hesitated, searching for the right word.

'As trustworthy as you? I agree. I shall keep my eye on her. Well, there is a first-floor flat — fully furnished, central heating — which became vacant yesterday. I will let you have a lease on that, and who you sublet to is your business. It's situated in the next road, in a big house similar to this. No access to the garden, I'm afraid. But then, I don't think Diana is a gardener, is she?'

'Ah. Have you let Roy have a flat in the same house?'

'No. He's in a different house in another road. Did he tell you I'd let him have a flat?'

'No. I guessed. And the rent for Diana's flat?'

'Do you care?'

'No, I don't think I do. Anything to get her out of my hair.'

'You're a terrible businesswoman, Ellie. Well, I'll be fair. I'll instruct the estate agents to let you have the keys tomorrow. I have only one stipulation to make. Diana must not know that I own the house, or indeed that I own anything apart from the riverside flats. You will tell her that you have discovered the flat for yourself, and are renting it to her.'

'Agreed.'

'Do you think Stewart will get a transfer to the London office?'

'Gut reaction says no, but I think Diana is determined to move down here. I suppose she might insist on Stewart giving in his notice and looking for another job down here, but . . . he's a nice lad, you know.'

'He's not up to her weight. Ellie, your advice please. As you may have guessed, I own not only the riverside flats, but also a dozen houses converted into flats and let out on short leases. I don't wish Diana to know about them, or to manage them. As you know, I have not been satisfied with the estate agents who have been managing my affairs. Do you think — if the worst comes to the worst — that Stewart might be a possible manager for those other properties, if I set up a dummy company as a front and got them to employ him as manager?'

'He is meticulous and honest, yes. No decorative flair, no driving ambition. He might do well.'

'I'll think about it. You're looking very smart today. You also look as if you have been crying. Have you had any more of those dreadful letters?'

'No, but I found out who was sending the typed letters . . .' She told Aunt Drusilla what had happened at the solicitor's office that morning. 'It's strange. I was frightened by the letters when they came from unknown hands. Now I know who sent them, I'm not frightened, but I do feel distressed for them. What sad, empty lives some people live! The damage those two women have done! And where has it got them? Pills and more pills for Sue. And for Harriet the loss of a job which has meant everything to her.'

'So it's finished, then? You've done a good job, Ellie.'

'I hope so. I hope it was Harriet who sent the wax figures and made those threatening phone calls. I shall find out tonight when I have supper with Bill.'

Ellie took the tea things out to the vast, unheated kitchen, and washed up. A tray with a meagre supper stood ready on the table for Aunt Drusilla. Ellie took that through

227

and left it on the side table. Aunt Drusilla did not appear to have moved since Ellie left the room, but one of the silver-framed photographs had migrated from the drawer to the table at her elbow. Ellie said nothing about that. She kissed the old lady and bade her goodnight.

Going down the drive, she thought how strange it was that she had come so close to someone whom she had always regarded as the cross in her life. She had actually kissed the old lady with affection! That was something that would have been inconceivable even a short time ago. But there it was. Ellie understood her better now.

* * *

It was later than she had thought. She walked home quickly, wondering if she had time for a shower before Bill came to pick her up. She walked straight into a party being hosted by Diana. Stewart was pouring drinks for wall-to-wall people, but Ellie could see cigarette ash all over the carpet, and nibbles tossed around everywhere. The noise level was appalling, as the guests competed with deafening music from the stereo. There was no sign of Midge.

'Oh! Who are you?' An ultra-thin woman in black bumped into Ellie. 'Where's the loo?'

Ellie tried to hang up her coat, but there was no room on the stand in the hall. Carrying it, she went into the kitchen. Someone popped their head around the door. 'What fun! Freddie's just sicked up in the fireplace. Have you got any more ice?' The head disappeared.

Ellie looked in the fridge. The fish she had bought for Stewart's supper was still in its wrapper. She went up the stairs. Two men seemed to be having a wrestling match on the double bed, which — thank goodness — had been returned to the back bedroom. On her own single bed in the front room lay a pile of coats. A woman was seated at Ellie's dressing table, primping.

'Oh, are you the daily? There's no more loo paper.'

'Hurry up, Vanda!' Ignoring Ellie completely, a man appeared in the doorway, zipping up his flies. 'I say, this is very boring. I thought you said this woman knew everyone, but it's a crowd of nobodies. How soon can we get away?'

'I only met her a couple of times at the museum or something. Can't even remember what she does. I wouldn't have come if we weren't due just down the road at eight.'

Ellie panicked, worrying about little Frank, but he was lying fast asleep in the cot, clutching Gog. She went into the bathroom and locked the door. The bathroom was in chaos, not a clean towel or any loo paper in sight. She piled the towels into the laundry basket, got out some new loo paper, and had a shower. Several people came banging on the door, but she ignored them. There were shouts and loud goodbyes from below.

Suddenly the house went quiet. Venturing out of her sanctuary, Ellie found her bedroom empty of clothes and people. Everything on the dressing table had been knocked over or pushed on the floor. She made a leisurely toilet and went downstairs to find Stewart rather cack-handedly trying to clean up. Diana was lying on the couch, complaining of a headache.

'Sorry, mother!' said Stewart. 'I didn't know we were going to throw a welcome back party till this evening. I said I didn't think you'd like it.'

'No, I don't,' said Ellie crisply. 'I know it wasn't your fault, Stewart, but whatever happens at your interview, this has proved that we can't all live together. I have to have my house to myself again. Diana, I have found a flat for you locally for six months, furnished, which should do you until you can sell your own house up north. You can have the keys tomorrow and I want you to move in the following day. I will pay the rent, but you will cover all outgoings and repairs. Understood?'

'What? But this is my home!'

'No, it isn't. It's mine. You're a grown-up girl now, with your own lifestyle, which is not mine.'

Stewart picked up the pieces of a broken wine glass. 'I told you she wouldn't like us having a party, Diana.'

'But you'll pay the rent?' Ellie nodded. 'Well, I suppose . . . where is this flat? Local? Big enough for an au pair? It will have a garage, of course.'

'I wouldn't think so, not in this area. You shall have all the details tomorrow. Meanwhile, you'd better cook that fish for Stewart's supper, or it will go off. I'm out this evening, remember.'

'With that no-good Bar-tick, I suppose!'

'Don't speak ill of your cousin . . .'

'Cousin?'

'Second cousin,' amended Ellie. 'He's Aunt Drusilla's long-lost son, put out for adoption at birth.'

Diana flushed. *'What?'*

'Don't shout, dear. Yes, he came looking for his mother, after all these years. Touching, isn't it?'

Stewart was gaping. 'You mean, he's after her money too?'

'Stewart!' Diana was appalled, not that her husband had been tactless, but that he had spoken the truth.

'Yes, dear. That's right. He's after her money too. But he does care for her in his own way. And no, I'm not going out with him tonight, but with Bill Weatherspoon, my solicitor.'

Prompt on cue, the front doorbell rang and Ellie wafted herself out of the house, leaving Diana to clutch her head and pace the floor.

'I'm glad someone can find something to laugh at,' said Bill, ushering Ellie into his car. 'What a day! You're looking very chipper, Ellie.'

* * *

She had hoped that Bill would take her somewhere quiet and expensive, where they would run no risk of being recognized. Instead, he took her to the local carvery, which, though good in its way, was also frequented by Archie and Roy. As his guest, however, Ellie felt she must be appreciative and keep her misgivings to herself.

She had roast lamb with four different vegetables, and when she was offered a Yorkshire pudding with it, she only hesitated for a moment before accepting that on her plate as well. In the old days, it would have been a social solecism to have pudding with anything but beef, but nowadays, apparently, anything goes.

'. . . so I called my partner in, and we got Melanie to cancel all our appointments and tried to get to the bottom of the matter. I don't know that we succeeded completely, but we did get Harriet to write out a confession in the end. I had to call a taxi to take her home; she was too upset to drive her own car. After all these years! I can still hardly believe that Harriet could do such a thing.'

'Did she say who else was involved, apart from poor Sue?'

'No. She denied even knowing Sue, in spite of having tried to destroy the evidence against her.'

'Did she admit to making threatening telephone calls to me? And sending the wax figures?'

'No. She said you were imagining things. We pressed her hard, but . . . she was so distressed, begged me to forgive her for not putting your calls through, said the letters she had written were only meant to be a joke, reminded me of her long years of service. Said she needed a holiday, that she'd been under a great deal of stress at home — she looks after her aged mother, you know. She offered to get some pills from the doctor, go for counselling, anything, so long as she could keep her job. But my partner, sound sort of chap, he said we'd never be able to trust her again, and that's true, of course. Still, it's a wrench, parting with someone who's worked for you for so long. We had to stand over her while she cleared her desk. Nasty.'

He sighed, and selected a sticky toffee pudding for afters.

Ellie said, 'So she's gone, and we're no nearer clearing up the last of the mystery.'

'She wouldn't talk about it. Believe me, I tried, but she turned obstinate, wouldn't listen, said it served you right. Floods of tears throughout.' He shuddered. 'Luckily, I remembered she always used to complain about her mother being able to cry at will in order to get her own way. Even so, I wouldn't wish to go through that again. Just as she was going, she turned on us. Said she'd sue the pants off me for wrongful dismissal, etc.'

'She can't, can she?'

'Not after signing that confession, no. And before you ask, my partner took all the evidence in the case to the bank and lodged it in a safety deposit box.'

Ellie tackled her cheese and biscuits. 'I feel sorry for her, a little. I had no idea she felt like that about you.'

Bill looked self-conscious. 'I just hadn't noticed. Or rather, I suppose I had noticed at one level, but . . . I suppose I was flattered, but I didn't do anything about it because . . . well, I'd never thought about her that way, and I didn't realize I was so desperately important to her. I blame myself for that.'

'Like Gilbert, our vicar. He realized Nora was dependent on him and I suppose he was flattered, too, in a way. He certainly didn't take it seriously enough. I don't think he had any idea at all that Sue was a grenade with a loose pin.'

'Coffee? Liqueur?'

An angry voice broke in. 'So there you are!' Archie, flushed with wine from having dined in an inner room. 'You can't find the time to come out with me, but you will eat out with anyone else!'

Bill stared. Ellie tried to retrieve the situation. 'Archie, this is Bill, my solicitor. Bill, this is Archie, a very good friend of Frank's from the church, you know. Do you think we could all have coffee together in the lounge? Archie, Bill here has just been telling me that he's solved the mystery of the poison-pen letters. We should all be able to sleep better tonight, don't you think?'

Bill understood that Archie was to be mollified by being Told All, and was ready to oblige. They all had coffee while

Bill and Ellie explained what they had discovered, without naming any names.

'No, Archie. We won't name names. They're two very sick ladies with desperate lives and I don't want them to suffer any more than they do already. I know you have such a kind heart that you will want to keep their names out of the gossip, and it's probably best we don't tell you who they are. You have such an expressive face, you might give them away without realizing it.'

Archie beamed under the influence of this delicate flattery and agreed that Ellie knew best, but he still shot wicked looks at Bill, and said pointedly that he hoped to speak to Ellie about church affairs when she had a minute. Ellie remembered the difficulty she'd been having with the church notices. She really didn't know what to do about them. She said she'd have a look at them tomorrow morning and would ring Archie as soon as she'd got them sorted out.

Bill drove her home. Ellie was tired, holding back a yawn. 'You know, Ellie, you're a honeypot. You don't mean to be, but that's what you are. I remember when Frank first met you, he said to me that you were a honeypot with lots of men buzzing around you, but that he thought he could capture you for himself.'

'Goodness! I thought the men were all over me now because of my money.'

'That, too. But there are lots of women with money who don't attract so many followers. Me, too, I shouldn't wonder.' He said this so lightly that Ellie realized he meant it, but was not proposing to embarrass her with a declaration.

She gave him a feather-light kiss on his cheek. 'Dear Bill. I adore you, and I've loved our evening out. We must do it again sometime. Which reminds me: I'm going to need some help sorting out a lease on a flat for Diana, and advice about helping a young man set up as a jobbing gardener, and oh, lots of things. Don't laugh, but my neighbours want to commission me to redesign their garden for them, and I haven't a clue about costings.'

'Mm. I have a client who does landscape gardening. You might find it worthwhile to meet him. Ring me, any time, and we'll discuss things.'

She waved him goodbye, thinking: And this time there'll be no Harriet to divert the call. Oh dear, poor Harriet. And now I suppose I have to puzzle out how Sue and Harriet are connected, and who the third person might be.

CHAPTER SEVENTEEN

Ellie woke slowly, with a feeling of impending doom. Little Frank was wailing. She'd been up to him twice in the night and was feeling distinctly off her grandchild. She wondered if Diana was perhaps feeling the same way about her offspring. Oh dear.

Midge nuzzled her ear. He had slunk into the house on her return and hightailed it up the stairs to her bedroom to sleep at her back. Dear Midge. What a comfort he was. She informed him that he would be wisest to stay where he was until Diana had left the house, and he seemed to understand.

Breakfast was a silent meal, with Ellie trying to coax Frank to eat and Diana immersed in *The Times*. As soon as Diana had gone, Midge appeared for his breakfast, only slipping out through the cat flap as Stewart descended, looking washed out. Ellie cooked him breakfast, but he could hardly face it. 'I'm dreading this interview,' he said.

Ellie tried to be bracing. 'Oh, I'm sure you'll sail through it.'

'I love my job up north. I really don't want to be tied down to an office job, and that's what promotion would mean. If only Diana weren't so set on moving.'

There was no answer to that, so Ellie just smiled, patted him on the shoulder, and waved him off as young Betty arrived to collect Frank for the day. Ellie let Midge back into the house and made much of him. Nice to have him around the place again — although Midge evidently disapproved of the stains on the carpet in the living room.

Ellie wondered whether she should get down on her hands and knees and scrub at the pile, but decided to get a professional carpet-cleaner in instead. Let the Yellow Pages take the strain, or something. What to do next?

First she rang Gilbert and told him what had happened when she had confronted Harriet.

'I don't think I know this Harriet,' said Gilbert. 'Maybe by sight? All these middle-aged women with hormones spinning out of control! You won't believe it, but I've already got a couple of them here in my new parish, calling round at all hours with problems that only the vicar can solve.'

'What are you going to do about it?'

'Liz suggests I appoint a couple of older women as pastoral assistants to visit and report back to me. That should do the trick.'

'Knowing you, you'll soon be keeping a complete harem going. You're a sucker for a sad story. Now Gilbert, I've discovered the identity of two of the ladies, but there's still one to go. Any ideas? Someone you counselled in the past? Someone who went through a bad patch?'

'Have you got all year to listen? No, Ellie. I don't think I can give you any names. Confidentiality, you know. Besides, if I don't know this Harriet, I might not know your third lady. There's no one who springs to mind exactly . . . or is there?' He sounded puzzled.

'A name did spring to mind? Can you give me a clue?'

'Animal, vegetable or mineral? No, I'm not going to say. The person I was thinking of . . . absurd. Not one of your weepy-wailies.'

'Then what do I look for?'

'Perhaps, a mischief-maker? No, it's I who am guilty of mischief-making now. Can you not let it drop? You've found and dealt with those two sad cases. The third member of the team — if there is a third — will surely hear that their cover has been blown and quietly fade away. Let it lie, Ellie.'

'Leave it in the hands of the Lord?'

He laughed. 'You sound sceptical, but it does work.'

'Hmph! Oh, someone's at the door. Speak to you later.'

It was a messenger with the keys to the flat for Diana, plus a standard rental form for Ellie to fill in. Good.

The phone rang and it was the doctor's surgery, saying that Ellie's blood-test results had come through. The doctor would like to see Ellie and could fit her in at the end of the day. Was that all right?

'You can't give me the results now?'

'Afraid not. Can you make it, then? Half-past six; it's our late surgery. All right?'

'Yes,' said Ellie, thinking that this meant bad news. Something had shown up on the blood tests, which she had forgotten all about. It would be just her luck to have all this on her plate *and* to go down with something nasty.

The doorbell. This time it was Neil, needing payment for clearing out her bits and pieces the other day and wondering if there was any more work she could recommend for him to do. Midge pranced out of the living room and started playing with the laces on Neil's trainers. They had a mug of coffee and talked gardening, and discussed how to make a stream run downhill and then get the water pumped back up again.

Ellie settled down at last to make a start on the church notices, but then Stewart arrived back, looking despondent. Ellie abandoned her own work, made him a coffee and let him talk. As she had half-anticipated, he had been turned down for a transfer to London. He said Diana wanted him to give up his job altogether if he didn't get it.

'Of course she's right,' said Stewart, looking miserable. 'We can't afford that big house and there's so much more opportunity down here. It's silly to think I can stay on up there in a dead-end job.'

Ellie dangled keys in front of him. 'Let's go look at this flat, shall we?' So they looked at the flat, which was spacious, light and clean, with modern furniture, kitchen and bathroom. Stewart was gloomy about it, though. 'She'll gripe because there isn't a bidet. Or a garage.'

'Remember it's rent free for six months.'

'I feel such a failure! Diana deserves better than this. I feel I've let her down.'

Ellie reflected that it was impossible to help someone who believed Diana was always right. She suggested she took Stewart out for lunch, but he was too dejected to be good company. It was the busiest time of the lunch hour, so Chloe was not free to talk, either — something which proved to be unfortunate.

Ellie suggested that Stewart take himself off for a good long walk while she did some work of her own. Stewart blinked at the notion that his mother-in-law might have something to worry about apart from him, but, good-natured as always, he did as she suggested. Ellie turned her attention back to the wretched church notices. And there it was.

As soon as she leafed through the notices, she saw it.

ST SAVIOUR'S SPRING FAIR
St David's Day
1 March
11 a.m.–4 p.m.
Refreshments — Face-painting — Story-telling
Crèche — Parachuting
CRAFT STALLS
Needlework — Glass-painting — Candles
Homemade cakes — Plants

Candles. Who at church made candles for sale? Gwyneth did.

Oh no. It wasn't possible that bossy Gwyneth could have been responsible for making those wax figures. Or was it? Gwyneth, the waspish, bosomy soprano who thought herself God's gift, worked part-time as the doctor's receptionist and so would know all about Sue and her 'difficult' times. Nora had been a patient at the same surgery, and probably

Mrs Guard was too. Gwyneth could easily have read their notes and played upon their fears.

Was there a connection between Gwyneth and Harriet? Ellie couldn't think of any. Besides, why should Gwyneth, respectable pillar of the church, on every important committee, stoop to sending anonymous letters and wax figures? It was so out of character, it was ridiculous.

Hang about. The letters had all been accounted for by Harriet and Sue. The phone calls, the killing of the cat and the wax figures were something else. A different sort of mind. A mind that had septic corners in it.

Mrs Dawes had once told Ellie that Gwyneth's husband had deserted her years ago, which might make any woman bitter. Where had Mrs Dawes got her information from? One of her cronies? Mrs . . . can't remember her name, who walks with a Zimmer . . . *and is an aunt of Gwyneth's.* Why hadn't she remembered that earlier? Hadn't there been something, ages ago, about Gwyneth making eyes at Archie? What a giggle.

A mischief-maker, Gilbert had said. Gwyneth was certainly that. But no. It was surely out of the question.

Ellie could ask her at the surgery tonight, if she were still there when Ellie arrived. She probably would have gone home long before. Perhaps Ellie might sound the doctor out, tell her in confidence what had been happening, check that someone was attending to Sue. Yes, that would be the best thing to do.

Meanwhile, Ellie decided that she would not worry about the blood-test results. No. She would occupy herself in preparing supper for the three of them, and playing with Midge. What is this life if, full of care, we have no time to play with a cat?

Diana, Stewart, Betty and little Frank all arrived back late, just as Ellie was putting on her coat to set off for her doctor's appointment. As the front door opened, so Midge made his exit. It's a wise cat that knows his friends.

'Sorry, darlings; must dash. Back in half an hour, I should think. A nice beef stew in the oven, veg ready to put on.'

'Really, mother . . . !'
But Ellie had fled.

* * *

The waiting room at the surgery was empty, but there was a light on in the doctor's room. She must be the last patient to be seen that night. Ellie thought her watch might be a trifle fast. She picked up a magazine and sat down to wait. Gwyneth came out of the doctor's consulting room, turning off the light behind her and locking the inner door. She was wearing a heavy black car coat over black trousers. Her eyes protruded slightly.

Ellie frowned. 'Has the doctor gone, then? I didn't think you were on duty today.'

'I do half-days, Wednesdays. I noticed in the appointments book that you were coming in, so when the doctor had to leave for an emergency, I volunteered to stay on and clear up. There was another patient supposed to be coming in tonight for an urgent prescription, but he hasn't turned up, so we won't be disturbed.'

Ellie put the magazine down with hands that shook. Gwyneth was unsmiling, focused on her. And much, much larger in every way. Ellie tasted fear. She stood up. 'I'd better ring tomorrow for another appointment about the results of the blood tests.'

'No need. The results were all within the normal parameters. It'll be easier for you if you just sit down again and keep still. That way it won't hurt too much. I promised I'd get you, and I always keep my word.'

Ellie tried to slow her breathing down to normal. 'It was you who encouraged Sue and Harriet to target Nora and then me? It was you who made the wax figures and killed the cat? But why, Gwyneth? Why?'

'Nora lost us our vicar. She deserved to die and so do you, flaunting yourself with all those men. Archie would have married me if you hadn't made eyes at him.'

'I didn't . . .'

'And now you've upset Sue so much that she's had to go back into hospital . . .'

'Oh, dear. That's awful.'

'. . . and you've lost Harriet her job!'

'She lost it for herself. Why did you hate Nora so much?'

'I didn't hate her. I despised her. I tried telling her, face to face, what people thought of her, but she wouldn't listen, and Gilbert told me I was meddling! I wasn't meddling. I was telling her — as it says in the Bible, if one of your members sins, you should go to her and rebuke her.'

It was hardly a sin to cry out for help, thought Ellie. And you did it without the necessary love. She said, 'Tell me, how did you three get together?'

'I see Sue at the creative writing classes. We were having lunch together afterwards one day at the Sunflower Café when, quite by chance, Harriet joined us at our table because there were no other seats free. I knew her, of course, because we both belong to the National Trust locally. We found we had similar views on matters of concern to the community, and continued to meet. We decided that where the law could not or would not act, then we would.'

One question to Chloe, thought Ellie, and I'd have had the answer. She said aloud, 'You formed yourself into a vigilante group? But what you've done is terrible. You drove Nora to her death!'

'And you, my dear Ellie. And you! You're going to be found unconscious tomorrow with a load of drugs inside you. Poor dear Ellie, still pining for her husband! We'll all be so sorry, and ask ourselves if we couldn't have done more to help you through your depression . . .'

'I'm not depressed!'

'Oh yes, you are. Your notes say you are. I've seen to that. There was a locum doctor here last week and he saw you. You said you were so depressed you didn't know how to cope. The records will show that you were prescribed anti-depressants. That was Harriet using your name, by the way. Haven't I arranged it all beautifully?'

'You'll find it difficult to get me to take any drugs.'

'Oh, I don't think so. A little prick with this needle, and you'll be like wax in my hands.'

Gwyneth reached out a hand and switched off the light. 'I've always been able to see in the dark, Ellie. Can you?'

> *From things that go bump in the night,*
> *Good Lord, deliver us . . .*

Turn the lights off, and the name of the game changes to Danger.

The click of the light switch sounded unnaturally loud. Darkness enclosed them. Ellie could hear her own breathing. And another sound. A whistling. Gwyneth was whistling through her nose.

Then came the whoosh of heavy coat over trousers. Ellie thought: I must move, or I'll be trapped. She tried to move sideways, away from her chair, but was brought up short by the wall behind her.

She blinked to accustom her eyes to the dark. A dim light seeped around the edges of the blind at the window. Something — someone — was standing between Ellie and the window.

Ellie slid to her knees, trying not to make any noise. She told herself not to panic. But which way was the front door?

A key snicked. She was locked in.

The shape was moving around the desk. Feeling the way. Arm raised.

Light caught the edge of a weapon, the hypodermic that would render Ellie 'like wax' in Gwyneth's hands. Ellie would have screamed, if there had been anyone to hear.

The heavy arm fell, stabbing. The cloth of Ellie's new coat caught the needle and held it. Gwyneth swore and tried to withdraw her weapon, which was stuck in the thick fabric. Ellie undid the button with her left hand and slid out of the coat.

She felt her way along the wall of the waiting room. Chairs against the wall. Whoops. She banged into one and heard the other woman snort with satisfaction.

Ellie lunged for the inner door, the one that led to the doctor's room. That door was locked, too. Of course, Gwyneth had locked it behind her when she came out. All the doors in a surgery should be locked at night.

Her eyes were getting accustomed to the darkness, which was not quite as black as she had thought at first. A weapon. But what? Gwyneth whistled through her nose and lashed out, as Ellie ducked and fell sideways across a chair. Kicking out with her feet, Ellie heard Gwyneth grunt in pain.

The hat stand! Ellie found herself bumping into it and, twirling it around, she brought it down where she thought Gwyneth's head might be.

'Bitch!' Something had struck home.

The stand was wrenched from her grasp and gone. Was this the receptionist's desk? Yes. A phone. She could dial 999 for help. If she had time.

No time. Gwyneth was up and after her again, whistling through her nose as she came. Was this the end? Someone banged on the front door. 'Hello, there! I've come to collect my prescription!'

Ellie froze. So did Gwyneth.

'Not a peep out of you!' whispered Gwyneth. 'The surgery's shut for the night. It's after hours. They'll go away in a minute!'

Someone banged on the door again. A man. A large, heavy man. 'Come on, come on! Open up!'

A woman's anxious-sounding voice. 'Fred, they're closed for the night. You can get it in the morning!'

'I need it tonight, woman! The doctor knows I'm coming for it tonight. If it hadn't been for that effing hold-up on the tubes, we'd have been here hours ago!'

'But you can see no one's there.'

Ellie felt around behind her, moving back . . . back . . . back to the wall.

243

'Don't tell me what I can see and what I can't see! There's someone in there. I saw her as we got off the bus on the corner. The doctor was in her room, and she didn't switch off her light till we were nearly here. If you hadn't been wearing those stupid high heels, we'd have been here before now!'

Ellie found one of the chairs that lined the walls and lifted it with both hands. She could no longer hear Gwyneth's breath whistling. Ellie hoped Gwyneth was now on the other side of the room, but she would have to risk it. There was no alternative. Brrring! Brrring! The man had found the bell, and was leaning on it.

Using the chair like a battering ram, Ellie lunged with all her weight at the window. The glass shattered with a horrifying crash. Pain spat at her hands, cut by the glass. She dropped the chair with a gasp. Gwyneth shrieked.

So did Ellie. 'Help, help! Get me out of here!'

The man said, sounding uncertain. 'There you are! There is someone in there! Who's that?'

'Help! Don't go away. I'm trapped in here!' Panting, holding a hand on fire, Ellie darted away from the window. The phone rang.

'Leave it!' hissed Gwyneth.

Ellie had no intention of touching it. She fell over another chair. Picking it up, she pounded with it on the outer door . . . and again . . . and again. Any minute now, Gwyneth would be upon her and . . .

'Christ, Fred! What do we do?'

'Don't leave me!' cried Ellie. 'Get the police!'

'How can I fetch the police without leaving you?'

'Use your mobile, you fool!' the woman said.

The light came on. Gwyneth stood there, looking as calm as if she had just arrived for a day's work. She went over to the front door, produced a key and opened it. There was no sign of the hypodermic. A large man, seriously overweight, and a sparrow-thin, bottle-blonde woman on stiletto heels peered in. Uncertain. Ready to flee.

Gwyneth said in her best receptionist's voice, 'I'm sorry you've been troubled. A false alarm. This woman came in at the end of surgery, turned off the lights and proceeded to make a nuisance of herself. I expect she's forgotten to take her medication again. I'll ring the hospital to come and collect her. She'll have to be sectioned again, I suppose. I'll report the incident to the police myself; it's a case of criminal damage, as you can see.'

Ellie realized that she herself looked far from calm, with her coat discarded and her clothing disarranged from her tumbles over the floor. There were cuts on both her hands from the glass.

The large man and the tiny woman craned their necks to see inside the surgery, but didn't enter. They looked with apprehension at the mess Ellie had made of the window. Both avoided meeting her eyes. Gwyneth was indeed calling the police. 'I only came for my prescription,' said the man, now apologetic and anxious to be gone. 'Fowler's the name.'

'Certainly, Mr Fowler.' Gwyneth sought in a file and produced the prescription for him. 'I'm so sorry you've been put to all this trouble to collect it. This woman locked the door on me, you see. Quite alarming for a moment or two.'

'It must have been,' said the woman. 'Come on, Fred. We must be on our way.'

'Don't go!' said Ellie, trying to speak as calmly as Gwyneth, and failing. 'The police will want to know exactly what you heard and saw.'

'Yes, but . . .'

'We don't need to detain you any longer, I'm sure,' said Gwyneth.

'Oh yes we do,' said Ellie. 'I'm not being left alone with you again, even if I have to commit another act of criminal damage to make sure they remain!'

Gwyneth's eyes rolled upwards and she shrugged. 'You see how it is,' she said to the Fowlers, who were now edging towards the door. 'Mad as a hatter.'

'We should be going, really,' said the woman.

Too late. The police car had arrived.

'I wish to file a complaint against this woman,' said Gwyneth. 'She suddenly went mad and smashed a window.'

'My name is Ellie Quicke. That woman there threatened me with a hypodermic syringe. She said she was going to stupefy me, and then fill me with drugs to make it appear I had committed suicide.'

'Fred . . . !' Mrs Fowler whispered piercingly to her husband. 'Let's get out of here!'

The two policemen, one male and one female, looked at Ellie and then looked at the massively calm Gwyneth. Ellie could see who they were going to believe and prepared herself to be arrested and carted off to the police station.

'Hang about!' said the woman officer to Ellie. 'I know that name. My mate Bob told me all about you. Nosy old . . . er . . . elderly lady with a nose for crime, he said. Didn't you bring in some poison-pen letters recently?'

Gwyneth protested, 'She threatened me!'

'She had a hypodermic in her hand a moment ago,' said Ellie. 'See if she's still got it on her. Or she may have hidden it somewhere in this room. She hasn't had time to dispose of it.'

Gwyneth lunged for her desk drawer and yanked it open just as the male policeman got her in a bear hug from behind. There was a sharp scuffle which Gwyneth gradually lost. As the policeman reached for his handcuffs, Gwyneth toppled slowly over onto her desk and lay there, inert. The policeman took out his handkerchief and gingerly withdrew the shining hypodermic from Gwyneth's thigh, where she'd accidentally stabbed herself in the struggle.

'I say, Fred!' said the sparrow-like woman. 'Who'd have thought it?'

'I rest my case,' said Ellie. 'Now I'll phone for my solicitor, who I think may be able to give you all the evidence you need.'

* * *

The house lay calm and quiet around her. It was the morning after. Diana had taken her family off to inspect the new flat. No doubt she would find fault with it, but there was also no doubt that she would accept free accommodation in the long run.

Stewart was still looking hangdog. Ellie wondered how long it would be before he had to give up his job in the north and come down south to be a house husband. Unless Aunt Drusilla rescued him, that is.

I must go shopping this afternoon, thought Ellie. Three new coats in two days is a bit much — but worth it, to clear up that mess. Midge jumped up to sit on her lap, purring. He smelt of chicken this time. Where on earth had he got chicken from? Which neighbour had he conned into feeding him?

Ellie thought about the word processor. She really didn't like being beaten by a mere machine. She might or might not start her driving lessons again, because she feared Frank had been right in saying she had no road sense. Yet a competent secretary ought to be able to master the word processor sufficiently to produce the church notices. Also, she would need some sort of professional-looking machine for her correspondence if she were to set herself up as a landscape gardener.

She looked up the number of the typing agency, and enquired if they knew someone who could give her some private tuition on her computer. Then she made herself some strong coffee, broke open a box of Belgian chocolates, and settled down with her notes to plot out a design for the garden next door.

THE END

THE JOFFE BOOKS STORY

We began in 2014 when Jasper agreed to publish his mum's much-rejected romance novel and it became a bestseller.

Since then we've grown into the largest independent publisher in the UK. We're extremely proud to publish some of the very best writers in the world, including Joy Ellis, Faith Martin, Caro Ramsay, Helen Forrester, Simon Brett and Robert Goddard. Everyone at Joffe Books loves reading and we never forget that it all begins with the magic of an author telling a story.

We are proud to publish talented first-time authors, as well as established writers whose books we love introducing to a new generation of readers.

We have been shortlisted for Independent Publisher of the Year at the British Book Awards three times, in 2020, 2021 and 2022, and for the Diversity and Inclusivity Award at the Independent Publishing Awards in 2022.

We built this company with your help, and we love to hear from you, so please email us about absolutely anything bookish at feedback@joffebooks.com

If you want to receive free books every Friday and hear about all our new releases, join our mailing list: www.joffebooks.com/contact

And when you tell your friends about us, just remember: it's pronounced Joffe as in coffee or toffee!

ALSO BY VERONICA HELEY

THE ELLIE QUICKE MYSTERIES
Book 1: MURDER AT THE ALTAR
Book 2: MURDER BY POISON PEN

THE BEA ABBOT AGENCY MYSTERIES
Book 1: A FALSE CHARITY
Book 2: A FALSE PICTURE
Book 3: A FALSE STEP
Book 4: A FALSE PRETENCE
Book 5: FALSE MONEY
Book 6: A FALSE REPORT
Book 7: A FALSE ALARM
Book 8: A FALSE DIAMOND
Book 9: A FALSE IMPRESSION
Book 10: A FALSE WALL
Book 11: A FALSE FIRE
Book 12: A FALSE PRIDE
Book 13: A FALSE ACCOUNT
Book 14: A FALSE CONCLUSION
Book 15: A FALSE FACE

Made in the USA
Coppell, TX
25 April 2024

31722589R00148